———————— ★ ————————

Eyes hardly blinking, I worshipped *Sunrise at Royan*. Had there ever been a dawn as young? A sea as flawless? All apricot, peach and turquoise, the water gently lapped at the shore, not marring the scene with so much as a wave.

With a sigh, I tore my gaze away. I had to save some adoration for *Sunset at Royan* on the opposite wall. I swiveled to the left and saw—oh my God!—an empty gilt frame.

The knockoff Chanel bag slipped from my arm and plunged to the floor.

I crept closer. Someone had sliced the canvas out of the frame. Only jagged edges still clung to the wood. Not daring to trust my eyes, I stared, unbelieving, at the sacrilege—a masterpiece cut and changed forever. Worse, it was gone, maybe for good.

The police. I had to notify the police.

———————— ★ ————————

THE MONET MURDERS

JEAN HARRINGTON

W🌐RLDWIDE ®

TORONTO • NEW YORK • LONDON
AMSTERDAM • PARIS • SYDNEY • HAMBURG
STOCKHOLM • ATHENS • TOKYO • MILAN
MADRID • WARSAW • BUDAPEST • AUCKLAND

To my dear friends, the BB's:
Eleni, Fran, Kati, Nancy and Ramona, for all the fun
and facts we've shared over the years.

Recycling programs
for this product may
not exist in your area.

THE MONET MURDERS

A Worldwide Mystery/August 2013

ISBN-13: 978-0-373-26859-7

Copyright © 2012 by Jean Harrington

Printed in U.S.A.

Acknowledgments

To Peg Longstreth of Longstreth & Goldberg Art for her insights into the international art world; Robert K. Wittman, founder of the FBI Art Crime Team, for his informative book *Priceless*; Kati Griffith for the Hungarian phrases and for allowing the use of her family name; Attorney Carolyn Alden for her legal expertise; my friend and critique partner Sharon Yanish and Lethaladies of KOD for their fabulous cyber critiquing; Houston's 2010 Lone Star Writing Contest for choosing *The Monet Murders* as a finalist; and to the Carina Press Executive Editor, Angela James, and my gifted manuscript-doctor editor Deborah Nemeth, who have welcomed Deva and company into their midst. Thank you, one and all.

CHAPTER ONE

I PUNCHED IN the code to the Alexander mansion as if I owned the place. Not wishful thinking. Familiarity. I'd been in and out of the house so often lately, it felt like home. Ha! My entire condo would fit into the dining room I'd just finished—my first ever high-end interior design project.

A gardener wearing a Devil Rays cap was clipping shrubbery by the stone portico. I waved to him, opened the door and stepped into the foyer. Though the Alexanders were in Biarritz for a week, I helloed like mad anyway. Staff might be around, and I didn't want to startle anyone.

The odor of lemon wax and gardenias floated through the air but not a single sound. Maria, the cook, and her husband, Jesus, the estate's major domo, must have taken the afternoon off. Perfect. I'd have the Monets to myself.

Heartbeat thudding, I tiptoed across the cavernous living room into the dining room. The new draperies I'd installed were closed, shutting out the light. I fumbled for the wall switch, flipped it, and the fabric swished apart, revealing a room magnificent enough for Arab sheiks. To give the paintings star billing, I'd kept the décor opulent but discreet with ivory-colored paneling and heavy matching silk at the windows. The Baccarat crystal chandelier and wall sconces added the only glitzy touches, except, of course, for the glowing Monets.

I turned to the wall on the right. Ah…eyes hardly blinking, I worshipped *Sunrise at Royan.* Had there ever been a dawn as young? A sea as flawless? All apricot, peach and turquoise, the water gently lapped at the shore, not marring the scene with so much as a wave. My business needed every dime I could earn, but seeing this painting was almost payment enough. With a sigh, I tore my gaze away. I had to save some adoration for *Sunset at Royan* on the opposite wall. I swiveled to the left and saw—omigod!—an empty gilt frame.

The knock-off Chanel bag slipped from my arm and plunged to the floor.

I crept closer. Someone had sliced the canvas out of the frame. Only jagged edges still clung to the wood. Not daring to trust my eyes, I stared, unbelieving, at the sacrilege—a masterpiece cut and changed forever. Worse, it was gone, maybe for good.

The police. I had to notify the police.

Hands trembling, I grabbed the bag off the floor, plunked it on the mahogany table, for once disregarding its polished surface, and rummaged for the cell. My fingers fumbled, as limp as overcooked spaghetti. I couldn't find a thing. In desperation, I dumped out the contents. No phone. It was sitting on the Audi's front seat.

I remembered seeing a phone in the kitchen. Abandoning the mess on the tabletop, I pushed open the swinging door and rushed through the butler's pantry into the kitchen.

I grabbed the receiver and dialed 911.

"My name is Deva Dunne. I want to report a theft."

That was when I saw Maria—stretched out on the

floor beside the food prep island—the toes of her ox-fords pointing at the ceiling, a bullet hole in the middle of her forehead.

The phone slipped from my hand and dangled at the end of its cord.

A distant voice squawked, "Hello? Hello? Please verify your location."

Heart pounding, I stared at Maria in disbelief.

"Hello. Hello. Your name, please?"

I yanked on the cord and pulled the phone back up to my ear. "There's a dead body here. On the kitchen floor. A woman with a bullet in her head."

"Please verify—"

"1570 Gordon Drive."

I had to get out of there. The killer could be lurking in the house. The phone dropped out of my hand again and clunked against a cabinet.

I pushed open the swinging doors to the butler's pantry and raced through to the hall, glancing up at the staircase as I ran. No one. Nothing.

Hurry.

My heel slipped, my ankle gave way, and I fell, striking my head on the foyer wall.

I CAME TO with a start, right into the glare of Lieutenant Victor Rossi's deep-set, penetrating eyes.

Uh-oh, déjà vu.

"You okay, Mrs. D?" he asked, kneeling beside me, rubbing one of my hands between his own. His blunt fingers were firm and warm, caressing. Someone moaned. That couldn't have been me, could it?

"You hit your head pretty hard," he said. "You've been out for a while."

The room swam back into focus. "How long?"

"I don't know. You were out when Officer Batano got here. I was in the neighborhood so I came right over. Not to worry. The doc's on his way. He'll take a look at that lump."

"*The coroner?* No thanks."

Rossi frowned and blew out a breath.

I waved a hand in front of my face. "You been eating garlic?"

He reached into a pocket, took out a mint and popped it. "Think you can sit up?"

Fingering the lump on my head, I eased into a sitting position against the wall. Three months earlier, Lieutenant Rossi of the Naples PD had investigated the murder of Treasure Kozlowski, my neighbor at Surfside Condominiums. Looked like he'd be on this case, too. I'd been scared of him then, but not this time. This time… oh God…this time…

"Maria's dead, isn't she?"

He nodded. "The woman in the kitchen? I'm afraid so."

"I hoped I'd imagined it."

"No, it looks like a homicide. You need to tell me what happened. Why you're here. What you saw."

I struggled to my feet and must have stood up too fast. The room turned fuzzy, but Rossi grabbed me before I landed back on my head. It was the first time he had ever put his arms around me, and his embrace was amazingly strong and comforting.

"Let's get you a seat," he said.

Resisting the urge to cling to him, I pulled free and, a little shaky, walked into the living room ahead of him and sank onto a sofa.

Rossi peered at me with what looked like concern on his face. "You feel up to answering a few questions?"

"Of course."

He reached into a pocket of the pink Hawaiian shirt he wore loose, hanging over his white slacks. With his wall-to-wall shoulders, the casual outfit looked as intimidating as a military uniform. Using a gesture I remembered all too well, he removed a notepad and a pencil stub.

Like death and taxes, there was no way out, so I told him everything I knew, which was next to nothing. He kept the pencil going as if he were whipping out a bestseller. Except when I asked, "Why did the thief only take one Monet? Why not both?"

That wasn't an idle question. I really was puzzled. Why steal the larger of the two paintings and leave the smaller one? Was the missing one more valuable? To me, both were equally beautiful, equally precious.

He stopped writing for a second. "There's a reason for everything, Mrs. D." He jabbed his pencil stub in the direction of the dining room. "That's what I'm here for, to uncover the reasons why a masterpiece has gone missing. And why a woman is dead." He held the stub over the notebook again. "You notice anything else gone?"

"No, but I didn't have a chance to look."

A fleshy police officer barged into the room. "The cook's husband is here," he told Rossi. "A Jesus Cardoza. Batano's got him on the terrace with the gardener. And the doc's outside."

"Tell Batano I'll be right there. You can send in the doc." Rossi flipped his notebook closed. "You sure you don't want him to take a look at you?" he asked me.

I shook my head and regretted it. The room swayed then slowly steadied.

Rossi reached back into his shirt pocket, withdrew a business card and held it out to me.

"I have one, Lieutenant, and I remember the drill. If I think of anything else I'll call you. Ditto if I leave town in the next few days." My recital over, I asked, "Now may I leave?"

He tucked the card back in his pocket and gave me a sweeping head-to-toe glance. "You're looking pale, Mrs. D. How about you go to the ER? Get that lump checked out? I'll have one of the officers drive you."

"Thanks, but no thanks. I'm feeling fine now. I'll just get my handbag and go home."

He huffed out a sigh. "I could insist."

"No, you couldn't. I'm not under arrest."

He shrugged. "Feel free to leave."

On my way home, I did intend to go to the ER at the Naples Community Hospital, but I didn't want to make a big deal out of it by pulling up in a squad car.

I was halfway to the door when he said, "You know something, Mrs. D?"

Exasperated, I turned around. "What?"

"We've gotta stop meeting like this." He grinned. Right in the middle of a murder scene.

How crass. Not a word about the victim, or the missing Monet, or my clients' loss. I shook my head. A big mistake. I couldn't take another step until the room stopped spinning.

"One more thing," he said, as I reached the door. "You'll need to come to the station tomorrow and sign a witness statement." He frowned and added, "I know tomorrow will be a tough day for you, but I have to ask."

I nodded then hurried away before the tears blinded me.

Tomorrow. He had remembered.

Maybe he wasn't so crass after all.

CHAPTER TWO

THE NEXT DAY, my spirits lower than the price of a garage-sale rug, I opened my shop, Deva Dunne Interiors, promptly at nine as usual. Though the MRI hadn't shown signs of trauma, my head pounded anyway. It had every right to.

This was December fifteenth, the one-year anniversary of my husband Jack's death, and as Rossi had guessed, a day I'd been dreading. But no whining allowed. I intended to meet it dry-eyed and chin up, as Jack would have wanted. No sobbing. No groaning or carrying on about how much I missed him. How much I'd lost. How much I wanted him back in the circle of my arms, so I could reach up and sink my fingers in his thick Irish thatch, and warm myself in the sparkle of his eyes and his smile. No moaning about how every cell in my body would come alive each time he said he loved me…in a lilt more enchanting than music, more wonderful than…

I glanced out the display window. No, not again! What a nerve! I jumped up and yanked open the shop door. I'd had it with being dumped on.

"Hey, you! Dreadlocks!"

In his early twenties, with latte skin and dozens of loosely wound braids to his shoulders, the guy turned and pointed a finger at his chest. "Me?"

"Yes, you. I saw you through my window. I want you to quit that."

He stared at me, a baffled look on his face. "I don't know what you're talking about, lady."

"Stop dumping your empties in my planters. I've been finding them there all week."

He shrugged. "That's what they're for."

"Like hell they are."

I stepped outside. Plucking a dead soda can out of an English boxwood next to the entrance, I held it up. "The planters are for decoration. For customers. *This* is for you." I threw the can at him. It bounced off his foot. "No more Cokes. No more Buds. Got that?"

In the distance, traffic pulsed along Fifth Avenue, Naples's version of Rodeo Drive, but no one ventured down the alley. Dreadlocks and I were alone. Over six feet tall, with pecs like Arnold, he could easily have knocked me down, but I stood my ground. I was struggling to create a little bit of beauty in the world and wasn't about to tolerate any trashing. Not today of all days.

He picked up the empty, crumpled it and dropped it in the gutter. "That better?"

I sighed. "Better. Not good."

Silver rings mounted the edges of his ears. He'd cut the sleeves off his sweatshirt; a tattooed snake rippled on his right upper arm.

"Thanks for the compassion," I said.

His eyes narrowed. "What's that mean?"

"I'm trying to get a business started here. Why make life tough for me?" Tears stung my eyelids, but I willed myself not to cry. Not here. Not now. I'd done enough of that all year. No more. Definitely not in front of this hostile stud with muscles, hooded eyes and 'tude.

He stepped in closer. "You crying?"

"Of course not."

His voice rose an octave. "Over a can? That's nothing to cry about."

"The nothings add up."

"Yeah, I know." He frowned. "Look, I don't want to make an old lady cry."

Old? "I'm only thirty-two, for Pete's sake."

Forehead creasing, he peered at me. "Whatever."

I didn't have a single gray strand in my frizzy red hair—at least not a new one—or a wrinkle that mattered. But in that minute I celebrated my hundred and tenth birthday. It was a pity party. Despite my resolve not to cry today, the tears flowed in earnest. I swiped at them with an open palm and turned back to my Boston green door.

"Hey, I'm sorry, ma'am," Dreadlocks called after me. "No more empties in your plants. If I see any, I'll fish them out, okay?"

Not trusting myself to say more than "Thanks," I gulped down the last of my tears and went into the best little design shop in Naples. The one practically nobody knew existed. But thanks to Channel 2 and the *Naples Daily News,* by now everybody probably knew about the missing Monet and the murder and my role in the whole ugly affair. What the reaction to that would be, I dreaded finding out.

The phone rang. Hoping the call meant business, I grabbed the receiver before the second ring.

"Deva Dunne Interiors."

"Deva, I just read about the crimes. I should never have sent you to the Alexanders."

Simon Yaeger, a Surfside neighbor. We were friends. No more than that. Though I had the feeling Simon would like to up the ante, I was far from ready for a relationship.

"What happened yesterday wasn't your fault, Simon. Who could've guessed I'd be involved in a murder?"

His voice lowered. "I mean it. I'm so sorry."

For some reason, maybe the effect of Simon's suave voice, I sat up straight and eased the linen sheath over my knees. At least the green dress—an homage to the season—gave off the understated vibes a designer should project. Despite the good dress, I was relieved he couldn't see me at the moment with what were no doubt red eyes, a red-tipped nose and out-of-control hair. A bit of vanity that shot my guilt through the roof.

"I appreciate your concern, Simon, but I'm confident the police will find the killer."

While Simon had given me the Alexander tip with the best of intentions, he *had* landed me in the middle of a murder investigation. But why tell him what he already knew?

A pause hummed through the receiver. "There must be something I can do. Take you out for dinner?" A moment of silence, then a whispered, "I can do more than dinner."

"No, I'm afraid you can't." I wanted to say, "I belong to Jack," but I couldn't bring myself to speak of him.

"Okay, your loss."

No question, ice dripped from his words. I'd seriously annoyed him. Terrific. In an attempt at damage control, I asked, "Want to come for Christmas dinner?"

"That might work. I'll let you know." He hung up.

I stared at the dead receiver in my hand. *Damn.*

Only two months ago, Simon had phoned with a great tip. "How would you like an A-list client?" he'd asked, his voice as smooth and silky as his custom-made clothes.

"Oh? You have one for me, do you?" I liked to play cool with Simon. Tall, tanned and Tampa bred, he had to be most girls' idea of a dream guy, but the man filling my dreams remained rumpled, charming Jack Dunne. I doubted the void he left in my life could ever be filled. But I gave silky Simon credit for trying. He could really work the phone, and that was saying a lot for a tax attorney who charged by the minute.

"Their name's Alexander," he told me. "They're newbies in town. Rich as sin. Trevor's a client of mine. Lives on Gordon Drive."

I clutched the receiver to my ear. Gordon Drive, Naples's most luxurious neighborhood. Snagging a design project in one of those mansions would lift my struggling business out of the red. My pulse rate rocked. "This is music you're singing, Simon. Do go on."

"Ilona, the wife, is Hungarian. Quite the looker. Very trophy." He cleared his throat at that little indiscretion. "They want to redo their dining room before the holidays."

"Just the one room?" Disappointment must have crept into my voice.

"Deva, the dining room's as big as your condo. They've got Monets on the walls."

"*Monets?* You're sure?" Playing the cool game had gotten harder.

"Two of them. People don't lie to their legal counsel."

"Ha! Why me? I'm not a name."

Simon sighed. "Because I recommended you. Highly. I told them you're from Boston, know all about classical furniture and art, and understand the effects of tropical light on interiors."

"You oversold me." My turn to sigh. He'd exaggerated my credentials. Not the best way to approach prospective clients. Could I, truly, create a design to showcase a Monet? Two Monets? Torn, I hesitated, wondering what Jack would have said. The answer came winging right at me. *Of course you can.*

"So, would you like the Alexanders' phone number?" Simon asked.

"Of course I can. I mean, of course I would."

After scribbling the number on a notepad, I thanked him, and the rest, as they say, is history.

Snapping me out of my reverie, the antique sleigh bells on the shop door went into a cheery ding-a-ling frenzy. My first customer of the day? I glanced up. Oh. Not quite.

"Lieutenant Rossi." I stood and strolled over to greet him. "You found my shop."

"I am a detective, Mrs. D."

He took my outstretched hand. His was as warm and firm as I remembered. His dark eyes flicked over me, a complete body check. I remembered that, too, and glared at him, pretending to be irritated, though I really wasn't.

"Has there been a break in the case, Lieutenant?"

He shook his head. "Not yet."

"So you're not here on official police business?"

"No. I had a few minutes free. I wanted to remind you to stop by the station and sign your witness statement, and ah, to see how you were doing." He yanked his glance away from me and looked around the shop. "I like it in here. It's got, you know, class." His glance swiveled back to me. "Like that dress." He peered into my eyes. "You been crying?"

My guess was that Rossi liked to spring questions.

Catch people off guard so they'd blurt out the truth. Well, that wouldn't work on me.

"No," I lied.

Staring at nothing in particular, he picked up a mercury glass Santa from a display table, put it down then reached for a crystal snowman. He cleared his throat. "When we met a few months ago, you mentioned that the date of ah…ah…"

I forced myself to say, "Jack's death."

He nodded. "Yeah. It's today, so I wanted to ah…"

"Cheer me up."

"Exactly." He looked relieved that I had fleshed out his sentence.

"Well you have, Lieutenant." I meant it and gave him what no doubt was a wobbly smile. "Your shirt alone does that for me."

He glanced down at himself and grinned. "You like it, huh?"

"I didn't say that."

He was sporting another Hawaiian number today. Green palm trees swaying in orange sunsets. Many trees, many sunsets.

"Do you own a suit jacket?" I asked. "You know, a blazer? In navy blue?"

"Yeah," he said, his expression guarded.

"Well?"

"Well, what?"

"Do you ever wear it?"

He shook his head. "I'm saving it for my wedding."

"Your wedding? You have a girlfriend this time?" Six months ago, he had me convinced he was engaged. Maybe this time he really was. I tamped down what felt strangely like a stab of disappointment but I wasn't fast enough. His detective's eyes flashed over me and his lips curved into a knowing smile.

"No, there's no girlfriend, but I let women think there is. Otherwise they're all over me."

I felt like slapping him. "That remains the most egotistical thing I've ever heard."

He shrugged and grinned again. "You never know, my M.O. could change."

A rugged, dark-haired forty-something, he had apparently evaded every trap known to womankind. Why let his guard down now? To hit on me? How did he know I wasn't the thief? Or the murderer?

"Want to take a look at my bedroom?" he asked, blowing my silent question out of the water.

Arms akimbo, shrew style, I said, "Rossi, you have the gall of ten men and the finesse of none. For five cents, I'd throw you out of here."

Smiling, smirking actually, he waggled a finger under my nose. "Your imagination's jumping ahead of the facts, Mrs. D."

"Don't give me that forensic mumbo-jumbo. I just heard you say—"

"You don't decorate bedrooms?"

"Oh." My face went from flushed to hot. I deserved his smirk. "I apologize. I'm not myself today."

"I figured this would be a bad day for you." He cleared his throat. "Wilma, that's my cleaning lady, she'll be at my place Friday morning. If you want to take a look, she'll let you in."

"I found a dead body yesterday. How do you know I'm not the killer?"

"Years of training, Mrs. D. Plus gut instinct." That grin again. "Besides, you were out cold. No smoking gun in your hand, either."

"My father was a Boston cop. He taught me something about police procedure. Aren't you supposed to avoid personal contact with witnesses?"

He nodded. "What I'm suggesting isn't personal. It's business."

"Oh? True." For some reason I felt deflated.

Amusement glimmered in his eyes. "You want the job or not?"

Not only did I want it, I needed it. Swallowing my pride, I nodded. "What's your favorite color?"

He shrugged. "I like 'em all."

"I'll take a look. Thank you."

He reached into his shirt pocket and removed his notepad and pencil stub. Apparently, he didn't go anywhere without them. After scribbling for a few seconds, he ripped off a sheet and handed it to me. "My address and phone number."

I glanced at what he had written. This was his private number. Not the one at police headquarters.

I tapped the paper with a fingernail. "Privileged stuff here, Rossi. You can be reached day or night. Correct?"

"Yeah, I'm leaving myself wide open, Mrs. D. Remember, I've got a murder to solve. Don't be calling me at all hours looking for a hot date."

"Rossi, I—"

His expression sobered. "And don't take any chances. Call 911 at the slightest suspicion of trouble."

"You think I'm in danger?"

He shook his head. "I doubt the murderer has you in his sights, but it's best to be careful. Gotta go. Don't forget to come in and sign your witness statement." His face relaxed into a smile. "When this is over, maybe we can try cruisin' for burgers."

"Is that an invitation or an order?"

"I never give orders to beautiful women."

I stared at him tongue-tied. He winked and exited the shop, leaving me alone with the jangling sleigh bells. And my guilt. Somehow, Rossi had managed to press my buttons, and on this day of all days.

Not only that, he could be jeopardizing his job by hiring me. Why? A clever ploy to keep me close, to get to know me better, to see if I could be a killer and a thief? Or all of the above? Bottom line, I couldn't believe a tough guy like Rossi cared a hoot about interior design. No, he had another motive. Me, myself and I? Was the reason as simple as that?

The sleigh bells were still jangling. I strode over to the door and ripped them off the knob. This Christmas season sure was murder.

CHAPTER THREE

AT FIVE, I closed the shop and drove to the NPD station where I signed my witness statement for a young female officer. Lieutenant Rossi was nowhere in sight, nor did I ask for him. Afterward, figuring that though the sleigh bells and the tree hadn't lifted my mood, maybe a glass of wine would, I drove back to Fifth Avenue and dropped in at the Irish Pub.

I sat at one of the little metal tables on the terrace overlooking Sugden Square and soaked up the cool evening breeze. As their children scampered about, tourists in shorts and T-shirts leisurely strolled the open square. Tiny white lights encircled the palm trees, adding a note of festivity to the scene. In this peaceful place, it was hard to believe that only a few blocks away a world-class masterpiece had been snatched into oblivion and a woman shot to death.

A slim blonde server approached, pad and pen in hand. "Evening, ma'am. What would y'all like?" she asked in a lilting southern drawl.

I'd heard that soft southern drawl before and glanced up from the menu. "Lee Skimp, is that you?"

"Y'all know me?" A hand flew to her mouth. "The decorating lady."

"I've been called worse things," I said, laughing. "How *are* you?" A sweet girl, Lee had been instrumental in finding Treasure's killer, and for that I'd be eternally grateful to her.

"I'm just fine," she said, adding shyly, "I looked in your shop window the other day. It sure is pretty."

While she spoke, she kept glancing over one shoulder then the other as if searching for someone.

"Is anything the matter, Lee?"

She nodded. "I shouldn't be telling a customer, but since you asked…it's my daddy. I moved out a month ago and heard tell he's been looking for me. If he finds me here, I don't know what all will happen."

"Anyone of legal age has the right to strike out on her own."

"I'll be twenty-one and a half come Friday."

Of course. To serve liquor she'd have to be, though truth to tell, she hardly looked that old. More like a lovely waif with her long, shiny hair and big Loretta Lynn eyes.

"Then your father can't force you back home against your will."

"You haven't met my daddy." She attempted a smile. "You're not here to listen to me yammer on. What all can I get you, Ms. Dunne?"

"Please call me Deva. And a glass of house chardonnay would be lovely." I was on a budget. My palate would understand.

"Coming right up."

As Lee hurried off to fill my order, I scanned the menu. I'd have a burger, the pub specialty, affordable and filling.

Maybe the man's hurried gait was what caught my eye. And his wintry clothes. Amid the scantily clad tourists, his blue jeans, cowboy boots and flannel shirt were as exotic as a bikini on an Eskimo. He trotted around Sugden Square, darting with a jerky step between clusters of sightseers. A nervous squirrel on a hunt for nuts, he looked vaguely familiar somehow. Strange.

Lee came back with the wine and took my order.

"A burger, well done, no onions."

She wrote it down. "Anything else, Ms. Dunne?" I never got to answer. "Oh, no," she whispered. "He's found me." Terror filling her eyes, she dropped the pad on the table. As if her fear drew him like a beacon, the strange man spotted her and came at her full tilt, in his haste elbowing a woman out of his way.

"Hey, quit your shoving," she yelled.

He ignored her and hurried toward the terrace. Trembling, Lee shrank against the pub wall.

I knocked my chair back and jumped up. "Daddy?"

She nodded, panic in her eyes. "He'll make me go home."

"You don't want to?"

Too terrified to speak, she shook her head.

I hate bullies, and judging from Lee's fear, this little, skinny guy was a bona fide bully in the flesh. No way could I sit by and let him push her around. A grizzly protecting her cub, I stood in front of Lee, my purse clutched in both hands.

"Get out of the way," her father ordered, his body fairly quivering with rage.

I squared my shoulders, drawing myself up to my full five feet six. "I'll do no such thing."

"My name's Merle Skimp, this gal's daddy. I'm telling you to step aside."

"I'm telling you to leave her alone."

"You got no right to come between kin." Skimp's hand, quick as a snake's strike, darted out and clutched my arm. For a skinny man, he had a powerful grip. I couldn't shake him off.

Food forgotten, the diners at the nearby tables stopped eating to stare at us.

"Let her go, Daddy," Lee begged. "I'll come with you."

"No, you won't," I said. "You," I shouted to a startled diner. "Get the manager. Hurry." To my relief, the man jumped up and rushed into the pub.

"That won't do you no good." Skimp tightened his hold on my arm, bruising it. "You heard her. She's leaving this godless place. Come on, gal." The pressure of his fingers increased, shooting pain down to my fingertips.

Shaking, ashen-faced, Lee took a step toward him. Where the hell was the manager?

As Lee moved away from the wall, Skimp let go of me to lunge for her. *The tyrant.* My Irish temper flared sky high. Before he could grab her, I swung my handbag and clobbered him. Combined, my cell phone, keys and makeup kit had enough clout to knock him off his feet for a second. But only for a second. He rallied, beckoning to her. "Come on."

I struck out again, this time knocking the baseball cap off his bald head. As he bent to retrieve it, I realized why he looked familiar. "I know you!"

He was the gardener I'd seen stooping over the shrubbery on the Alexanders' lawn.

Before he could admit or deny it, a tall, chesty man with the heft of a barroom bouncer hurried over, trailed by the flustered diner.

"I'm Brad, the pub manager. What's the problem here?" the big guy asked.

"Ain't nothing to worry about, sir," Merle Skimp

said, tugging the Devil Rays cap back on his head. "It's a family matter."

Brad turned to me. "You called for help, ma'am?"

There was that "ma'am" again. First Dreadlocks, now Brad. Clearly, I needed to change my image—lengthen my hair, shorten my skirt. *Something.*

"This man—" I pointed a finger at Skimp, "—attempted to abduct your server."

At the direct accusation, Skimp found his spine. "She's my gal. I just want to do the right thing by her. She don't belong in here. Servin' drinks like a common hussy."

His eyes on Lee, Brad upped his hefty chin in her father's direction. "You know this man?"

Trembling, Lee stepped out from behind me and nodded.

"You want to go with him?"

Without lifting her gaze from the concrete pavers lining the terrace, she shook her head. "No, sir."

"You heard her," Brad said to Skimp. "I have to ask you to leave."

Skimp shot a venomous glance at me then held out a hand to Lee. She made no move to take it.

"Come on home, gal. Think of what your momma would say."

Lee shook her head. "No, Daddy."

Brad reached into his pants pocket and removed a cell phone. "Your choice, mister."

"I'm goin', but I ain't happy about it. I'll talk to you another day, gal."

"Come back, I'll call the police." Arms crossed over his green Irish Pub T-shirt, biceps bulging, Brad held the phone, watching as Skimp darted across the square and disappeared around the corner of the Island Grill.

"I'm so sorry," Lee began, teary eyed. She got no further.

"No need to apologize, Lee. You're a good employee." Brad turned to the gaping diners. "Show's over, everybody. Drinks on the house."

As a pleased buzz went up, he asked me, "Your name again, ma'am?"

Ma'am. "I give up."

"What was that?" Brad asked, a puzzled look on his face.

I shook my head. "Sorry. Just thinking out loud. My name's Deva Dunne. I opened a design shop on Fern Alley a few weeks ago."

"We're neighbors, then." He held out his huge hand, pumping mine up and down with a surprising gentleness. "You're a friend of Lee's?"

"Yes," I replied without a moment's hesitation.

Lee rewarded me with a tremulous smile.

"We're not busy right now," he said to her. "Why don't you take an hour off? Have a burger or something. Talk to your friend…ah…Deva. I'll have Nancy cover for you."

"What a nice man," Lee said as Brad strode off.

"Absolutely," I agreed, stopping short of adding, "One out of two ain't bad."

With a grateful sigh, Lee sank onto the steel mesh chair across from me. Her lips quivered, but she didn't cry. "Daddy means well, but I had to leave home all the same. He wouldn't let me do anything. Except go to work at Kmart. He didn't want me to have friends, either. Not even girlfriends. And I've never had me a boyfriend. Not one. Not ever."

"He wanted to keep you for himself?"

"I guess so. Since Momma passed, he's been lonely but..."

"You have your own life to lead."

She nodded, her eyes misty. "I stayed, though, till he told me to quit school. That's when I left."

"School?"

"FGCU. Florida Gulf Coast University," she added, sitting up straight. "I'm an art major. Got me a scholarship, too. I plan to be a decorator just like you."

Just like me. I wanted to cry. I'd seldom had a finer compliment.

"I'm renting a room two blocks over on Third Avenue, so I can walk to work, and I get a ride to class with a girl I know. Everything's going just fine, except for—"

"Daddy."

"Yes."

Working nights and going to school days couldn't be easy. She looked so frail and burdened I reached across the table to squeeze her hand. "Let's order burgers and Cokes. You'll feel better after you eat something." She had a long way to go until the pub closed at midnight.

We had nearly finished eating when she surprised me with a question. "Deva, would you like some help in your new shop? When I peeked in the window the other day, I told myself I'd surely love to work there."

I rested what was left of the burger on my plate. "I'm barely getting started, Lee. I can't afford to hire anyone."

Her eyes flared wide. "Oh, I don't mean for pay. I mean kind of like a—what's the word?—internship. Yes, that's it. Internship. For the experience, like."

I shook my head. "That would be taking unfair advantage of you. Besides, you have enough to do as is."

"I worked at Kmart all through high school and after.

I got to know the Martha Stewart line real good. Martha's another decorating lady," she added, "just like you."

Just like me. I sighed and gave in on the spot. "What did you have in mind?"

The last bites of her burger abandoned, Lee leaned forward, eyes aglow. "Well, I'm free Wednesday and Friday afternoons from two to five. I kind of thought if you're working all alone, you might need to leave, you know, to go to customers' homes and stuff. I could keep the shop open. At least two afternoons a week."

"Lee, has anyone ever told you that you're a steel magnolia?"

Her brow furrowed. "No. What do y'all mean?"

"You're strong."

"I wish my daddy thought so," she said, looking as wistful as an abandoned child.

"If he didn't before, chances are he does now. Though you'd better be careful walking home at night. He might follow you."

"It's okay, Deva. He won't hurt me."

Hoping she was right, I glanced out onto Sugden Square. Couples strolling arm in arm had replaced the tourist families. As night deepened, the lights on the tree trunks transformed the palms into glimmering sculptures. A lovely sight, but I couldn't keep staring at it without answering Lee's question. Yet how to answer her? The last thing I wanted was to hurt her feelings, but with my entire future at stake, the truth was my only option. I pulled my gaze from the square and looked across the table.

She was a beautiful girl, anyone could see that, but I suspected her wardrobe consisted of jeans, Reeboks and T-shirts. Loose T-shirts. Daddy wouldn't have allowed anything else.

"Well, for openers, interior designers sell the sizzle. The steak comes later."

"Y'all confusing me, Deva."

"What I mean is it's an image business."

She nodded, her brow creasing as she waited for me to make my point.

Oh boy, this wasn't going to be easy, but I had no choice except to plunge ahead. "To put it in as few words as possible, you need a signature look."

"A what?"

I blew out a breath. "Clothes."

"Oh. I don't have any," she said, sagging back onto the metal chair. "Nothing but jeans and tops."

She looked so upset, I quickly added, "I can help you with that. So say we agree…you work in the shop Wednesday and Friday afternoons." I held up a warning hand. "On three conditions."

She nodded before I could count them off.

Index finger: "You bring your homework. When the shop's quiet, you get in some studying."

Third finger: "As soon as I'm out of the red, you go on the payroll."

Ring finger: "Before you start, I buy you a black dress and high-heeled sandals. Black is fabulous on blondes. Wait and see. And a string of chunky faux pearls."

"I've never had no black dress before."

We'd have to work on those double negatives, too, but not tonight.

"Tomorrow's Wednesday, why don't you stop by at two, and we'll shop for a dress?"

The smile on her face drove away any misgivings

I might have had—except for one. "If you're going to work with me, there's something I should warn you about." I hesitated. What I had to tell her might kill our association before it began. I gave a mental shrug. No way to avoid that. She deserved to know. "I'm involved with the police."

Before I could say another thing, she raised her right hand then dropped it, palm down. "Don't you go worrying yourself one little bit, Deva. I read the newspaper this morning. I know all about that dead body you found."

CHAPTER FOUR

So, APPARENTLY, DID everybody else in town. On Thursday, for the second day in a row, the *Naples Daily News* headlined the double crimes. By Friday, local TV channels were focused on little else. Even CNN gave the story a mention, but except for questioning me at the scene, the police hadn't contacted me.

I'd hung the bells back on the shop door, and each time they jangled I expected to see a cop in the doorway. So maybe it was a good thing for my nervous system that walk-in business was practically nonexistent.

Anyway, Friday was Rossi Day, and I was curious to see his place. How he lived, the colors on his walls, the furniture—the pictures of his old girlfriends—would all have a tale to tell, and I couldn't wait to hear it. Anyway, considering his execrable taste in clothes, whatever his motive for hiring me, I probably had my work cut out, which was fine. A healthy person didn't need a doctor, right?

At eleven I changed the arrow on the Open sign in the shop window to two o'clock and locked up.

It was good to know that if I didn't make it back by two, Lee would reopen for me. As expected, she looked breathtakingly beautiful in her new black dress, her blond hair shimmering over her shoulders, her long, slim legs showcased in the new high-heeled sandals. What were a few double negatives in light of all that?

She'd be a wonderful, reliable asset to the business, I was certain of it. Now I just had to drum up enough business to keep her.

Rossi lived in East Naples, in Countryside, a gated community with a security system that rivaled the Kremlin's. When I finally got through the guard check at the entrance gate, I drove along a curvy street lined with mailboxes and well-groomed lawns. A single-story stucco like its neighbors, Rossi's house had curb appeal—new-looking beige paint, Mexican tile roof, shrubs trimmed to within an inch of their lives, walks swept clean of even so much as a fallen leaf.

I sat in the Audi staring at the property for a while. Not bad. I resisted the thought that Rossi had tidied it up just for me. Still, the possibility that he might have made me smile. Why, I had no idea. At least none I was willing to admit to. Now for the interior and a peek into Rossi's psyche, if not into his underwear drawers.

I climbed out of the car, walked up the brick path to the front entrance and rang the bell—a no-nonsense buzzer. The door flew open.

"Lieutenant! You're supposed to be at work." I eyed him suspiciously. Had he lied to me about Wilma, his cleaning lady? Was this a trap? I sighed and walked in anyway, telling myself every man in the world didn't find me irresistible. In fact, most didn't, and Rossi was probably in that vast number.

"I worked all night," he said. "Just came home to grab a shower." He looked so heavy-eyed and fatigued I believed him.

"I can come back later. You have more important things to do than—"

"No, no. Life goes on even during police investiga-

tions. Come in. Come in. I've been waiting for you."
He waved me inside with a wide swipe of his right arm.

"If you're sure. We can make it fast."

"Not to hurry, Mrs. D. I have time."

I walked through the small, bland foyer into a living room that was a virtual sea of light beige. Walls,
furniture, rug, lamps. Straight ahead, open glass sliders led to a pool sparkling in the morning sunlight, its
vivid aquamarine a jolt of visual relief. The only one.
I glanced around. Not only was everything beige, everything was immaculate. Not a newspaper, a coffee
cup, a discarded slipper or a wilted flower anywhere.

"Your cleaning lady just leave?" I asked.

"No, I told Wilma to skip this week."

"It's this clean after a whole week?"

"Two weeks." He let his glance roam over me and
changed the subject. "No dress today?"

"You don't like slacks?"

"Yeah, I do. They're a good tradeoff."

"What's that supposed to mean?"

"No legs, but—"

—ass. "Don't go there, Rossi."

"No." He ran a hand over his stubbly jaw. "I was
definitely out of line with that one. See what you do to
me, Mrs. D?"

He did look distracted. He must have the murder
on his mind. Not to mention the Monet. No doubt he
needed to get back to work as soon as possible. I didn't
want to waste his time. "Where's your bedroom?" I
asked.

He broke out into one of his big white Chiclets grins.
"Now you're talking." He cocked an index finger and
beckoned me down a short hallway with a closed door
at the end.

"You first," I said. No way would I walk ahead of him while he checked me out.

"No flies on your tail, Mrs. D."

"Lovely expression," I muttered and followed him down the hall. Telling myself not to be ridiculous, I squelched a sudden spurt of tension. I had surveyed men's bedrooms before, many of them. And without another woman present. What made this different? Rossi's attitude? Or Rossi himself?

He opened his bedroom door. Like the living room, it was textbook perfect. The king-sized bed could pass military inspection. Not a single object studded the sleek Art Deco dresser. The matching bedside tables each held a pottery lamp and nothing else. Nowhere did I see an alarm clock, a loving cup, a watch winder, or heaven forbid, a dirty sock flung into a corner. And not a single girlfriend's picture.

"You live here?" I asked, deadpan.

"What's that supposed to mean?"

"It means you're a neat freak, Rossi."

"That's good, right?" His brows collided. For the first time since I'd known him, I had him worried. It was such a good feeling, I increased the pressure.

"Do you ever sit on the bed?"

"After it's made? No. Why?"

I didn't answer. Let him stew. "May I see your closet?"

"Sure." He opened a set of shutter doors and snapped on the closet light.

I walked in to a store's worth of Hawaiian shirts. I recognized a couple—that pink one and the green one with the orange sunsets. Like a rainbow, he had them arranged according to the spectrum. Red, orange, yellow, green, blue, violet.

"Rossi." I turned around so fast, I bumped into him. As I moved back a step, the sleeve of a jacket brushed my arm. Navy blue. So he did have one. The cramped space, or maybe Rossi's proximity, was making me claustrophobic. "I want to get out of the closet."

"Yeah, you don't belong in one."

That grin again. He turned everything into—

"So what do you think?" he asked when we were back in the bedroom.

"California Closets could learn from you, Rossi, but as for the rest, may I be honest?"

"That's what I prefer."

"A house is not a crime scene. Fingerprints are okay. Ditto for used coffee cups and magazines. Even an empty pizza box isn't a felony. It's like you've got invisible yellow tape everywhere, cordoning everything off. Why don't you let down the police barriers in your mind? Loosen things up? Get some pizzazz, some fun, some excitement in here."

"Excitement I get on the job. Fun I don't get from furniture."

"Okay, I got carried away. Your home is commendably…ah…clean. Make that immaculate. But it lacks color and accessories."

"Accessories?"

From his puzzled tone, I wondered if he'd ever heard the word.

"Yes, for starters, the big three. Plants. Pillows. Pictures." I waved my arms around the room. "I like beige walls. I like beige furniture. I like beige rugs. I like beige coverlets. I like beige—"

He raised a hand, palm out. "Enough already. Barley's Paints had a sale. I stocked up, that's all. Then

I matched everything. It was easier than figuring out what colors I should pick."

I eyed his shirt. Turquoise today with yellow hibiscus blossoms. "You don't have that trouble with your wardrobe."

"I don't look at what I'm wearing. You do."

"Good point. So...to get back to why I'm here. What do you want from me?" *Wrong question.* I knew it the instant the words left my lips and ignited one of his grins. So why had I said them? Freudian slip? Maybe Rossi attracted me more than I let on—even to myself.

The claustrophobia rushed back. I hurried out of the bedroom and marched down the hall ahead of him. Let him check my butt if he wanted to.

In the living room, I sank onto the couch and glanced around. "You could use a little help out here as well. In fact, I suggest we start here, not in the bedroom."

Damn. There was that grin again.

"Maybe I should just leave," I said, picking up my handbag.

"No, no. Don't go. I want to hear your ideas. I mean it." He slid onto a beige lounger opposite the couch, leaning back like he intended to listen. Or judging from the look of his heavy eyes, fall asleep.

I put the handbag down and swallowed my pride once again. Right now, I couldn't afford to walk away from any job that came my way. "I'll take some measurements. Make some notes. If you have no objection, I'll photograph your interiors. Then, I'll submit a proposal and layer it to give you several options. We take it from there."

"Sounds good."

I was removing the tape measure from my bag when

he said, "Will you wait up a minute with that, Mrs. D? There's something I have to tell you first."

No grin. No humor. No innuendo.

A band tightened around my chest.

He leaned forward, focused and intense, all signs of sleep deprivation gone. "The Alexanders' insurance company wants the FBI involved."

"Understandable, considering the value of the missing Monet."

"Correct, if not exactly flattering to our local boys in brown." He blew out a breath. "I hope you also find this understandable—you've been asked to have a polygraph test."

My jaw went slack. "As in lie detector?"

"Yes."

"But I didn't kill Maria. I didn't steal the painting, either."

"I know that. You know that. Now the insurance company and the chief need to know. You were in the wrong place at the wrong time. We want to eliminate you as a possible suspect. Not incriminate you."

"Oh really? How comforting. Are these tests fool-proof?"

He glanced away from me to study a nonexistent spot on his wall. Body language doesn't lie. The answer was no.

"I refuse."

"Thwarting a police request isn't smart. I wouldn't do that if I were you."

He sounded so morally superior I wanted to fling the measuring tape at him. "Well, you're not me. You're not under suspicion, either."

"How you feel is only natural, but—"

"Is that why you're here today? Instead of Wilma? To tell me this?"

"Partly. I knew you'd be upset."

"Now you're a shrink as well as a detective." I grabbed my bag and leaped to my feet.

He leaned back in his chair, maddeningly a man at ease in his own home. "You're not alone."

Halfway to the door, I turned around. "What's that supposed to mean?"

"Everyone who knew the entry code is to be tested. For starters, you. The gardener. Jesus Cardoza. And the Alexanders."

"The Alexanders? That's ridiculous. They were in Europe at the time."

He cocked an eyebrow at me but didn't respond.

"Okay, not ridiculous, but farfetched." I stomped back to the couch and sat on one of the arms, defying it to break off. "When?"

"What's the matter with today?"

CHAPTER FIVE

ROSSI CALLED AHEAD for an appointment. Then, insisting I was too nervous to get behind the wheel, he drove my Audi to the Florida Polygraph Services office on Airport Road. We made good time along the Tamiami Trail but with minimal small talk. I really was too nervous for that.

Bob Butterworth, the polygraph analyst, met us at the reception desk. He topped six-three, carried at least a hundred extra pounds, and was dressed in black from head to foot. His Darth Vader look didn't make me feel any easier.

"I'll be waiting outside, Mrs. D." Rossi took out his cell phone as he headed for the front door. Before it swung closed behind him, I heard him say, "Yeah, I'll be in as soon as we're finished here."

Police business, I surmised, wishing he had followed me into the cubicle with Darth, who said, "Please have a seat and let me tell you how the polygraph works."

He indicated a straight-backed wooden chair in front of a small table. The stale air in the windowless room reeked of fear and tension, or maybe it was just my imagination working overtime. I took the seat he indicated. With nothing on the industrial tan walls to attract my attention, I concentrated on the table and its black box. Roughly the size of a briefcase, the box bristled with wires, some of which led to a blood pressure cuff. A graph printer was attached to one side of the box.

"There's no right or wrong to this test," he said as I sat down. "What the polygraph does is record your physiological responses to the questions I'll ask. These responses are involuntary. In other words, they can't be controlled."

I was about to ask, "What makes you so sure?" when he handed me a sheet of graph paper. "This is a sample printout." Jagged vertical lines marched across the page. "The longer the lines, the greater the emotional response to the question."

"Those are the lies, then?"

He stiffened. "Possibly."

Bingo.

He removed a sheet of paper from a manila envelope Rossi had handed him when we came in. He glanced at it briefly then gave it to me. "Read these over and when asked, simply answer truthfully with a yes or a no. All questions are factual about events that did or did not occur. None are based on emotion or opinion."

Straightforward enough, but still I could feel my blood pressure shoot up, and my palms go sweaty. Rossi must have written the questions before I got to his house. Knowing he had did nothing to calm me down. In fact, believing he'd set me up, I'd be taking the test mad as hell. As Darth stood there with the blood pressure cuff in his hands, I scanned the questions. He had been truthful; I could answer every one with a single yes or no.

I gave him back the page. He hooked me up to the machine and wrapped the cuff around my upper arm. "I'm also going to put a monitor on your finger to measure pulse and breathing rates, so try not to move your fingers or toes. Movement can affect the results. Okay so far?"

I nodded though I wasn't okay with this at all. Far from it. Maybe I should have contacted a lawyer before getting in so deep. I heaved a sigh. A fine time to worry about legal counsel now that I was hooked up like fish bait.

"First, I'll ask you some basic questions," Darth was saying. "They're not relevant to the case, but they'll give me a baseline for your responses. I'll be marking the sheet as you respond. Don't worry about that. It's standard procedure. Just answer truthfully. Then I'll ask a final question, and I want you to lie."

I nodded. The fake lie would establish a sample of my reactions when I really was lying.

He stood behind the table, turned on the polygraph machine and asked, "Ready?"

I nodded.

"Is your name Devalera Dunne?"

"Yes." *I love the Dunne part.*

"Are you married?" *Oh, I was, I was.*

"No."

"Divorced?" *From Jack? Never.*

"No."

"Widowed?" *Dear God in heaven, that has to be a...*

"Yes."

"Have you ever stolen money?"

"Yes." *When I was seven, a dime from my grandma's change purse.*

"Final question. Have you stolen anything in the last six months?"

"Yes." *That's my lie.*

The long sheet of graph paper spewing out of the printer spilled over the table edge. Darth examined it then picked up the list of relevant questions Rossi had prepared.

"All right, Mrs. Dunne. We'll do a practice run of the lieutenant's questions. Simply answer as truthfully as you can. Then we'll do the test a second time. That's the one that'll count. Understood?"

I nodded, ignoring the trickle of sweat between my shoulder blades.

The questions began. "Did Mr. and Mrs. Alexander employ you as an interior designer? Did you steal the Monet seascape? Do you know Mrs. Alexander's maiden name? Did you know the Alexanders' cook, Maria Cardoza? Did you find the Monet cut from the frame? Do you know who stole it? Did you contact the police? Did you find Maria Cardoza's body? Did Maria Cardoza ever cook you a meal? Did you kill Maria Cardoza? Do you know who did kill her?"

On and on, he droned. All told, with periodic stops while he marked the graph sheet, the practice test lasted for nearly an hour. In between the benign queries there were four lethal ones—did I steal the painting; did I know who had? Had I killed Maria; did I know who had? Those were no, of course. After we ran through the list once, Darth examined the printout then he turned off the polygraph machine, removed the cuff from my arm and the monitor from my finger.

"You did very well," he said.

I looked at him in surprise. "What's the matter, Mr. Butterworth, aren't you going to give me the test?"

His smile said it all. "I have, Mrs. Dunne. We're finished."

"Wasn't that a practice run?"

"Well," he said, his smile growing broader, "if you

put me on the machine and asked that same question, the needle would spike."

"You lied."

"Yes," he said, "I did. But I'm sure you didn't."

"So I PASSED the test, but dammit, Rossi," I said when we hit the parking lot and headed for the Audi, "that guy lied to me. I bet you knew he was going to."

"Pretty standard procedure, Mrs. D. If the subject thinks it's only a practice test, he relaxes. It goes better."

"So now I'm a subject. Of what? Speculation? All I did was check on my design job. I *found* the crimes. I didn't commit them."

Rossi stopped midstride and, planting his feet wide apart on the tarmac, stood facing me. "It looks like a woman. It moves like a woman. I'll bet it feels like a woman. Too bad it sounds like a child."

"You have a hell of a—"

He held up a warning hand, palm out. He had a long lifeline. "Stop there. This is a murder investigation. I'm sorry you were lied to, but I'm sorrier Maria Cardoza is lying on a slab."

Heat rushed into my face. If I had a mirror, I'd be looking at a boiled beet.

Rossi stared at me without blinking, waiting, no doubt, for his pound of flesh. I gave it to him. "I'm truly sorry. You're absolutely right. Forgive me for losing sight of what matters."

He grinned. "Maybe. All depends. Want to hear the terms?"

"Why not?" Though I could guess.

"After the investigation is concluded—not before— you'll have dinner with me."

"Where? Mel's Diner?"

Mel's was the local greasy spoon. I let my voice purr with disdain, but I was faking it. Fact is, though I hadn't been out with anyone since losing Jack, at least not on an actual date, I was surprised to realize I'd enjoy going to dinner with Rossi. And somehow, I knew that would be okay with Jack.

"No, not Mel's," Rossi said calmly, not letting my disdainful tone affect him. Or at least not enough to let it show. "Someplace where I have to wear a jacket. The one in the closet on the fifteenth hanger."

"I know the one." I heaved a sigh to make him think the decision came hard. "St. George and the Dragon?"

"Great. It's dark as a cave in there."

"You've been?"

"I'm the detective. I ask the questions. And there's something else. I spoke to the chief while you were taking the test. He'll recuse me from the case if you and I…ah…give the appearance of impropriety."

Relief flooded through me. So he *had* been sincere in hiring me. There was no trap, after all. Still I asked, "What does recuse mean, Rossi, in plain English?"

"It means just the suspicion of collusion can prejudice the outcome."

"That's English?"

He put a hand on my shoulder and said, "Except for police business, I won't be contacting you until the case is resolved. No dinner. No house redo. No nothing."

"But that's all it's been. Nothing." I'd only told one lie all day, and this wasn't it.

He slammed a fist against his chest. "That cuts, Mrs. D."

"You know it's true."

"So far." His mouth tried for a smile but failed. "I also know a detective has to be above reproach. Like

Caesar's wife. See how much you made me forget?"
His expression sobered. "I'm sorry to put off the re-
decorating. But it's not forever. Now let's get going.
I've got work to do."

I DROVE BACK to Rossi's house and dropped him off so
he could pick up his car, a dusty, dinged Mustang.

"That's quite a vehicle," I said, "for Mr. Clean."

"Part of the disguise, Mrs. D." He climbed out of
the Audi, taking the scent of his aftershave with him.
I would have asked what it was but didn't want to give
him the satisfaction of knowing I'd been aware of it
for the whole damn drive. Before closing the door, he
leaned across the front seat. "Not to worry. For my social life, I have different wheels."

Does he think I'm a snob? For some reason, that
bothered me. It bothered me a lot. "I only mentioned
your car because it doesn't fit your squeaky-clean
image. Besides, Jack always had dirty cars. I'm used
to them. There's something very liberating about tossing a banana peel on the backseat and leaving it there."

"To *rot?*"

"Precisely." The shocked look on Rossi's face made
my day. *"Ciao, ciao, bambino."*

I waved goodbye and laid rubber, the screech of the
tires on his quiet street music to my ears. Halfway down
the road, I eased my foot off the gas pedal. Maybe Rossi
had been right earlier. I *did* have a childish streak. To
make up for my outburst, I drove back to the shop five
miles under the limit. I was disappointed not to be able
to tackle his bedroom right away. I sure could use the
business, but I was surprised to realize how much I'd
miss seeing Rossi. He was growing on me. Like moss.

I laughed and checked my watch. Two-thirty. If all had gone according to plan, Lee would be at the shop now.

On Fifth Avenue, I spied an in-season rarity, a parking space. I nosed into it, holding up a parade of traffic as I pulled in, pulled out, pulled in, pulled out, until, finally yanking on the wheel for the last time, I nestled that baby in place. Triumphant, I waved thanks to the row of waiting cars, locked up and crossed the street to Fern Alley.

Off Shoots, the junior clothing shop next door where we'd found Lee's new dress, buzzed with customers. Good for Irma and Emma, the hard-working twins who owned it. Their ad for holiday dresses in the *Naples Daily* had attracted a lot of interest. A green strapless gown in their display window caught my eye. It would be perfect for New Year's Eve, but I wasn't going… and then I saw him. Dreadlocks. The handsome young guy who promised not to drop his empties in my planters. Why was he hanging out in front of the shop? Sitting cross-legged on the sidewalk with a clipboard on his lap?

He was so intent on what he was doing he didn't hear me approach until I came alongside him. When he spotted me, he looked up and gave me a dazzling smile.

"Hey, design lady!"

"What are you doing crouched in front of my shop window? You'll scare people away."

"I'm drawing. Have a look."

With a sigh of irritation, I peered over his shoulder and gasped in amazement. I couldn't believe my eyes. His drawing was masterful. He had captured her. Lee Skimp. Her very essence, not just her beauty, lived on that page.

I glanced from the clipboard into the shop window

where Lee sat near the entrance at a desk—an antique bureau plat actually—looking stunning in her new black clothes, her hair a shimmering curtain to her shoulders.

"It's beautiful," I told him, looking back at the clipboard.

"Yes, she is," he said, glancing from the page to the window…his glance lingering there…then back to the page.

"Listen," I said, hands on hips, "I can understand your fascination, but for the second time I have to tell you I'm running a business here. And it's not a dating service."

"What?" He glared up at me as if *I* were the encroacher. "I'm not trying to make out. I'm an *artist.* I specialize in portraits."

"Right."

"Yeah, right." He scrambled to his feet. "This drawing is a study for an oil painting."

"How do you know she wants you to paint her?"

His annoyance fled, replaced by something else. Uncertainty? "I don't," he said.

I peered at his sketch again. The lad had a talent that leaped off the page. Lee looked alive in his rendering, her gentleness, her serenity, her strength uncannily revealed in a few bold lines.

I waved at Lee inside the shop. She returned my greeting with an uncertain little waggle of her fingers.

"Have you two met?" I asked Dreadlocks.

He shook his head.

"Would you like to?"

That smile again. "Is the pope a Catholic?"

"Okay, wise guy, come on." I had my hand on the door knob before I thought to ask, "What's your name?"

"Paulo St. James. It's Jamaican."

"I'm Deva Dunne. It's Irish."

Clipboard in hand, he followed me into the shop. When the Yarmouthport sleigh bells stopped their jangling, I said, "Mr. Paulo St. James, this is Miss Lee Skimp."

I think they both heard me, but I couldn't be sure. I wonder if the moment you fall in love you're aware of anything except the beat of your heart banging against your ribs?

Lee recovered first and, still seated behind the desk, she held out her hand. Paulo wiped a palm on his jeans before reaching across the desk to her. When they touched, I half expected to see a lightning bolt shoot across the shop, but no, he took her fingers gently, bowed and placed a kiss on the back of her hand.

So French. Or so Jamaican. Whichever. I was impressed.

And Lee? Well, Lee damn near fainted.

"I declare," she said. "I've never had my hand kissed before."

"You should have," Paulo said. What he left unsaid would fill a volume.

I cleared my throat. Startled that I was still there, they both looked at me, wide eyed.

"Mr. St. James wants to paint your portrait, Lee," I said. "Are you willing?"

She looked at me as if I were crazed for asking. "That's a mighty fine compliment."

"Then it's yes?" Paulo asked.

She nodded, her heart in her eyes.

"I've made a preliminary sketch," he said, holding up his work for her to see. "To establish the composition. I'll refine it tonight and be back tomorrow with an easel and canvas."

"Oh, it's wonderful," she said, staring at the sketch as if she couldn't believe what she was seeing. "But I'm not here except for Wednesdays and Fridays."

His face fell. "Wednesday's good. I won't bother you. I'll be outside." He pointed to the alley then swiveled his attention to me, a stricken expression on his face. "As long as Mrs. Dunne doesn't object."

"No, that's fine." I said. "Actually, an artist with an easel might bring people down the alley. And that might be very good for business."

He nodded, his smile wide enough to include both Lee and me. "I'll paint you through the window, Lee, like today. Seen through its gleam, you'll be mysterious, unattainable. Like in…what's that passage?…'through a glass darkly.'"

"St. Paul. From the Corinthians," Lee said, her voice spiking with pleased surprise. "You read the Bible, too?"

I wondered if Paulo could pass a polygraph on that one.

"No. Not really," he said, regret tingeing his tone. "But I think I'll begin. Starting now."

"I love St. Paul. He's my favorite of all the New Testament writers."

"Then I'll definitely begin with him." Obviously reluctant to leave, Paulo stood clutching his clipboard, his eyes devouring Lee.

I suppressed a smile. "Perhaps we could hold Bible class at another time."

"Oh. Sorry, Mrs. Dunne." With a visible effort, he tore his gaze from Lee. "I'll be back on Wednesday. I promise I won't interrupt your business."

With a courtly little bow for each of us, he left, setting the sleigh bells jangling. This time, looking at a radiant, pink-cheeked Lee, I thought they sounded positively jolly.

"Well," I said. "What do you think of all that?"

"Miz Dunne…Deva…I'm so frazzled, I can't think hardly at all."

I laughed or I would have cried remembering the impact of Jack Dunne's presence the first time we met. "Can you come back down to earth long enough to tell me if there were any calls?"

"Oh. Oh, yes, ma'am. Two. One from a Mr. Simon—" she glanced at a note pad, "—Yaeger. He wants to talk to you about Christmas dinner. He said he'll call back this afternoon. And Mrs. Ilona Alexander called. She wants you to drop by her house tomorrow. She needs your decorating advice for their Christmas Eve party."

A party? And poor Maria's remains hardly scooped up from the kitchen floor? *Unbelievable.*

CHAPTER SIX

"WHY ME?" ILONA Alexander asked when I arrived at the Gordon Drive house the next afternoon. "This morning I must take lie test. Can you believe? Me?" She pointed a French-manicured fingernail at her spectacular breasts. "They say I pass. Of course I pass. Instead why they not tell me who stole my painting? Or why my cook is killed? Why? Why my cook?" She pronounced her *w*'s like *v*'s, the heavy Hungarian accent adding to the allure of her blonde supermodel looks.

Simon had been right. Everything about her shrieked *trophy*—the long tanned legs, the highlighted hair tumbling past her shoulders, the aura of Opium perfume floating around her. And, of course, the breasts. *I'll bet they're fake,* I'd sniffed the first time I met her. She had stepped out of her home gym in workout gear, her spandex top challenged to the max. And did I mention her face? Perfection. She made the average female— *moi*—acutely aware of all my flaws: my frizzy hair, my every freckle, my mere size-B cups, my generous hips.

Today, in a leopard-print sheath and spike-heeled gold slides, she paced her living room's marble floor, asking, "Why?" *Vhy?*

"It is tragic," I said, mystified as to the reason I had been summoned there.

"Yes, tragic. To think I cannot find cook. No one

will come. Not after this...this *katasztrofa!* They're too afraid."

"Perhaps a bonus."

"I try that. No woman will touch it. And I want female cook. My mother had woman for cook. My grandmama had woman for cook. I am Szent-Gyorgyi. Woman cooks are family tradition." She heaved a sigh. "Also Trevor must be happy. He is so jealous, he wants no men living here. Only Jesus because he is married man." Her diamond-studded fingers flew up to her mouth. "No more he is. I suppose now Trevor will say he must go."

She sank onto the down-filled cushions of her double-length sofa. "Why this happen? Why?"

"The police are asking that same question, Ilona. I'm sure they'll find the reason."

She nodded but didn't answer. She didn't invite me to sit, either, but I thought, *what the hell,* and did anyway, on an exquisite bergère across from the sofa.

The original owners of the house had hired Holland Sally, Naples's premier design firm, to create the interiors. They had chosen white and ivory for the public rooms with yellow silk brocade on the French chairs and touches of gilt on the ormolu tables and accessories. A masterful plan, it enhanced the formality of the high-ceilinged rooms yet managed to keep them light and playful. It was a look strangely at odds with Trevor's blunt practicality, but one that suited glamorous Ilona perfectly. Though looking at her lovely, discontented face, I was struck by the realization that all this opulence hadn't made her happy. Far from it.

"Now what I will do?" she asked. "Fifty guests for Christmas Eve and no chef. *What?*"

She looked like she really wanted to know, so I decided to tell her what I honestly thought. "Well, in light of the investigation and Maria's death, you could cancel."

She bolted upright on the cushions. "Absolute not. Once given, invitation never is withdrawn."

"But under the circumstances?"

"*Nem.* No. But where to find chef, even male, in so short time? Is half impossible."

"True," I said, annoyed enough to agree. Not a word of sympathy for Maria had yet escaped from those sculpted lips. Ilona acted as if Maria had never existed, never boiled her an egg, never prepared her special local meals, her *après* pool parties, her lavish dinners. Sweet Maria who had called me Señora Dunne in her soft voice and had smiled so warmly each time, almost as if she knew how much I loved being known as Jack's wife. What a shame her life had been snuffed out so savagely.

Ilona heaved a sigh. "I'm desperate woman. Desperate."

I thought of Chip, who lived in the condo next to mine. A retired executive chef, he could probably use some extra cash. "Well, if you're really at wit's end, a chef I know might consider pitching in. He's retired but—"

Ilona sat up straight, bristling with interest. "Who this marvel is?"

"My next-door neighbor, Chip."

"Cheep?"

"Yes."

"What is his specialty?"

"Italian."

"Northern Italy?" Hope leapt across Ilona's chiseled features.

"Southern." I was enjoying myself.

"*Jaj Istenem!* Oh, my God! Not tomatoes."

"Exactly. Everybody loves his lasagna. He passes extra sauce around. And wait till you taste his anti-pasto." Touching my thumb and forefinger to my lips, I sent her a little pucker of gastronomic bliss. "Gelato for dessert. Homemade. Vanilla is his *forte*."

Ilona heaved a sigh that sent her breasts aquiver. Hmm, maybe, just maybe, they weren't implants. "Never can I face my friends again." She wrung her hands, the stones on her fingers clicking together. "You know I'm Szent-Gyorgyi?"

"You mentioned that, but I don't understand."

"Szent-Gyorgyi. I descend from noble family. Kings, queens, intelligentsia. You heard of Albert Szent-Gyorgyi? Yes?"

I shook my head. "No."

"My great uncle. My *Albert Bacsi.* He won Nobel Prize for Medicine in 1936. For green peppers."

"Green peppers?"

"*Igen.* Yes. Hungarians love them. Uncle Albert iso-late vitamin C from peppers. It was big medical break-through for my *bacsi.*"

"Ah. Fascinating."

"Of course. My family is one of oldest in Europe. And now I cannot even hire cook, a menial."

Okay. For that crack, Chip's price just doubled.

"Well, should you decide to ask Chip for Christmas Eve, his fee would be two thousand dollars. You'd pro-vide the food as usual, of course."

"Two thousand? That is ridiculous. Who he is? Wolf-gang Puck?"

I shrugged. "Chip's retired, so he may not want to get back into a kitchen." But I knew he would. Chip adored cooking and had only retired to please AudreyAnn, his love buddy. While not exactly a trophy, AudreyAnn required a lot of TLC. Chip, I suspected, enjoyed dishing that out as much as he did lasagna. Still, for two grand, AudreyAnn would no doubt be willing to sacrifice a cozy Christmas Eve around the palm tree.

Ilona slumped deeper into the down cushions, staring through the glass wall out to the Gulf of Mexico sparkling turquoise all the way to the horizon. As Ilona stared at the view, I wondered why on earth I'd been called here. I was grateful to the Alexanders for hiring me but also worried that the scandal would kill fledgling Deva Dunne Interiors before it had a chance to fly. But there wasn't much I could do about that except hope the case would soon be solved. So, nerves on edge, I waited, my design time clock clicking away at a hundred dollars per hour.

Finally, Ilona tore her attention from the view, heaved a sigh and said, "You know something, Deva, I never should have married him." She threw her hands up in the air. "That yenta should be shot."

"I'm not following you, Ilona."

"No? You never heard of yenta?"

"I have, but what has that got to do—"

"You want I should tell you?"

Uh-oh. Here it comes. Something I shouldn't hear. The same thing happened on nearly every sizable design project. Somehow, when you pick out people's drapery fabric, you morph into a confessor, and they tell you stuff their own mothers don't know. Usually I dread these confidences, but this time I was as alert as a bunny in an open meadow.

In fact, I aided and abetted. "So tell me. What's a yenta?"

Another dramatic sigh. "A matchmaker. This one I should never have listened to."

"No?" I leaned forward so as not to miss a word.

"It's no secret. When Trevor drinks, Trevor talks. Everybody knows. Everybody." She swept her arms wide encompassing the room, the Gulf, the world. At least the world that counted socially.

"Ilona, I have no idea what you're talking about." I *did* have a glimmer, but curiosity had seized me in its sharp teeth, and I was dying for the fangs to sink in deeper.

"He buy me."

"You're kidding, right?"

"I no kid. For three hundred thousand dollars."

"No!" If my jaw hadn't been attached to my face, it would have hit the floor.

"Yes, I tell you truth. That's what that yenta charge him. Her clients search everywhere but cannot find what they want in wife. She finds. All over world. Only the best, the *crème de la crème*. She comes to Budapest and interviews me many times, and I tell you, Deva, she asks questions your mama never would. Terrible."

"You answered?"

Ilona's eyes widened with a frisson of surprise. "Of course. In strange way, it was honor. And I want to marry. It was time."

I was amazed that her noble family would have allowed such bartering for one of their own. Centuries earlier, rulers did so out of political expediency, but today there could only be one reason. You couldn't live on a noble name alone, and Trevor Alexander was an extremely wealthy man.

Interesting that he couldn't find a woman without a yenta, but, no, I dismissed the idea as soon as it popped up. Though a portly fifty, what Trevor lacked in physical stature—and hair—he more than made up for in fiscal assets. Women would fight to nail him. He didn't need a high-priced marriage broker to find a mate. But he obviously hadn't wanted a garden variety female; he'd wanted a twenty-something aristocratic hothouse plant. *Hot* being the operative word.

"Anyway, that is past what I speak of," Ilona said. "Now I must look to future, or—"

"Sounds ominous, darling," a male voice boomed from the doorway.

"Oh, Trevor. Dearest, you're here at last. We wait for you."

Without moving from her cushioned comfort or revealing the slightest guilt at what she'd just admitted, Ilona held up her arms and raised her face for a kiss. When Trevor bent over the couch to embrace her, she clung to him as if she never wanted to let go. An Academy Award performance. Trevor loved it, and the kiss lingered on. And on. I was about to excuse myself when he finally broke loose and stood upright. He removed a folded handkerchief from a pocket of his linen slacks and wiped the trace of Ilona's pink lipstick from his mouth.

When he lowered the handkerchief from his lips, Ilona gasped. "You have blood. Is something wrong with mouth? With teeth?"

"Nothing I can't handle. I think you bit me, darling."

"Yes? See what power you have over me. I forget myself."

He smiled, probably in anticipation, an expression Ilona must have understood all too well, for she immediately changed the subject.

"How did lie test go, darling?"

His smile disappeared. "As well as can be expected. At least we've got that behind us."

Ilona turned to me. "Can you believe, Deva? In Europe we are when the Monet is cut. Yet still we must take this detector test. Ridiculous!"

Trevor patted his mouth once more before putting the handkerchief back in his pocket. "I take it you ladies haven't addressed the design problem yet."

"Not yet, darling. I told you, we wait for you." Ilona unfolded her lovely curves from the sofa and crooked a finger at me. "Come, Deva. We look. You tell us what you think."

More puzzled than ever, I followed the two of them to the dining room. I hadn't been in there since the day I found the Monet missing, and my heart pounded as I walked in. Though the room looked its best at night under the glow of the Baccarat chandelier, the wall sconces, and the flicker of candles, I was grateful for the afternoon sunlight. In it, the remaining oil of the beach at Royan took my breath away once more.

At my side, Trevor said, "The insurance company returned the painting to us just yesterday. They had insisted on having an appraiser examine it. It's intact, thank God."

I forced my attention from the painting and glanced over at him. "I love looking at it, Trevor, but frankly I'm puzzled. Why am I here today?"

"To settle a dispute between my beautiful wife and me. We're at odds about what to do in here."

I laughed. "A family spat? How can I possibly help with that?" Truth be told, though, husbands and wives often had different design ideas. When they did, my job involved negotiating a solution that would satisfy both. This had to be one of those times.

Trevor pointed to the empty gilt frame on the opposite wall. Shorn threads of canvas still clung to the wood.

"I think we should remove the empty frame and leave that wall bare for now. Some bastard took the larger painting, but the remaining one's strong enough to dominate the room on its own."

"Of course, it is," I said.

"I disagree with dear husband." Ilona softened the sting in her words by slipping her arm through his. "Is dramatic to leave frame in place. Why try to hide truth? Everyone knows."

"Our house is perfection, darling." Trevor's glance ran over her saying without words, *and so are you.* "It distresses me to have this desecration on our wall. Don't you agree, Deva?"

A loaded question. I was King Solomon with a naked baby lying in front of me. Cut it in half or leave it intact? Not wanting to give him a blunt yes or no, I asked, "Have you been to the Isabella Gardner Museum in Boston?"

His lips thinned in displeasure. "How is that relevant?"

"A multimillion-dollar theft occurred there a few years ago." I pointed to the plundered frame. "Same scenario. Pictures were cut from their frames. They've never been recovered."

Trevor's already thin lips tightened to a slit. *Uh-oh, a mistake to mention that. Oh well, too late now.*

I plunged on. "The Gardner left the empty frames on the walls with notes explaining what had been stolen. I wouldn't tack up a note, but I would leave the frame in place. It's gorgeous on its own, and besides, it's dramatic. Think of the dinner party conversation it will generate."

His slitted lips settled into a frown. Obviously, he disliked my suggestion.

"You see. I say same. For drama alone is worth keeping." Ilona winked at me over Trevor's shoulder.

"Very well. I can't fight you both," Trevor said, his frown disappearing as he drew Ilona to his side.

A discreet cough sounded from the open doorway. We turned to see a solemn-faced Jesus standing there.

"The bartender is here, sir, awaiting instructions for Christmas Eve."

"Ah, good. Come along, darling," Trevor said to Ilona. "I want to discuss the setups with him. I'm thinking of putting the bar on the terrace this time. I hope you'll agree to that, at least."

My opinion rendered—for two hundred dollars in design time—I followed them out to the living room where Jesus waited with the bartender.

"Oh my," I said when I saw him. "I can't believe it's you."

His startled expression told me he was as surprised as I was. "Hello, there, Mrs. Dunne," he said, giving me one of his signature bows.

It was Paulo St. James.

CHAPTER SEVEN

"YOU KNOW EACH other?" Trevor asked, glancing back and forth at us.

I nodded. "We've met. Paulo's an artist. He's painting a young woman who works in my shop."

"Is that so?" Trevor said. "What makes you think you're an artist? You have something unique to say?"

I looked over at Paulo. Though the silver studs rode his ears, he had tied his dreadlocks together at his nape with a black cord, and a starched white shirt concealed the snake tattoo. A spark flared in his eyes.

"Time will tell." Paulo held up his large, strong hands. "And these."

"Humph," Trevor replied. "This house is full of art. You've worked here before. You must have noticed?"

"Certainly, sir."

"The Monets, of course, are the stars of the collection. You've seen them?"

"Yes. They're glorious."

"Well, one still is anyway. You'd like to paint like that?"

At Trevor's mocking tone, caution crept into Paulo's expression. I stole a glance at Ilona. Intent on watching Paulo, she didn't notice.

"Well," Trevor goaded, "no answer for me?"

"I have no wish to imitate the great Monet," Paulo replied. "Portraits are my passion. I want to paint people and reveal what is hidden within…the secrets they keep from the world."

"Very ambitious. Very." His words courteous, his voice patronizing, Trevor cocked a finger at Paulo beckoning him toward the terrace. "Well, as to the bar…"

The two men strolled outside and, after giving Ilona "Chef Cheep's" phone number, I left for the shop.

All the way back to Fern Alley, I mulled over the surprise meeting with Paulo. A multimillion-dollar painting was missing, a woman dead, and, like me, Paulo had been in the house many times. He knew its layout, its treasures, and, to some degree, its owners' comings and goings. No doubt, he well understood the value of the Monet. But I didn't want to go down that ugly road, not with Lee's radiant face shining in my mind.

Surprising, too, that Trevor hadn't said if he'd been to the Gardner Museum in Boston. He obviously loved Impressionist works, and the Gardner had several major examples. But I hadn't been surprised to learn that Ilona had regrets. From what she'd revealed about the yenta, her marriage was one of convenience, nothing more. At least on her side. After watching her eyes feasting on Paulo, I suspected that Trevor might have reason for jealousy.

With my head spinning, I opened up the shop to another surprise; Simon came in right after me with a big happy-to-see-you smile stretched across his face. Easily the best-dressed man I'd ever known, he looked wonderful, as always. In recent months he'd abandoned his dark business suits for Naples casual wear, though he had his slacks custom tailored and bought only imported Italian silk shirts.

To Jack, clothes had been just a means of protecting himself from the elements—and public view. "A history teacher is supposed to be rumpled," he'd told me once. "You know, the absent-minded professor look." The colors and patterns of his clothes were always at war. For some reason, I had found that endearing. Rossi's execrable Hawaiian shirts struck me the same way. But Simon was different, and I wasn't sure how I felt about the difference. While clothes didn't make the man, they sure did make him pleasant to look at. That wasn't enough, not even close to enough, but I doubted I had learned all there was to know about Simon.

This was his first visit to the shop, and he nodded in approval as he looked around. "Very nice. Very nice, indeed." He pointed to the lime green rear wall. "I like that, and the white garden bench you set in front of it. Looks like a piece of sculpture."

My turn to smile. "That was the whole idea. I hoped it would show how much can be done with a little imagination."

"It does." He circled the Christmas tree, sniffing the pine aroma. "This is great, too. Right out of my childhood."

"I meant it as a reminder of old times. Going to Grandma's house for Christmas. That sort of thing. But there've been days I wish I hadn't bothered."

"The holidays can be hell," he agreed, his voice warm with understanding. "My parents both died in the same year. That Christmas I stayed drunk for two days. It gets better, Deva."

Unwelcome tears rushed to my eyes. I blinked them away, hoping Simon hadn't noticed. He stepped closer, stopping an arm's length away. For a moment, I thought he'd enfold me in an embrace, and for that single moment, I hoped he would. But he gave me a rueful little smile and said, "You will be happy again. I promise you."

"I'm happy now," I insisted. "Sort of."

He laughed. "There's hope for you and…" His voice trailed off. Had he meant to say "for you and me"? If he did, I never found out. He changed the subject to, "I'm here on a mission. I need some Christmas gifts. For my two partners and my secretary. It's either Deva Dunne Interiors or the Total Wine Store."

He strolled over to one of the four skirted display tables I'd placed against the side walls. Two were covered in bright red and two in a gold-and-white paisley print. I planned to keep them on through Valentine's Day then switch them for something that said spring. Maybe lavender for Easter, later a blue-and-white awning stripe for summer. It would be a simple and inexpensive way to keep the shop looking seasonal year round.

Simon picked up a bronze golfer in midswing. "One of the guys plays golf. What do you think of this?"

"Ideal." We spent the better part of an hour making his selections, which I wrapped in festive paper tied with glitzy bows—the golfer, an ormolu desk box, a crystal ice bucket with silver tongs.

On his way out, almost as an afterthought, he asked, "Are you free tomorrow night? There's a gallery opening, and I promised a client I'd drop by."

This was the second time this week he'd invited me somewhere, and I hated to refuse him again.

"We could do a late dinner afterward," he said.

I flecked some imaginary dust off one of the tables. Accepting was stage one. Stage two would probably be a kiss. Stage three would be a hand on my thigh. Stage four would be… I wasn't ready for that, not with Simon. He was a good friend and neighbor, but—

"Or we could just have a nightcap," he was saying. "Or only do the gallery," he ended lamely.

He had stopped short of begging, but the pleading note in his voice decided me. Besides, I couldn't hide out forever, turn into a professional widow. Above all, Jack wouldn't like that. The unexpected realization swept through me like a healing drug, and I blurted out, "I'd love to go to the opening, Simon."

His eyes took on a shine. *Over me?* "Wonderful. Pick you up at quarter to eight."

"I'll be ready," I said. It would be networking, I told myself, not a date.

WITH CLASSES at FGCU over for Christmas break, Lee's hours at the Irish Pub had increased from three nights to five. Still she insisted she was free on Sunday afternoon and showed up for work at two, her usual time. She must have informed Paulo, for he arrived promptly at two as well. While Lee sat at her desk by the entrance greeting people as they walked in, he sat outside on a folding stool behind his easel engrossed in the portrait. When a customer needed her help, Lee would leave her place by the window. Each time that happened, Paulo waited patiently for her to return to her seat. As she did, he nodded, smiled, and resumed painting, the attention turning her pink as a rose.

The sight of an artist at work drew people down Fern Alley, and for the first time the shop buzzed with activity, the sleigh bells on the door pealing every few minutes. In a few hours, I'd sold more than I had all week. One woman wanted her powder room redone right after the holidays and left her name and phone number. A small job, but a good omen for the future.

Lee had to change into her server's uniform and be at

the Irish Pub by six. So at five, she retrieved her purse from the storage room, and with a soft, "See y'all on Wednesday, Deva," she stepped outside.

The lure of the painting brought her, as it must, to Paulo's side. As I watched, she stared at the canvas, a hand covering her mouth to catch the gasp escaping from her lips. Paulo smiled up at her, causing my heart to turn over. I remembered the same light shining in Jack's eyes when he looked at me so long ago. A lifetime ago.

"Deva, how much is this glass bowl?" a woman asked, and when I glanced out to the alley again, Paulo and Lee were gone.

SIMON PICKED ME up right on time, quarter to eight. Since we both lived in Surfside, he didn't have far to go, just a quick elevator ride from his third floor condo to my garden apartment on ground level. When I opened the door, he let out a wolf whistle and made a circle with an index finger. "Turn around." I obliged. "Arm candy," he declared.

I laughed. "High praise coming from the best-dressed man in Naples."

"It's not the dress, it's the body," he said, bestowing a light kiss on my cheek.

"I won't argue with that," I said, laughing even more. A woman knows her flaws better than anyone else, so to have them overlooked by an attractive man has to be high praise. I'd worn my one and only Armani suit, black shantung, the skirt slightly too short, the heels slightly too high, and Jack's mother's pearls, exactly right.

With every parking spot on Broad Street taken, we parked a block away on Third Street South. Before we walked to the Adler-Meek Gallery in the mild December air, Simon popped open the BMW's trunk and removed an Hermès briefcase.

"Yours?" I asked. "An Hermès? I'm impressed."

"No, a client's. It's been in my office since last week. He was rushing to catch a plane to L.A. and forgot it. He'll be here tonight and asked me to bring it along."

Simon left the case at the reception desk, and we skimmed the gallery's catalog before shoehorning our way into the showrooms.

"It's jammed," Simon whispered in my ear.

"Figures. Opening night. Free champagne and hors d'oeuvres." It looked like every art buff in town was here. I wondered if Ilona and Trevor would be as well.

Simon plucked two champagne flutes from a tray and handed one to me. "To my lovely lady," he said. We clinked glasses.

The "lovely lady" was nice, but I wasn't sure about the "my." To hide my confusion, I strolled ahead of him. Perfume and aftershave swirled in the air along with the buzz of talk and laughter.

I glanced back over my shoulder. Simon had stopped to speak to someone he knew. I should take a lesson from him and chat it up. That was why I had come, after all, to network. Judging from their clothes and jewelry, this was a high-end crowd who might well be interested in the talents of a good interior designer. Trouble was, I'd have to interrupt a conversation to be heard.

I sipped my champagne and, squeezing through tight clusters of people, strolled into the next room. Into an explosion of color. A bit dazed by the visual impact bouncing off the walls, I wandered over to a large nude of a female torso. A Sizov. One of the Russian surrealists the catalog mentioned. It was surreal, all right, with magnificent breasts and swollen nipples, the paint swirled on in wild combinations.

A tall, lean whippet of a man with a high fore-head and receding hairline stood engrossed in the oil. He wore a double-breasted suit and a jaunty bowtie strangely at odds with his serious demeanor. I stood next to him, trying to see what he found so fascinating. If he noticed me, he didn't let on.

"What's the focal point?" I finally asked of no one in particular.

He glanced over at me. "Does there have to be one?"

I shrugged. "Surrealism's a ball game without rules."

He took his attention from the oil to rivet it on me. His keen glance appraised my suit and lingered at the pearls I'd clasped around my throat. Assessing their value? He extended his hand. "Morgan Jones."

"Deva Dunne."

"I'm in love with this painting," he said.

"You have the eye of an artist."

"More likely that of a surgeon."

"Oh?"

"Surgery's my work. Art is my love. But to get back to the Sizov. You seem conflicted about her."

I took another sip of champagne. "Green nipples take a little getting used to, but what tears you away from them is that third eye." I laughed. "The one in the middle of her forehead."

He looked back at the painting. "Why do you sup-pose it's there?"

"Does there have to be a reason?"

"Let's assume there is."

"All right." If he wanted to play mind games, I was willing. "Let's assume the breasts are bizarrely colored to capture our attention, but once we're captured, it's the eye that holds us. It pulls our glance upward, away from the physical to the mind. To the intelligence. Hence, we have two focal points. One stronger than the other. And the stronger is mind over matter."

He cocked an eyebrow. "Very good. You're no idle gallery groupie."

Maybe he didn't mean to be condescending, but I stiffened. "My degree's in art history. I guess that helps."

His eyes, glossy as agates, flashed over me again, missing nothing this time, openly appraising what I wore, my makeup, my hair, my jewelry, and estimating the cost of my suit down to the penny.

"Interesting" was all he said, but he made no move to walk away.

I opened my purse and took out the sterling silver card case Simon had given me when I opened the shop. I handed Dr. Morgan Jones my business card.

His glance flicked over it. "So you're an interior designer? That's how you used your degree?"

I nodded. He didn't need the story of my life.

He snapped the card with an index finger. "I'm buying the Sizov. She'll be an exciting addition to my collection." He tucked the card into a pocket. "Tell me," he said, "if you had to work this lady into a house—" he gestured to the painting, "—how would you go about it?"

It was an impossible question, and he knew it.

"I haven't seen the house," I said.

"Exactly." His lips parted a bit over even white teeth in what might pass for a smile.

I glanced at the gorgeous nude and took a mental leap. Why not? What did I have to lose? "I'd hang her where you would never expect to see her. Let her play with the observer. Shock him. Take him by surprise."

He laughed, his smile increasing for a fraction of an instant before it disappeared. Somehow I got the impression laughing and smiling were rare indulgences for him. "I'm going to find a salesman before someone else decides he can't live without a woman with green nipples. Stay," he said in a voice accustomed to giving orders and having them obeyed. "I'll be back."

Stay, like a puppy in obedience training. A waiter passed by with a tray of bacon-wrapped scallops. I took two and munched them, glancing around for Simon. I finally spotted him at the far end of the room, deep in conversation with a handsome, tanned couple. For someone who'd only been in town for six months, he'd already made a lot of connections. Well-heeled ones, no doubt. No sign of Ilona and Trevor. They probably didn't care for surrealism.

Dr. Jones elbowed his way through the crowd, a young clerk with a choirboy face, in a black silk T-shirt and slacks, following in his wake.

"Andre, this is Ms. Dunne," Dr. Jones told him.

Andre greeted me warmly enough, but he wasted no time in swiveling his attention back to Dr. Jones. I didn't blame him. How many people here tonight would buy in the five figures?

"Send the painting to my new address, Andre, and I'd like photographs of all my gallery purchases. Include sizes as well."

"Certainly, Dr. Jones. Our pleasure."

"Ms. Dunne will need that information when she does the interiors of the house."

"HE DIDN'T EVEN *ask* me," I said to Simon when we left the gallery. "He *told* me to meet him at his house tomorrow morning. If he likes my design suggestions, I'm in. What do you think of that?"

"I think you need the business."

I sighed. "True. My stupid pride keeps getting in my way."

"The guy's arrogant, no doubt about it. He's forgetful, too, so get some money upfront."

"You know something I don't know?" Though if he did, Simon would suddenly become Mr. Legal and clam up.

"No, not really. It's just that he forgot the damn briefcase. My client couldn't make it tonight, after all. He called and asked me to give the case to Morgan Jones. He'll be seeing him tomorrow. I told Jones it was at the front desk, but he walked off without it."

"Not surprising. He was all excited. He had a nude on his mind."

"What! That cold fish?"

Simon sounded so disbelieving, I laughed. "It's a long story."

"All I know is I'm tired of babysitting this briefcase. You want to do me a favor?"

"If I can."

"Bring it with you tomorrow and give it to Dr. Jones?"

"Happy to."

"Thanks, I'll call my client first thing in the morning and tell him Jones will have it."

The winter night had turned chilly. I was grateful for Simon's sheltering arm around me as we strolled along Third Street toward his car. At the corner I spotted a beat-up Mustang parked at the curb, a dark figure behind the wheel. *Rossi.* What on earth was he doing here? I resisted the urge to go up and talk to him, hop in the front seat, ask him how the case was coming… ask him…

No, not if he missed me. Why the surveillance? Over a hundred people had attended the exhibit. Surely, he couldn't remember all those faces. Or was he hoping to see one particular person? Someone of interest in the Alexander case? A suspect?

Me?

For an instant, the possibility chilled my blood, but Rossi wouldn't think of me that way. I was sure he wouldn't. Furthermore, I had passed the polygraph with flying colors. I told myself to relax, and the fear slowly faded.

Besides, I had something more immediate to consider. Simon. After all the finger food and champagne, I begged off making another stop. As we approached Surfside, I began to tense. What now? A good-night kiss like a couple of teenagers on prom night? A handshake? Or the whole Monty? His bed or mine? As he pulled into the carport and doused the headlights, to my disgust a fit of virginal panic seized me.

I had my palm on the door handle when he said, "Wait for a minute, Deva. It's still early."

"It's been a long day."

"They're all the same length. Twenty-four hours apiece."

In the dim glow from the lights lining the parking lot, I could see the humor flitting across his features. *He knows.* I hoped he wasn't aware of the flush heating my cheeks.

When he rested a staying hand on my left arm, I forced myself not to flinch. "I wanted to tell you how beautiful you looked tonight. How proud I was to have you with me."

"Thank you, I—"

His hold on my arm tightened. "There's more."

The fingers of my right hand clutched the door handle.

"Your business will succeed beyond your wildest dreams. You have the skill to make that happen. And you will. What I'm truly sorry about is getting you involved with the Alexanders, with that whole investigation thing."

"Don't blame yourself, Simon. Who would have guessed? Besides, I have confidence the case will be solved soon."

"I agree." His hand slid up my arm and wrapped around my shoulder. "Why don't you take your hand off the door handle?"

I stared at him without moving a muscle.

"Go ahead, take it off."

Wary, reluctant, I let my hand drop into my lap.

"Now put your arms around my neck."

Quickly, before I had a chance to refuse, he leaned toward me and gathered me in his arms. He lowered his mouth to mine, the tip of his tongue darting out to touch my lips, urging me to open to him. To my surprise, I succumbed to his urgency and opened my mouth, sucking him in, clinging to him, my own sudden need a shocking recognition of how lonely I had been.

But was this what I really wanted? Or was Simon a Band-Aid on my bleeding heart? I squirmed in his embrace, and his arms loosened around me.

"That was amazing, Simon. Thank you, but—"

He reached out and put a finger over my mouth. "No, don't say any more. If it was good, that's enough for now." His smile returned. "There's more where that came from, but not tonight."

He opened the driver's side door and stepped out. Weak-kneed, I slid out the passenger side, not sure I was disappointed or relieved as he walked me to my door, handed me the briefcase, and with a quick kiss on my forehead said, "Good night. See you on Christmas Day. I'll bring the wine."

I keyed my way in, dumped the briefcase on a chair and headed for the shower. A cold one.

CHAPTER EIGHT

ALL NIGHT I had long, vivid dreams of Simon, but toward dawn, Rossi entered the picture and drove him away. Interesting and annoying. What was Rossi doing in my psyche? Even more important, what was he doing in the Alexander case? No clue either way.

At ten o'clock I set the arrow on the shop window sign to two, locked up and drove to Dr. Jones's house in Bonita Bay, an upscale gated community a few miles north of Naples.

The Bonita Bay gate guard admitted me and gave me directions to the Jones property. The day couldn't have been more beautiful, full of sun, full of promise as I followed a winding road through a lush, jungle-meets-Palm Beach landscape. Every acre or so, a sprawling house, usually faux Tuscan in design, studded a well-groomed lawn. When I spied a boxlike stark white structure in striking contrast to its neighbors, I pulled onto the curved stone driveway.

Figures. Anyone who liked surreal green nipples would like sleek deconstructionist architecture. Judging from its exterior, the house would be fascinating to work with and, not to be crass about it, a big empty place that needed *everything* was a designer's dream come true. Well, one of them, anyway.

Pulse pounding, I climbed out of the Audi and rang the front entrance bell. Waited, rang a second time, waited, rang a third. No answer. My pulse rate dropped back to normal, and I returned to the car and sat behind the wheel. Our appointment was for ten thirty. I'd give him until eleven. If he didn't show by then, I'd leave. Whether I needed the job or not. A girl has her pride.

To my relief, Dr. Jones didn't put me to the test. Shortly before eleven, he roared up in a marine blue Porsche Boxster. The car door swung open, and he jumped out frowning. I yanked the key out of the ignition, picked up my handbag, clipboard and the Hermès briefcase, and exited the Audi.

Dr. Jones nodded and flicked his glance over me, running it from my hair down to my Jimmy Choos—one of the best investments I'd ever made. In neutral leather, they went with everything. Everything today being a gold tank top and pencil skirt over which I'd tossed a new purchase, a short fitted jacket, hand-quilted in squares of coffee, orange, green and gold. It even sported chunky wooden buttons that looked a lot like Oreo cookies. I hoped it would signal to Dr. Jones that while I do classic black I do flashy funk too. After all, he *had* bought that bizarre painting, who knew where his tastes might lie?

As Dr. Morgan's glance crawled over me, I felt nothing sexual in his stare. Like last night, he gave me the impression he was merely appraising the dollar value of my attire. Creepy. And I was about to enter an empty house with him? I gave a mental shrug. Simon knew I'd be meeting Dr. Morgan this morning so that was a safety valve of sorts. Besides, the man was a well-respected physician. Creepy didn't mean dangerous, did it?

I held up the briefcase. "Your friend's?"

"Yes, thank you." He took it from me, and with his

free hand jabbed a finger at the house. "Shall we? I only set aside an hour for this."

No apology for being a half hour late? Reining in my irritation, I followed him to the front door. Anger didn't pay well. *Be charming,* I muttered to myself, *even if it kills you.*

He coded off the electronic security locks and held open one of the double doors. His frown disappeared, and a smile flitted across his face. Unexpected as a flash of sun at midnight, it startled me. But I was in for another shock. I stepped inside, walked through the foyer into the great room and gasped.

"The house is full of art!" I said, whirling around to face him.

"I wanted to surprise you," he said.

He had, all right. In the bare white interior, a row of stunning oil paintings was propped against the walls. I stood in the center of the empty, echoing space and stared at them in amazement. Eight in all, they ranged from a smallish Jim Dine, a mere two feet by four, to a monumental Rosenquist. At nine by twelve, through sheer size alone it ruled the room.

Dr. Jones walked up to the massive abstract, studying it as though it were a beautiful woman—with lust glowing in his eyes. Then he turned to me. "I had to have the Rosenquist. I couldn't resist. The color is exactly right for the house."

Shades of blue, pierced with thunderbolts of silver and black, shot across the canvas.

"Which color is right?" I asked.

"The blue. It's my favorite color in the world."

Blue for a post-modernist structure? This was a house on the cutting edge, and it called for cutting edge colors to play up the form. "Blue as an accent, perhaps, but—"

"Blue," he said, his eyes piercing mine with the sharpness of a scalpel, "is the only possible color. Period. End of story. Design around that premise, Ms. Dunne, or don't design at all."

Of course he liked blue. Shame all over me. I had forgotten the principles of my design bible—color dynamics. Blue was the coldest shade in the spectrum. No wonder he adored it.

"Blue it is," I said.

"Yes, blue it will be. I have a copy of the architect's plans for you. And these photographs from the gallery." Dr. Jones pulled an envelope from his breast pocket and held it out. "I thought photographs of the art would help you select the palette for the rooms."

My defection apparently forgiven, he favored me with a smile as I flipped through the snapshots.

I didn't smile back. "No, I'm afraid they're of no help. They distort the colors in the paintings."

His gemlike eyes widened at being contradicted, but I had to hold my own. Once I started playing obedient nurse to his commanding doctor, I might as well flush my credibility down the toilet. He'd won the blue round. Now I had to win one. Either that or walk off the project, a luxury common sense told me Deva Dunne Interiors couldn't afford.

"I need to match swatches to the paintings themselves. That's the only method that results in perfection, Dr. Jones."

"Call me Morgan," he said, "and, if I may, I'll call you Deva." He held up a warning finger. "Remember, keep blue in mind."

"How could I forget…Morgan?"

He waved a dismissive hand, as if my words were gnats dive-bombing his nose. "I want the blue inter-preted with sophistication. Do you understand?"

"Yes, I believe I do. Subliminal. There, but not there."

"Good girl." He actually patted my arm. "Now come, I'll show you the rest of the house. Let's start with the master suite."

When we reached a ballroom-sized bedroom, he said, "I want this room luxurious. When the lights go on in the evening, everything must be bathed in a lu-minous glow." He pinned me with his eyes. "Tender-ness, softness, is what I'm after."

I nodded. "Now that I have a better idea of—"

He cut me off. "Put in several levels of lighting. Sconces, chandeliers and muted lamp light on the bed-side tables. The wall color is to be the most delicate blue-gray you can find, and make it shimmer. As I said, softly."

I couldn't believe what I was hearing. *This* from the Ice Man? Maybe I had him pegged all wrong. Maybe he hid his passion from view, but like a beating heart, it pulsed steadily out of sight. For what Dr. Jones wanted was a bedroom oozing sex. The kind of fantasy room that would cause a woman to strip off her clothes, stretch out on a satin sheet, spread her hair like a cur-tain over the pillows and wait…

I took notes as we toured, my handwriting deterio-rating into pictographs as Morgan spewed out demands faster and faster. He trashed a few of my ideas but re-tained most. Then, when it came to the placement of the Sizov nude, I won another round.

"It belongs in the kitchen," I said.

He recoiled like I had hit him. "No, absolutely not. It'll be wasted in there."

"It'll be unexpected in there." I tempted him. "It'll be intelligent in there."

He hesitated. "A nude in the kitchen?"

"Positively. She's perfect for the kitchen. Apple cheeks, eyes like purple grapes, nipples like unripe cherries. She's good enough to eat."

I let him gnaw on that one, and he did. A smile creased his face. No word of a lie, the third smile in the past hour.

"Fine," he said, shooting an overly starched cuff, checking his Rolex. "I have five minutes left. I want to see color samples and sketches as soon as possible."

"I'll get on it right away, but with the holidays so close, should we plan to meet after the New Year? January second?"

He nodded. "That'll do." Reaching into a kitchen drawer, he removed a silver ring with two attached keys and gave it to me. "The small one is for the security system."

"Thank you. Before I leave, I think I'll take another look around."

"Take all the time you need." He glanced at his watch again. "I was expecting someone else, but he's late, and I've got to leave. Be sure to turn on the alarm when you're finished."

"Of course."

As we left the kitchen, the chimes sounded. His habitual frown in place, Morgan strode to the foyer and yanked open the front door.

"Do you have my briefcase?" a man asked.

"Yes."

"Christ, I've been worried sick about it."

"Then you should have shown up last night."

"I had good reason not to. Whose Audi is that in the driveway?"

Curious to see the caller, I strolled toward the foyer. The visitor was a middle-aged man with the tanned, fit look of a dedicated sportsman.

"George Farragut, this is Deva Dunne, my interior designer," Morgan said. "George is my financial advisor, Deva. He's known for keeping creative books."

"I'll ignore that crack, Morgan." George peered at me. "Haven't I seen you somewhere?" he asked as I held out my hand. "Ah, now I remember. In the Naples paper. You're the woman who discovered the art theft at the Alexanders."

Not a word about Maria. I lowered my hand. "That's correct. I discovered the theft. I didn't perpetrate it."

"I didn't mean to imply you had," George said, his expression implying plenty.

"You know the Alexanders?" I asked, annoyed enough to question him.

"I'm Trevor's financial advisor."

"Then we have something in common. We both work for him." Borrowing one of Rossi's ruses, I sprung a surprise question. "The Monets are marvelous, aren't they? Which one is your favorite?"

"Sunset at Royan." He stopped short as if he'd said the wrong thing.

"The one that's missing." My turn to insinuate. You could say I do bitchy really well.

Anyway, the smug expression fled George's face. "Yes, so I understand."

"I've never seen the Alexanders' Monets," Morgan said with a shrug. "No matter. My preference is late twentieth century. Here's your precious briefcase,

George." Morgan picked up the Hermès case from the foyer floor and handed it to him.

George clasped it to his chest. "I got in eighteen holes at Pebble Beach, but other than that, the trip to L.A. was damn near a bust without this. The office faxed most of what I needed, but still…"

"You shouldn't have been so forgetful," Morgan told him. "Are you slipping, George?"

This from the man who'd forgotten the same case last night.

Without waiting for an answer, Morgan clasped George's shoulder and drew him toward the front door. "I'm seeing patients this afternoon, and I know you have to get back to work. So let's leave Deva alone to do her thing. Don't forget to turn on the alarm," Morgan said, glancing back and tossing me a wink. I couldn't believe it. A wink from the Ice Man? Would wonders never cease?

And would the list of people who had access to the Alexander mansion keep growing? Rossi had his work cut out for him. Socially prominent, the Alexanders entertained constantly. Scores of people, most of them wealthy and well connected, had been guests in their home and had seen the Monets. But being a guest in the company of others was one thing; having access when the house was empty was another. Except for family and close friends, that would be business people like George and me, and service personnel, the laundress and maids who came in several times a week, floor polishers, window cleaners, and the party temps who helped Maria and Jesus serve invited guests.

Even the gardeners had limited access. On several occasions I saw Maria open the kitchen door and hand bottles of cold water to the men sweating in the sun.

Men like Lee's father. Alone that fatal day, had she opened the door to the wrong person? To someone she recognized? Surely not to Paulo, but to Merle Skimp, perhaps? Or to George Farragut? Or to someone I had never met and would never know?

That was the hell of it, not knowing. But someone did. The killer, who had walked in bold as brass and walked out—to borrow Simon's phrase—as rich as sin.

CHAPTER NINE

On the drive back to Naples, my mind swirled with Morgan's demands. For the sake of both my business and my sanity, I needed to concentrate on his project and stop obsessing about the crimes—to trust in Rossi and the Naples P.D.

To help me get a grip, and to lighten my mood, I decided to use a little psychology on myself and tally all the pluses in my life.

Okay. First and foremost, I passed the one year anniversary of Jack's death without a total meltdown.

After years of dragging my heels, I finally summoned the guts to start my own business.

The Jones project promises to be a shot of fiscal adrenaline.

Last night, a handsome man kissed me breathless.

I passed a slowpoke driver and switched into the high-speed lane. To even the playing field, I'd count the negatives, too.

Though the hurt ebbs away a little each day, each week, each month, the bitter truth is I've lost Jack forever.

Morgan might not like my ideas and refuse to hire me.

A kiss is not a life.

I miss seeing Rossi.

Whoa! Where had that come from? A red light flared

in front of my eyes. I jammed on the brakes. God, I had nearly sped through the stop. What was the matter with me?

A lot.

I was in emotional recovery.

Lonely.

Broke—almost.

I had discovered the theft of a twenty-million-dollar painting and found a woman with a bullet in her head.

Things couldn't be much worse. Then, like some kind of urban miracle, the stop light turned green. An omen. *Go.* I stomped on the gas pedal and my self-pity at the same time.

I was still young and healthy and worked in one of the loveliest towns in America. The sun shone, the palm trees swayed, the hibiscus bloomed. And all this in December.

What did freckles and frizzy hair matter? My B cups were filled out pretty well, and more than one man had mentioned my sensational legs.

I felt better already. The psychologists were right, counting your blessings was a good thing.

Tonight after work, I'd go grocery shopping for Christmas dinner. The Irish Pub would be closed on the holiday, so I'd see if Lee might be free—Paulo, too. For I couldn't believe, didn't want to believe, he was anything but a young man in love.

We'd have roast prime rib, Yorkshire pudding—Jack had loved it—baked stuffed tomatoes, steamed asparagus and two kinds of pie, pecan and pumpkin. I'd lace the whipped cream topping with a little brandy. Cold shrimp for the first course. Some simple cheese snacks with wine before dinner. Not gourmet but not bad.

CHRISTMAS MORNING THE dining table gleamed with Nana's Coalport china and Jack's mother's old Irish silver. Red decorations would war with my peach-colored walls, so, instead, I sent a wired gold ribbon cascading along the center of the table and topped the ribbon with a row of brass angels holding thick ivory candles. As if it were confetti, I sprinkled tiny gold snowflakes over the entire tabletop. When we sat down for dinner, the candlelight would make everything glittery and warm and festive.

I found myself humming. It had been over a year since anyone had come for dinner. What a good feeling to have a semblance of normalcy seep back into my life.

I lit the oven, and soon the roast filled the air with a heavenly aroma. Preparations complete, I stripped off my shorts and Jack's old BU T-shirt. Glamming it up a bit, I shrugged into a snug green crop top and matching wide-leg slacks. The fuzzy angora top played off the silky smooth pants. And the narrow swath of bare midriff added a little sauce to the mix. I dabbed powder on my nose, glossed my mouth with Revlon Peach and, for fun, put on dangly Christmas tree earrings. Swaying on either side of my face, they looked a little dumb, but oh well, "'Tis the season," my image in the bathroom mirror told me. It also said, "Be happy today."

"Good advice. I'll take it," I said out loud.

Promptly at two, the door bell chimed.

Da da da DA.

The opening notes of Beethoven's Fifth, Jack's favorite. Simon and Paulo had arrived together and stood outside on the stone walkway. From their smiles, they were clearly more than ready for a party.

"Come in! Welcome. Merry Christmas."

"Merry Christmas, Deva."

Simon held up two wine bags. "I covered both bases. Red and white." He gave me a discreet peck on the cheek, so discreet I wondered for a second if I had fantasized our encounter in the carport.

While I arranged brie and crackers on a plate, Simon put the red wine on the kitchen counter—we'd have that with dinner—and uncorked the Pinot Grigio.

Paulo asked for a Coke. When we carried our drinks into the living room, I sat where I could watch the clock. In less than an hour, the roast should be done to perfection. Above all, I didn't want to ruin it.

Paulo sipped his soda and glanced around my living room, his gaze lingering on the heirloom pieces I'd inherited from Jack's family, the tall case clock, the sideboard, the Tabriz rug in faded shades of apricot, taupe and muted green. He caught me watching him and grinned sheepishly.

"You have a good eye," I told him.

"You have nice stuff, Mrs. Dunne."

"Deva."

He nodded and sneaked a peek at his watch. I knew what he was thinking. Where *was* she? On the days Lee worked at the shop, she'd never been late. So why late today?

At three, I went out to the kitchen to rescue the roast. Simon followed me with our empty glasses and poured more wine while I transferred the meat to a platter to rest before carving. To keep it warm, I covered it with a sheet of aluminum foil. I was about to skim the pan drippings and start the Yorkshire pudding when the kitchen phone rang. Busy at the stove, I asked, "Would you get that, Simon?"

He answered. A second later, he asked, "*What?* Where are you? Are you at home?" At the edge in his voice, I looked up, alarmed. "Where are you?" he repeated, listening for a long moment before slowly lowering the receiver onto the cradle. "She screamed, then the phone went dead."

"Who?" I asked, knowing.

"That was Lee, wasn't it?" Paulo suddenly appeared in the kitchen, an empty Coke can crushed in his hand.

"Yes," Simon said. "She was crying. I think someone snatched the phone away from her. She said, 'Don't do that.' Next thing the receiver slammed down."

I turned off the stove. We wouldn't be eating dinner anytime soon. "Where is she?"

"She didn't have a chance to say, only that she's not at home."

"Someone's hurting her." Paulo looked like his world had shattered into a million pieces. "We have to do something."

"I'll call the police," I said, reaching for the phone.

"It's Christmas Day." Paulo raised his arms then dropped them to his sides. "They'll think she's partying or something."

"True." Simon blew out a breath. "It takes at least twenty-four hours for any action on a missing person. And we're not even sure she's missing…though she did say she wasn't at home." He paced around my small kitchen. That's when I knew he was as upset as Paulo.

"There is one other thing we can do," I said.

"What?" they asked in unison.

"Call Lieutenant Rossi."

Paulo looked at me with wide, scared eyes. "The lieutenant who questioned everybody at the Alexanders?"

"Yes."

"He's a *homicide* detective." Paulo looked ready to weep.

"Don't jump to conclusions, son," Simon said. "Lee's very much alive."

"Call him." Paulo's voice broke. "Call him now."

"I have his home phone number," I said. Ignoring Simon's raised eyebrow, I dug the slip of paper Rossi had given me out of my purse and dialed his number, hoping to God he'd answer.

He picked up on the first ring.

"Lieutenant Rossi, this is Deva Dunne."

"I've been thinking about you, too," he said.

"This is serious, Lieutenant."

"You wouldn't have called otherwise, Mrs. D," he said, unflappable as ever, giving nothing away.

"I need your help."

When I finished telling him about Lee's call, he asked, "Have you notified the station?"

"No. Just you."

A pause. I knew detectives weren't first responders. This was a violation of protocol. He could well refuse to get involved, especially after his chief had warned him about even a hint of impropriety. But all he said was, "I'll take my pizza out of the oven and be right over."

While we waited for Rossi, the three of us huddled in the kitchen, staring at the phone, willing it to ring again, but it didn't. Simon and I slumped in the chairs by the table. Paulo stood at the kitchen sliders looking out at the palm trees waving in the bright Christmas sun. For once, I felt sure his keen artist's eyes were seeing nothing. Only Lee's face streaked with tears. And fear.

When the chimes sounded, we all hurried into the living room. Rossi nodded but wasted no time in greetings. "Tell me what you know about the girl. For starters, where does she live?"

"In a room on Third Avenue South," I said.

"She said she wasn't there," Simon told him.

"Any boyfriends?"

"No," Paulo said. "No boyfriends." His firm tone left no room for argument.

Rossi shot him a keen look. "How about enemies?"

"Absolutely not. If you'd met her—"

"She's afraid of her father, though," I said.

Rossi switched his attention from Paulo to me.

"He works for Gro Green Gardeners. Merle Skimp's his name. He was working outside the Alexander house the day I contacted 911."

"I've talked to Merle," Rossi said, his jaw tightening.

"Merle?" Paulo exclaimed. "I know him. I've seen him there. He's Lee's father? Oh God." Paulo sank onto Nana's couch. "He hates me."

We all turned to him. "Why?" I asked.

He shrugged. "Isn't it obvious?"

"You're acquainted with Skimp's daughter?" Rossi asked.

Paulo nodded then stared down at his hands clenched in his lap.

"Has her father seen you together?"

"I don't know. It's possible. She works at the Irish Pub, and lately I've been walking her home when her shift ends. It's late for her to be out alone."

Simon looked across at me. Our glances tangled, caught up in the same thought.

"Since she told you she wasn't home, we'll start with the father," Rossi said. "I'm going out to use the car radio. I'll be back."

We waited without speaking. I was worried sick about Lee, but my heart went out to Paulo, too. He sat on the sofa, his shoulders sagging, his hands dangling between his knees. I knew without being told that

Merle's unearned hatred wasn't the first ill will Paulo had encountered in his young life.

After a few minutes that felt like an age, Rossi strode back in. "I have the address of a Merle Skimp in East Naples, off Rattlesnake Road. I'm officially off duty, but I'll be happy to pay a friendly social call on Mr. Skimp. If the girl's not there, we'll make a formal report at the station. But in light of what you told me, Mrs. D, this is worth a try." He met Paulo's panic-stricken eyes. "You want to ride with me?"

Paulo leaped off the couch.

"I'm coming, too," I said.

"Deva and I will follow you, Lieutenant," Simon told him.

Rossi darted a hooded glance my way, then nodded. "Let's go."

Christmas Day traffic was light, and within twenty minutes, we were outside a barrackslike condominium building that must have held a couple of hundred units. In the parking lot, Simon parked his BMW next to Rossi's beat-up Mustang.

"He's on the first floor," Rossi said. "On the end. Don't stand in front of the door," he warned as we reached Skimp's unit.

Pressing hard, Rossi ground his thumb on the bell. Shrill and clear, a buzzer pierced the air. No answer. He lifted off his thumb and pressed a second time. Still no answer. Using the flat of his hand, he pounded on the door.

"Open up, police."

Again he buzzed. Nothing. His hand was raised, ready to attack the door again when it squeaked open as far as the safety chain allowed. Merle Skimp's thin, worn face peered through the slit.

"What's all this noise?"

"Lieutenant Rossi. Naples Police." Off duty or not, Rossi flashed his badge. "We're looking for a Miss Lee Skimp."

Merle squinted at the badge. "What do you want with her? She's done no wrong."

"Can we come in and talk to you?"

"I've got nothing to say to the police." Merle broke the word into two syllables—*po-lice*.

"I have a few questions, Mr. Skimp. A short while ago, your daughter placed a distress call. We have reason to believe she may have been kidnapped."

"Kidnapped?" Merle snorted. "You can't kidnap your own kin."

"She's here, then?" Paulo asked, his voice rising.

Merle peered at him through the narrow opening. "What's it to you?"

"Remember me, Merle?" Paulo asked. "From the Alexanders? The big place on Gordon Drive?"

"Yeah, I remember you, all right. Stay away from my gal, you hear. I don't want her consortin' with the likes of you."

"Where is she, Merle?"

"None of your business, Blackie."

Ignoring his warning, Paulo shoved his foot in the opening and cupped his hands around his mouth. "Lee! Lee, are you in there?"

"I'm here, Paulo. I'm in here!" Lee's voice, muffled but unmistakable.

Before Merle could react, Paulo leaned on the door and, pressing against it with the flat of both hands, he raised his knee then slammed his foot forward. The safety chain snapped like a broken thread. The door banged open, knocking Merle to the floor.

In a flash, Paulo dashed inside. "Lee, where are you?"

"Here! I'm in here."

He raced to the sound of her voice. Tossing aside a chair that had been shoved under a bedroom doorknob, he twisted the handle, and she ran out, straight into his arms. He wrapped her in an embrace that said she was the one gift he'd always longed to have—for Christmas and every day. As they clung together, he bent down to brush a kiss on her hair.

"Get your hands off her," Merle shouted, scrambling to his feet. "She's not for the likes of you." Swift as a ferret, he darted forward and grasped Lee around the waist, his surprise move wrenching her out of Paulo's arms. "Your granddaddy's from Alabama. And *his* granddaddy fought for the Rebs. What would they say, seein' you so shameless, in the arms of this n—"

"Don't you dare. Don't you dare!" Lee shouted, raising her voice to her daddy for what I suspected was the first time in her life.

"This is my home, gal. You remember that." Merle waved an accusing finger at each of us in turn. "Breakin' and enterin' without a search warrant. That's a criminal offense. I intend to prosecute all of you. That includes you, lady." His finger lingered in front of my face. "This ain't the first time we've tangled. As for you," he said, a finger under Rossi's nose, "I'm reportin' you. I'll have your badge."

"You're within your rights, Mr. Skimp," Rossi said coolly, not a single one of his feathers ruffled. He turned and smiled at Lee. "I'm glad we found you well, Miss Skimp. Would you care for a ride back to town?"

Clinging to Paulo's arm, Lee nodded.

"Before we leave, I have something to say to you,

Mr. Skimp." Silent until now, Simon stepped forward. At the quiet control in his voice, Merle took a hasty step backward. "I happen to be an attorney as well as a witness to this…ah…incident. Lieutenant Rossi did not break in. When this man," Simon nodded at Paulo, "heard the victim cry for help, he came to her rescue. If necessary, I will testify to that in any court in the land. So pursue this beyond today and your ass is mine. Not that I want it, Merle," he added dryly.

"You got no right—" Merle began.

"Daddy," Lee said, tears running down her face, but before she could utter another word, sobs overtook her.

"I wouldn't hurt you, gal. You know that," Merle said, not looking as if he understood how much he already had. His pinched, sun-baked face bore the signs of a lifetime of hard work, yet glancing about the neat but shabby condo, I realized he hadn't profited much from his labors. I would have felt sorry for the guy, except for the sight of Lee leaning against the kitchen sink, sobbing into her hands, her shoulders shuddering. Paulo hovered close by, ready to catch her should she fall, but plainly not knowing what else to do other than sweep her back into his arms.

I found a tissue packet in my purse, pulled out five or six and pressed them into her fingers. She wiped her eyes, her sobs subsiding into quiet tears.

"I'm so ashamed, Daddy. And on Christmas Day. Momma wouldn't have wanted this."

"Your momma was a good, pure woman. She wouldn't have wanted you keepin' company with *that!*" He pointed a finger at Paulo.

Her tears dried up in that instant, and I could see her spine stiffen. "You're my father, and the Bible says to honor you. But you surely make it hard for me, Daddy."

Her eyes luminous with tears, she looked up at Paulo. "I want to leave now."

"Stay away from your daughter, Mr. Skimp," Rossi ordered. "When she's ready, she'll get in touch with you. Don't contact her before then. If I hear there's a problem, I'll nail you. Understood?"

Merle nodded, the sag of defeat in his lowered shoulders.

"I'll call you, Daddy," Lee said softly. "I promise. But I won't come out here ever again."

His glance focused on the linoleum floor, Merle didn't respond as she hurried past him.

In the parking lot, I called to Rossi as he was about to get into the Mustang. "Did you eat that pizza?"

"No, it's waiting patiently for me, Mrs. D."

"How many have you had this week?"

He shrugged. "I lost count."

"That's what I thought. Well, this is a holiday and you're off duty—after performing an act of mercy."

He had a quizzical expression on his face like he didn't know where this was heading.

"So...you think the chief would mind if you joined us for Christmas dinner? Prime rib. Yorkshire pudding. Two kinds of pie. Brandy sauce."

"What chief?" he said, grinning from ear to ear.

CHAPTER TEN

BACK AT SURFSIDE, striving for a little holiday atmosphere, I lit my Christmas candles and poured drinks for the men. A beer for Rossi, a Coke for Paulo, a glass of the Pinot Grigio for Simon.

Lee brought a cheese tray and a bowl of cold shrimp into the living room, set them on the coffee table, then joined me in the kitchen while I surveyed my wreck of a dinner. I told myself that in the nearly two hours since we'd been gone, the roast hadn't morphed from a Julia Child centerfold to roadkill. But looking at the meat sitting in its congealing juices, I had trouble staying positive about it.

Okay, Plan B.

"I'm bagging the Yorkshire pudding," I said to Lee. "Too fussy. Too time consuming. You like potatoes?" I peered at her, standing there pale and deeply troubled in her FGCU T-shirt and jeans.

"Sometimes." She sounded unsure. About potatoes, probably. About her future, for a certainty.

I opened the fridge and removed some Idahos from the vegetable bin. "If you want to tell me what happened," I said, "I can listen while I cook. I'll scrub these, nuke them for six minutes then put them in the oven with the roast."

"No potato for me, Deva, if y'all don't mind."

"Not for me, either," I said staring at the roast with distaste. "Maybe we should just have pie."

She gave me a halfhearted smile and sank onto a chair at the kitchen table. "It all started out just fine. Daddy picked me up yesterday so we could spend Christmas Eve together. I cooked supper for us and all, and we talked about my momma, how much we miss her. Then I made a mistake."

The Idahos scrubbed clean, I popped them in the micro and set the timer. "What did you do?"

"I told him how I felt about Paulo."

"Oh, I see." I wiped my hands on a kitchen towel and poured us both a glass of wine. Lee was about to refuse but I said, "Consider it medicinal. Under the circumstances."

She treated me to another wobbly smile and took a sip. "Nice."

"So you told Daddy…"

"He went crazy, Deva. Plumb crazy. Started raving like a madman. I calmed him down by saying nothing had happened." Lee's pale face turned pink. "Nothing has," she murmured with a quick glance out to the living room. "So the rest of the night was fine. Then today when I said I had to leave to come here, he started up again. That's when I called y'all, but he grabbed the phone and forced me into the bedroom. I was about to climb out the window when I heard Paulo's voice."

Thoughts of my own father, of how pleased he had been when I told him about Jack, flooded my mind. What a shame Lee wouldn't have a similar happy memory. "Your daddy needs to understand you're a grown woman now," I said as gently as I could.

Lee placed her glass on the table. Twirling the stem between her fingers, she stared at it as she spoke. "I'm not sure he ever will. Until he does, I have no Daddy." She sipped the wine. "It'll be better that way," she added, but from the pain in her eyes I could tell she didn't mean it.

"Be careful at night walking home from work."

She nodded. "When Paulo can't meet me, I'll get a ride home with Brad, the pub manager."

"Good." I doubted Merle would try messing with Brad again.

I lifted the meat off the platter and put it back into the roaster. No question, it would be overdone, but overdone would be better than room temperature. Though not by much. When the Idahos were nuked, I tucked them in the oven along with the meat and a foil-wrapped loaf of garlic bread. The tomatoes and asparagus would have to take their turn in the micro. Plan B had its flaws.

Simon sauntered into the kitchen. "I'm going upstairs for another bottle of the Pinot. Won't be a minute." He glanced from Lee to me then back again. "Girl talk?"

I nodded.

"Rossi wants another beer. I'll get it for him." Simon opened my fridge like he owned it, removed a can of Bud and disappeared from the kitchen.

"The food's under control for now. Let's join the men," I said.

"Gracious, I'm forgetting all the manners Momma taught me," Lee said, jumping up and following me into the living room.

I was eager to get back to Rossi. To see if he'd discuss the case. At least I told myself that was the reason. When we entered the living room, Paulo leaped to his feet, his eyes shining on Lee. Rossi? He remained sprawled at his ease in a club chair, looking perfectly at home. He raised his beer can in a silent salute but didn't say a word about the case. Or anything else, for that matter. Which, to tell the truth, was about what I expected.

Anyway, Simon returned with more wine and shortly thereafter, Lee helped me serve dinner. The meat had the texture of Goodyear rubber, but Simon and Rossi both had seconds of everything. Paulo ate very little, throughout dinner hardly tearing his gaze from Lee sitting across from him.

As we lingered over dessert, she said, "I want to thank y'all for what you did today, coming for me and everything. And for this beautiful dinner, Deva, that almost got ruint. But I have to tell you something y'all don't know." She drew in a deep breath as if talking about the "something" wouldn't be easy. "My daddy's a good man. My momma, she was sick for years, and he took mighty fine care of her. It cost him near every penny he had, but he didn't complain. Not once. So I owe him for that. For other things, too." She upped her chin, as if defying herself to go on. "I'm all he has left, but he really doesn't have me anymore. So I worry about him." Her voice faltering, she looked down at her lap. "There's more to Daddy than what he showed today."

Unbidden, a thought popped into my head. If Merle Skimp had spent everything he'd worked for on medical bills, would he—out of desperation—have dared steal the Monet? Watching Lee make a case for her daddy's goodness, I found it hard to continue the thought, yet it refused to go away.

When I glanced across at Rossi to try to guess what he might be thinking, he winked and picked up his fork. He had another piece of pumpkin pie to deal with. I should know by now that Rossi never gave anything away.

One by one, the candles guttered in the angel holders and died. I was about to light some lamps when Paulo rose from the table and came over to kiss me on the cheek. "Thanks, Deva. That was delicious."

Lee looked up at him, all limpid, inquiring eyes. "You're leaving?"

"Yes." Avoiding the plea in her voice, Paulo turned to Rossi. "Lieutenant, will you take Lee home?"

"My pleasure," Rossi said, smooth as silk.

"But Paulo..." Lee whispered his name like a prayer.

"I have to get back," he said, and with a little bow to all of us, he left, taking Christmas with him.

"He's ashamed of me." Lee sank against her chair back. "I'm white trash, and he knows it."

"Not so, Lee," Simon said. "You need to look deeper."

"You can't go any deeper than your family," she said, shaking her head. "You sprang from them. They made you what you are. Who you are."

Simon swallowed a forkful of brandied whipped cream. "Exactly. Think about it. Paulo may feel the same way about his own folks."

Lee stared at him, thoughtful and wide eyed. "You think that's what's troubling him?"

"Could be. He might be seeing himself through your father's eyes."

"Daddy's still fighting that war, isn't he?"

"Most likely," Simon said quietly. "Problem is, the battle's just beginning for Paulo."

"For me, too," Lee said, picking up her fork and polishing off her pie.

A steel magnolia.

Rossi pushed his empty dessert plate back from the edge of the table. "Mrs. D, that was the best meal I've had in weeks. No, make that months. I owe you one. And now, I think I'd better check my calls and get this young lady home. So—" he stood, "—if you'll excuse me, I'll be on my way."

He offered his hand to Simon, who grasped it. They didn't exactly Indian wrestle, just hand clasped, *mano a mano*.

Despite her distress, Lee looked over at me and grinned.

I shook my head, and her grin got wider. What was she signaling? The two men were vying for me? No way. I couldn't believe it, but I admit I enjoyed considering the possibility.

The macho handshake over, Rossi walked around the table to say goodbye to me. Did I have a kiss coming? Maybe a peck on the cheek? No. Just a quick smile— and a single finger secretly stroking my palm. "You made my Christmas, Mrs. D," he said in his best crime-busting voice.

Did he know his surreptitious signal had just sent my blood pressure soaring? No doubt. Nothing escaped Rossi.

Lee scooped up her backpack, hugged me tight, then with a "See y'all Sunday at the shop, Deva," she left with Rossi.

"Alone at last." Simon wore his biggest smile of the day. Definitely the biggest one since I'd invited Rossi for dinner. "How about a nightcap?"

"Sounds good, but first the dishes, okay?"

"Let me help."

Together we cleared the dining room table and loaded the dishwasher. After setting the roasting pan in the sink to soak clean, I found a bottle of Grand Marnier lurking behind a box of cornflakes. Simon poured us each a double thimbleful, and we carried our glasses into the living room. With a grateful sigh, I collapsed into a club chair's down cushions. It had been a long day.

Simon put his Grand Marnier on the coffee table. "Be right back. There's something for you in the bottom of that wine bag."

He returned a moment later. "For you," he said.

I looked up. Nestled in the palm of Simon's outstretched hand was a box in that unmistakable shade of Tiffany blue.

A tiny blue Tiffany box.

My mouth fell open. *Oh God, it's a ring.*

My heart began a rumba, pounding away as if I had a mariachi band in my chest.

I didn't want a ring. I didn't want a commitment. I didn't want a new love.

I didn't?

Did I want to go through life alone? A widow forever? Sleeping alone? Eating alone? No one caring if I lived or died? All potent reasons to marry again, but…

Fingers trembling, I undid the white bow. The ribbon rippled to my lap. I glanced over at Simon perched on the edge of Nana's couch, an expectant gleam in his eyes. What about the most important reason to say 'yes'? What about love?

"Go on, open it," he urged with a smile.

I heaved a sigh. *A ring, egads.* While I didn't want to erase the happy smile from Simon's face, I didn't know if I even wanted to go out with him. Never mind accepting a ring.

Removing the blue lid with care as if a joke box snake might leap out and bite me, I said, "Tiffany boxes are so exciting. Every woman loves them."

"You're not every woman, Deva. Far from it."

The rumba revved up a notch. Once I opened his gift, our relationship would change forever. We'd go from being friends to lovers…or enemies.

Trapped by Tiffany's, with no way out, I reached inside and lifted out the inner box. In one swift move, I pulled off its lush velvet cover. And gasped.

"A pendant! It's beautiful!"

"It's a Paloma Picasso," he said.

Fashioned of gold, spare yet intricate, retro yet new, the design was absolutely gorgeous. I loved it.

Relief like an exotic drug swept through my veins. I leaped up and, box in hand, threw my arms around Simon and kissed him. He swept me into a body hug and repeated his stellar performance of the evening in the carport. No question, the man had talented lips.

When we came up for air, he asked, "Does this mean I'm invited?"

I stared at him, blank faced. Though I knew, I asked anyway. "Invited to what?"

"To stay the night."

I could have kicked myself. Like a teenaged tease, I'd sent the wrong vibes. Now what?

Wriggling free of Simon's embrace, I stood, tugging his hand until he stood, too.

"Toward the bedroom?" he asked, one eyebrow arched hopefully.

"Toward the door," I said, trying out my playful turndown voice. "With an apology. The pendant was such a thrill I got carried away."

"But obviously not to the moon." He let me lead him toward the door, didn't complain, didn't try to change my mind. His lack of protest lessened my guilt. Wasn't he supposed to sweep me off my feet? Carry me up the steps of Tara? Or at least get pissed? *Nada.* Not even looking annoyed, he touched a finger to his forehead in mock salute and left with, "Thanks for everything, Deva. Be in touch soon."

Humph. I locked the front door and flicked off the living room lights. At least Christmas with all its angst was over.

And if my love life was over, too, whose fault was that?

CHAPTER ELEVEN

THE NEXT MORNING I tossed together a sandwich of left-over roast beef on leftover rye, grabbed a can of Diet Coke from the fridge and got to the shop an hour early. The day after Christmas traditionally brought out the bargain shoppers, and I wanted to be ready for them.

I planned to collect all the holiday items: the silk centerpieces, the needlepoint pillows with the clever mottos—"He knows where you've been sleeping"— the mercury glass Santas, the red and green dessert plates—everything seasonal—and arrange them on the two skirted tables nearest the entrance with a big white 50% off sign.

At eight-thirty I was about halfway through the re-arranging when the front door knob rattled. I looked up to see a big-hipped middle-aged woman banging on the window with the palm of her hand. The shop lights were on, but the closed sign leaned against the glass. Not ready to open up, I waved, pointed at my watch, and kept on with what I was doing. Another bang on the glass. Louder this time. Then she rattled the door handle several more times.

Can't the woman read?

A bargain hunter with a vengeance, she pressed her face to the window, cupped the sides of her cheeks with her hands and peered in. When she saw me look her way, she raised an arm and waggled her fingers, beckoning me toward her.

I strode over to the window, miming, "We open at nine."

Red-faced, she shouted, "Do you know who I am?"

Annoyed, I turned away without answering. I was a shopkeeper, not a slave.

In a voice shrill enough to shatter glass, she yelled, "I'm Mrs. Morgan Jones!"

That got my attention. I whirled around. The Great One had a *wife?* Why, he'd never let on. Didn't wear a wedding band, either. I'd assumed he was a bachelor.

Whatever this woman had to say, I wanted to hear. I unlocked the door and let Mrs. Jones inside the shop.

"Are you Deva Dunne, the decorator?" She eyed me up and down, her glance lingering on the Christmas tree earrings. I knew they were dumb, but I was trying to create a mood here.

"I'm Deva Dunne, the designer." I spoke in my iciest Boston voice. This was a woman I could learn to dislike, and it wouldn't even take one lesson.

"Well, I'm Jessica Jones, Morgan's wife."

"Yes?"

She obviously wanted something from me, but whatever it was, she'd have to work for it.

Still red-faced, she flung her arms akimbo, sending her outsized Ferragamo tote banging against one ample hip. "Is that all you have to say?"

"As you can see, Mrs. Jones, I'm busy." I put down a mercury glass snowman. "But I can spare a few minutes. How may I help you?"

"I want to know what's going on."

"What do you mean? Exactly?"

She rummaged around in the Ferragamo, pulled out

my card and plunked it on the sales table. "This was in Morgan's blue serge suit. With your home phone number on the back."

I picked up the card. "Yes, I gave this to Dr. Jones. My clients sometimes need to contact me outside of shop hours."

Her face went from beet red to bedsheet white so fast I thought she'd faint.

"Would you like a seat, Mrs. Jones?"

"Of course not," she snapped. "What I'd *like* is to know what your card...with your personal number on it...was doing in my husband's pants."

That was when I knew I was in trouble. "You need to ask your husband that question."

A big-boned woman packing thirty or forty extra pounds, she took a step forward. I took one backward.

"I demand an answer," she said, moving forward with the relentlessness of a Sherman tank.

"Then talk to your husband. I can't reveal—"

"Are you two having an affair?"

"*What?* Absolutely not. I'm designing the interior of his new house."

Her shoulders slumped, sending the Ferragamo sliding down her arm. "Shit! I was hoping he was having an affair."

Was she serious? My God, that was the last thing in the world I'd ever hope Jack was having.

Without further ado, she plopped onto a zebra-print settee, set the tote on the floor, and crossed her feet at the ankles. I wondered if her legs were too chunky to cross at the knee. Whatever. She obviously had no intention of moving until she found out what she wanted to know.

I glanced at my watch. Ten to nine and I'd only half

finished setting up the sales displays. The Christmas cookies I kept in a small dorm fridge in the storeroom hadn't been set out yet, either. But one look at Mrs. Jones's determined expression, and I knew the fastest way to rid myself of the woman was to tell her the truth. I pulled up a gold Chiavari chair and sat facing her.

"What do you need to know, Mrs. Jones?"

"Everything. Begin at the beginning."

If my association with Morgan was a secret, he should have mentioned the fact, yet with a sinking feeling I knew that wouldn't make a bit of difference when he found out about this meeting. And find out, he would.

Beginning with a sigh, I told her about the house in Bonita and what I had been asked to do there. Jessica sat unmoving on the zebra skin. It might have been my imagination, but the more I said, the more she seemed to shrink into herself. Nor did her face get back its beet-colored hue. No question, my news had upset her.

"You knew nothing of this house?" I asked at the end of my tale.

She shook her head. "Morgan doesn't want me to know. When the place is move-in ready, he'll pretend it's a surprise for me. But it isn't for me. It's not even for him…not really…it's for those damned paintings. He promised he wouldn't buy any more. But I guess he can't help himself. It's an obsession. He sees them, falls in love and has to possess them." She dipped into the tote, removed a tissue and swiped at a tear. "When I found your card, I was hoping this time he'd fallen in love with a woman."

"Really?" This was mind-blowing. I had to struggle to keep my mouth from falling open.

"A woman might have been cheaper." She took another swipe at a tear. "You don't know the half of it."

Uh-oh, here it comes. I leaned back on the chair and braced myself for the familiar client-to-designer spilling of guts. Or a version thereof—Jessica Jones wasn't even a client, for Pete's sake—but she sure acted like she needed to vent. I peeked at my watch. Nine-fifteen.

"Morgan's a cardiac surgeon," she said, "a gifted one. I can't tell you how many people he's pulled from the brink of death. It's no wonder our annual income is in the high six figures—some years seven. And you know what? We don't have a dime. Hardly a cent in savings. Not a single, solid investment." She paused to reach for a fresh tissue and blew her nose. "But I can tell you what we do have. Lots and lots of canvases. We live in an eight-thousand-square-foot house, and we've run out of wall space. So what's the size of this new place? Ten thousand? Twelve?"

"Twelve," I admitted.

"High ceilings. Right?"

Reluctantly, I nodded.

"And he wants the rooms decorated in shades of blue."

I tried for a smile. "You know your man."

"And he knows his bankers. They give him any loan he asks for. Problem is, he forgets they have to be repaid—including this latest extravaganza."

Now what? Would Jessica go home and confront Morgan, tell him I'd confided everything? Betrayed his secret? A secret I didn't even know he had? If so, he'd most likely fire me before I'd even been officially hired.

I leaned forward on the Chiavari until we were eye-to-eye.

"Jessica, you have to tell Morgan we've met and that you know about the house. Either you tell him, or I will." I smoothed my apple green skirt over my thighs.

"Once he knows, I'll offer to resign from the project. That's always better than being fired." The laugh I reached for came out a croak.

Her initial shock over, a little color had seeped into Jessica's broad cheeks. "Working on Morgan's house is important to you?"

I nodded. "The shop's only been open a few weeks. Every sale counts." I stood and moved the gilt chair back behind Lee's bureau plat. "So if you'll excuse me, I have to finish setting up the display."

"Let me help." Jessica heaved to her feet and surveyed my half-arranged bargain table. "Looks like you want to get rid of holiday items."

"It's either that or store them for a year."

"Why don't I go around and collect them? Then you can stay put and do the arranging."

Without waiting for an okay, she went over to a wall shelf and removed two red pillar candles embellished with wax holly. She brought them over to me and went back for two more.

Despite her considerable bulk, Jessica moved efficiently and soon had the two sales tables piled with items I arranged, smaller in front, larger in back. When she'd gone around the shop several times gathering up things, she asked. "What else can I do?"

Nine-thirty. I flipped the Closed sign to Open and unlocked the door. "There are some Christmas cookies in the storeroom fridge. They go on the hunt board against the side wall." I pointed to a Sheffield tray that had belonged to Jack's mother and, needless to say, wasn't for sale. "You can put them on that."

She arranged the cookies in neat rows on the silver tray, fanned some paper napkins to the right and placed a silver dish with my business cards on the left.

Munching on a cookie, she strolled over to the table where I was finishing up. "This is a cute shop, Deva. The displays look great. You'll do well here. You have a knack, I can see that. I'll do well, too. I'm going to divorce that obsessed son of a bitch. Then I'm going to lose fifty pounds and find a guy who hates art."

She grabbed another cookie, picked up her tote, and with a "Ta-ta" let herself out, setting the Yarmouthport sleigh bells jingling joyfully.

"Hey, wait a minute," I called. "Are you telling Morgan or am I?" Too late, her black-clad form disappeared out the door just as a group of three women entered.

By noon, the cookies were all gone, and by five, I'd sold two-thirds of the markdowns. I'd keep the sale going until New Year's Eve, though judging from today, there wouldn't any discounts left by then.

Happily weary, at six I turned the Open sign to Closed, snapped off the lights and sat behind Lee's desk near the entrance. The long shadows cast by the buildings lining Fern Alley darkened as the sun slipped lower. Faint rumbles of thunder echoed in the distance and, overhead, a streak of lightning flashed high across the horizon, silhouetting rooftops against the sky. A soothing, gentle rain splashed lightly on the front window.

I rested my arms on the desk and lowered my head to them. Just a few more days and the holiday season would be over. Thank God. I'd have to dismantle the tree…order some romantic Valentine-themed accessories…and call Morgan Jones. Too bad. I hoped I wouldn't lose his project. It would lift me out of the red ink I was awash in.

Although if what Jessica had said was true—and why would she lie?—his assets were tied up in his art collection. So even if I managed to keep him as a client, I'd have to be careful…request fifty percent upfront for any purchases…that would cover wholesale costs. For added protection, I'd ask him to sign a contract. The standard industry boilerplate. He shouldn't object to a straightforward business arrangement like that. Still, in light of what I'd just heard, I found it strange that Morgan retained George Farragut as his financial planner if he didn't listen to the man.

I raised my head off the desk. Why ponder these details? Most likely the job was lost. I leaned down to massage my foot. Tomorrow I'd wear flats. Standing in heels all day hadn't been smart.

Wait a minute! I let go of my aching foot and sat up straight. George wasn't just Morgan's financial planner, he was also Trevor Alexander's financial planner.

So what? What was I reaching for?

Think. Think.

According to Jessica, all of Morgan's money went to feed his art addiction. He was constantly short of funds. What did that have to do with George Farragut? Nothing. And yet Morgan must know George had access to the Alexanders. That still didn't mean anything. Morgan liked abstract, avant-garde art, not nineteenth-century Impressionism. He wouldn't covet the Monet. Ah, he might sell it, though. If he could get hands on it. A big *if*. But who knew?

I stared across the darkened shop, seeing only shadows. With George Farragut's help, maybe Morgan had somehow gained entrance to the Alexander mansion. Who was to say they weren't in on it together? Aiding and abetting? A thief and a murderer? They could have cut the painting from its frame and fenced it to a private collector. Morgan must have widespread connections in the art world. Valued at twenty million, even on the black market, the Monet would fetch enough to make both men wealthy. And go a long way toward covering the walls of a twelve-thousand-square-foot house with Russian abstracts.

Would Morgan stoop so low? Jessica had called him a gifted healer. Would a man like that murder a woman for any reason under the sun?

Hard to imagine, yet Morgan had deceived his wife, big time. Not exactly a sterling character trait. Agitated about where my thoughts were leading, I kicked off the heels and padded around the unlit shop in bare feet. My theory was an unsubstantiated idea, tantamount to character assassination. So maybe I should just forget about it.

In the dark, my foot struck a table leg. Pain shot up my leg. I yelped and hobbled back to my seat.

On the other hand, someone had killed Maria, a good, decent woman. Anything that might help find her killer, no matter how wacky, should be explored. As botched up as my thinking might be, I owed it to her to call Rossi and let him know what I'd learned— and suspected—about Dr. Jones and George Farragut.

To prove to myself this wasn't personal in any way, I'd contact Rossi at the station, not at home. Though at either location, his voice would come through abrupt and gravelly. Then, when he heard me on the line, there'd be a pause before he'd ask, "What can I do for you, Mrs. D?" I loved those little pauses.

I picked up the desk phone and glanced outside. The Fifth Avenue street lamps had surged on, lifting the alley's gloom a bit. Without warning, a bolt of lightning split the sky. Another wild flash, closer this time. The gentle rain turned vicious and pounded against the glass. The storm was getting nasty. After making the call, I'd head for home.

I'd punched in the first three digits of the NPD number when, with an explosive crash, something heavy struck the window. At the impact, the glass shattered, sending lethal shards spinning throughout the shop.

I screamed. For a split second, a lightning bolt like a streak of fire illuminated the alley, turning night into noon and revealing the rain-soaked figure of a man. Merle Skimp in the flesh.

CHAPTER TWELVE

A HUNK OF concrete as big as my head had landed on the shop floor. So much for Daddy being Mr. Nice Guy. Heart pounding, I looked out through the gaping hole. The alley was empty. But I *had* seen Merle. I was sure of it.

Even in the half light, glass fragments sparkled on the desk top. I fumbled around for my shoes. No telling where the other fragments had landed. They could cut my feet to ribbons. As my toes searched for the shoes, I felt something dripping along my left arm. The sleeve of my green striped shirt was slashed. A shard must have hit me; that was blood leaking onto the desk. My fingers trembled but managed to punch in the NPD number.

A no-nonsense male voice answered. "Naples Police."

"My shop's been vandalized," I said.

"You're calling from 555-8880?"

"That's correct."

"Your name?"

I told the official voice what he needed to know and sat still until the blue cruiser lights came flashing down the alley. The blood had soaked my sleeve to the wrist. I needed a tourniquet but somehow I couldn't think of what to use to staunch the flow. When I got up to open the door and snap on the lights, my head spun, but I clung to the entrance doorjamb. A part of my mind acknowledged that the rain had stopped. A good thing, with that big hole in the front window. I sniffed the air. It smelled fresh and clean, newly washed.

The biggest cop in the world came striding toward me. Officer Batano. Two weeks ago, he'd been the first responder at the Alexanders'. "You're injured, ma'am?"

"My arm."

He gave it a visual scan. "Why don't you come in and sit down? We'll call an ambulance."

"No, that's not necessary, but I will sit."

He helped me to the desk chair. "That arm needs attention."

I sat down heavily, an old woman suddenly. His female partner, a petite brunette, followed him into the shop.

"This here's Officer Hughes," Batano said. "Call for an ambulance," he told her in the same breath. "She's losing blood."

As Officer Hughes worked her cell phone, Batano went behind the counter that held the cash register and packaging supplies. He tore off a length of moiré ribbon, doubled it, came back and tied it around my arm above the gash. "You all right?"

"I think so." I really wasn't sure. I glanced around at my wounded shop. As if sprinkled with ice, it glittered in the light from the overheads.

Batano peered at my face. "You're the woman who found the murder vic on Gordon Drive? Right?"

I nodded.

"And now this?" He pulled his cell phone out of its case. "The lieutenant'll want to know what happened here."

To my relief, he asked for Rossi. I brushed the glass fragments off the desk and laid my head on the top.

"Hang in there, Mrs. Dunne. Help's on the way." That was the last I heard before I tuned out the world.

I WOKE IN the ER with an IV drip flowing into my right arm and Rossi hovering beside it looking distraught. A sight better than a tropical sunrise, it made me smile.

"Mrs. D, what am I going to do with you?" he asked.

I could have told him, but the effort was more than I could muster. "They drugged me," I murmured.

The curtains surrounding my cubicle parted. A tired-looking nurse in hospital greens stepped up to my bed, nodded at Rossi and checked the IV. "We'll be wheeling you into the OR in a few minutes, Mrs. Dunne. We're going to take good care of that arm."

"Is the plastic surgeon here?" Rossi asked her.

Whoa! "What plastic surgeon?" I asked.

"The one I requested," Rossi said.

"He's scrubbing now, Lieutenant," the nurse told him.

I raised my head off the pillow just enough to peer at my arm. It was so swathed in bandages, I couldn't see a thing. But at least the throbbing had stopped.

"Mrs. Dunne lives alone. I want her kept overnight."

Listen to that Rossi, I thought before I drifted away. *He sounds like a husband.*

WELL, AS IT turned out, the underlying muscle tissue in my arm had been damaged, and I'd needed over fifty stitches, from wrist to elbow. Batano's tourniquet had saved me from bleeding to death, and Rossi's plastic surgeon had saved the function and, not incidentally, the appearance of my arm.

"How're you feeling?" Rossi asked when he arrived in my throw-up-green hospital room the next morning.

His stubbled chin and heavy eyes told me he hadn't had much sleep.

"Weren't you wearing that same shirt last night?" I asked him. "I think I remember that beach scene."

He glanced down at one of the stars in his Hawaiian collection, Waikiki and Diamond Head repeated every ten inches. He rubbed a hand across his chin. "Didn't have time to change."

Lifting my injured left arm with my right hand, I moved it to my lap like the dead weight it was and turned in the bed to face him. "Thank you, Lieutenant, for being with me last night. I appreciate your concern more than I can say. But will you answer a question?"

Wariness flooded his hawk eyes. "Yeah…"

"When you insisted on the plastic surgeon, why did the ER staff carry out that order without asking me?"

"You were in no condition to answer."

I evil-eyed him. "Rossi. Come clean."

He cleared his throat. "I signed a form guaranteeing payment for his services."

I rolled back, flat out on the bed. He thought that much of me? For the first time since all this happened, tears leaked out of my eyes.

"Hey, stop that," Rossi ordered. "You've lost enough fluids. I'd have done the same for my sister."

"You have a sister?"

He shifted from one foot to the other. "Well, no."

I let the tears flow. They felt good running down my face, dripping off my chin. "I have excellent health insurance. It was Jack's from BU. Whatever the costs, they should be covered." I mopped my face with the sleeve of my jonny. "Thanks for saving my arm, Rossi. I love you for it."

At my words, his face flushed a deep magenta. What a sight. If I hadn't seen it, I wouldn't have believed it.

"Gotcha!" I said, flipping him a grin.

To cover his confusion, I swear, he bent over and picked up a Deva Dunne Interiors shopping bag—glossy white stock with the logo and handles in deep Boston green. "A change of clothes," he said, "for when you get sprung. Which should be later today, after the surgeon's rounds."

I could feel the grin melting off my face. "How did you get my clothes?"

He cocked an eyebrow.

"You've been in my condo?"

His shrug sent hurricane winds whipping over Waikiki.

I blew out a breath. "Okay, let's see what you brought."

He placed the bag on the bed. With my good arm, I lifted out a lavender tank, a pair of hyacinth slacks, flat sandals and my makeup kit. I left the lacy bra and panties in the bag.

"Good choices?" he asked, back in control again. Despite his fatigue, his eyes sparkled.

"Have you been in my underwear drawers?"

"Let me put it this way, Mrs. D. I know you don't wear cotton granny briefs. No padded bras either."

"You checked. And I'll bet you sniffed everything too. That's disgusting. You know that, Rossi."

He couldn't suppress a grin. "Actually, I accompanied your assistant, Miss Skimp, to the condo. She made the selections while I waited in the living room."

"You had a key?"

He sighed. "We can open any door in town. Remember that and keep your dead bolts on when you're home."

He arched an eyebrow. "I know you don't want any surprise visitors at midnight."

If that was a question, I didn't bother to answer it and glared at him instead.

"That's what I thought." He cleared his throat. "Now, if you're feeling well enough, we need to talk seriously."

"I'm ready whenever you are."

This time, suppressing yet another grin—at least it looked suspiciously like one to me—he sat in the faux leather chair beside the bed. With the two fingers he always used for the job, he extracted a notebook and pencil stub from his shirt pocket and wasted no time getting down to business.

"Last night, you said you saw Merle Skimp in the alley right after the attack. Correct?"

"Yes."

"That alley's pretty dark."

"There was a flash of lightning. It was Merle, all right."

"Did you see him throw the rock?"

"No. Right afterward. Then he disappeared."

"You're sure?"

"I'd swear on a Bible."

Rossi nodded and scribbled in the pad before looking up. "You realize it's your word against his. The allegation will be tough to prove."

"I understand, but what about—"

"Further vandalism?"

I nodded. "Exactly."

Rossi cleared his throat and shifted on the leather chair. "We can't rule that out, of course, but the probability is remote. Batano and I paid a call on Mr. Skimp last night. Batano scared the bejez—he warned Mr. Skimp we'd be watching him day and night from here on in. The police will increase patrols in the shop area also." Rossi lowered his note pad. "That said, I want you to park your car on Fifth Avenue, not in the lot in back of the shop. And close up nights before dark. It's doubtful Skimp would try anything in broad daylight. Above all, be careful. As I've told you before, call the minute you suspect something."

I moved the injured arm back onto the mattress. "The lights were out. He must have thought the shop was empty."

"A sneaky dude, all right, but you understand we can't prosecute him. There's no hard evidence he was the culprit."

"I know. And for Lee's sake I don't want this to escalate. But there's something else you need to know. I was about to call you at the station when Merle shattered the window."

He gave me one of his skeptical here-she-goes-again looks. I ignored it and launched into what I'd learned about Morgan Jones and George Farragut, muffling my guilt as I did so. True, I was ratting on a client and his friend, but Maria's silent form trumped my concern for them. I had to tell Rossi what I believed, however specious my theory might be. Either that or never sleep again.

He took notes with his scrap of a pencil before glancing up. "I'll consider this a confidential lead. We'll see where it takes us." He pocketed the pad and pencil and stood, pushing the chair into a corner. "I've got to get back to work."

"So do I."

"Not so fast."

"What do you mean, not so fast? I have a business to run. One with a gaping hole in the window. God knows what's happened to the inventory, and there were glass shards everywhere. I've got to get over there."

If Rossi hadn't been in the room, I'd have tossed the thin hospital blanket aside. But the short, blue-sprigged jonny hardly reached the top of my thighs.

Rossi paused in the doorway. "Not to worry. It's all been taken care of."

"What do you mean?"

He walked back to the foot of the bed. "A disaster cleanup service came in last night. Got rid of the glass. Boarded the front window." He glanced at his watch. "Lee Skimp should be over there now, letting in the glazier."

"What glazier? What disaster cleanup service?"

"The ones I contacted."

I sank back onto my pillow. "Were you up all night?"

"No," he said. But standing there unshaven, in yesterday's shirt, he sure looked like he'd just lied.

"When this case is over, Rossi…"

"Yeah?" he growled, his heavy eyes brightening.

"Mrs. Dunne," a deep voice boomed from the open doorway, "I'm Dr. Lemoine." A tanned man with the lean physique of a long-distance runner bounced into the room on the balls of his feet. "I operated on your arm last night."

"Doctor, this is—" I began.

Rossi and the surgeon nodded at each other. "We met last night," Rossi said. "And now I'm on my way. Before I leave, there's one other thing, Mrs. D. When you're released, your neighbors Chip and AudreyAnn will be here to take you home."

He had my entire life arranged. Torn between gratitude and irritation, I watched him make a quick exit then concentrated on what Dr. Lemoine had to say: I should retain full use of my arm and have minimal to no scarring.

What irritation? Deep, heartfelt gratitude won out.

"YOU'RE HAVING ITALIAN penicillin for lunch," Chip announced on the way home.

"Which is?"

"Minestrone soup. My mother's recipe. After you eat that, you'll probably want a nap. When you wake up, it's a filet mignon with Chanterelle mushrooms and roasted asparagus." He glanced across the seat. "You need red meat for strength."

I didn't have the heart to tell him I'd had beef for Christmas and a chunk of it still lingered in the fridge. "Chocolate tiramisu for dessert," he added.

"I'll go up a dress size, Chip."

"Just this once," he said. "It'll make you feel better."

Yeah, it would. Further protest died on my lips.

"Thanks to you both for all this inconvenience." I glanced over my shoulder at AudreyAnn in the backseat. Usually dour faced, she was actually smiling into the rearview mirror. She bent forward and ran a finger through the curly hair at Chip's nape. "Tell Deva your big news, honey."

Honey?

He took his eyes off the road to beam at me, his round face lit with a grin.

"The Alexanders want me to be their celebrity chef at the February Wine Festival. Imagine that. Me. Chip Salvatore. A celebrity chef at the biggest social event in Southwest Florida. There'll be fifteen celebrity chefs at fifteen different mansions, and I'll be one of them. We'll each cook for thirty guests. Altogether that's four hundred and fifty philanthropists." Eyes twinkling, he glanced across the seat again. "What do you think of them apples?"

"That's 'wow' news. I'm thrilled for you." A warm, bighearted guy, Chip deserved an ego boost. Somehow, I doubted he'd had many in life. For making him so happy, I owed Ilona a thank you.

"Yeah, I figured you'd be pleased. It's for a good cause, too. Raises millions every year for needy kids. And you made it possible for me, Deva, giving my name to the Alexanders and all." His chins began to wobble.

I hoped he wouldn't cry. "You've earned the honor, Chip. You make a killer lasagna."

"This time, I'm going fancy. No lasagna at a big event like this."

"But everybody loves it."

He shook his head. "Nah, I'll be competing with fourteen giants. My food's gotta stand up to a lot of competition."

"The chefs will be at fifteen different houses, Chip, so you won't really be competing, will you?"

"You don't understand. You know who these guys are?" Chip turned to me again, taking his eyes off the road so long, I gripped the arm rest with my intact hand and braced myself for another trip to the ER.

"No, Chip, I don't…but the road?"

"Oh yeah." He swiveled his attention back to his driving. "They're famous. The cream of the crop. Tony Mantuano from Spiaggia's in Chicago, Obama's favorite restaurant. Emeril, for gosh sakes. Wolfgang Puck." He raised his hands off the wheel. "Everybody!"

"And Chip Salvatore," AudreyAnn chimed in from the backseat.

I sent her a grateful smile over my shoulder. It was the first compliment I'd ever heard her give Chip. It was nice to hear, and when I turned back in my seat, nice to see him grip the wheel again.

"Mrs. Alexander..." Chip cleared his throat and took a quick peek in the rearview mirror, "...Ilona...called last night to tell me the news. She was going to call you next. She wants you to work on the festival, too." His expression did a one-eighty. "But after the publicity you got in this morning's paper, she maybe changed her mind."

CHAPTER THIRTEEN

THE PUNDITS CLAIM there's no such thing as bad publicity, but when I got home and read the newspaper account of last night's attack, I groaned. The *Naples Daily* had plastered Deva Dunne Interiors all over page one, including a photograph of the shattered window and an inset of me leaving the Gordon Drive house the day of Maria's murder.

The headline read Design Shop Vandalized. Owner Injured. They'd even included the shop address. Beneath it, the whole of last night's episode and a recap of the double crime at the Alexanders'. Chip was right. After reading all that, I did need a nap. I'd become notorious and the shop along with me. We were both doomed.

Under Chip's watchful eyes, I ate my soup then went to bed and slept like the dead until five o'clock. The phone woke me. I groped for it with my good hand.

"Deva? How y'all feeling?"

Lee. "Groggy at the moment. Did you have an awful day?"

"No, not at all. That's why I'm calling. People crowded the shop from nine o'clock until just a minute ago. All the sales items sold and a lot of the regular merchandise. Two ladies who want design work left their names and numbers. Oh, and Mrs. Alexander phoned. Something about a wine festival. She said she'd call back." Lee dropped her voice to a conspiratorial whisper. "Officer Batano's here. He's going to escort me to the bank with the proceeds. So I have to go now, but I'll be in tomorrow. Don't worry about a thing, Deva, the shop's doing just fine."

Just fine without me, she meant. I hung up and lay there limp as a discarded dishrag. Nobody needed me for anything…not even to run my own business. I was wallowing in self-pity when a knock sounded.

Gluing on a happy face, I called, "Come in."

AudreyAnn peeked around the edge of the door, stern as a cigar store Indian. "You all right?" Not exactly Mother Teresa but she meant well.

"Except for needing a shower, yes."

She eased the door wider. "I'll help you."

Get naked in front of AudreyAnn? Not in this life. I tossed off the covers and sat up, a little lightheaded, on the edge of the bed. "Tell you what. If you'll bring me the plastic sleeve the *Naples Daily* came in, I'll slide it over the bandage. After that, I can manage alone."

A frown creased AudreyAnn's forehead. "You strong enough to stand?"

She really was concerned for me. Severe, no-nonsense AudreyAnn. Who would have guessed?

"It won't take long. Besides, the water will revive me."

"Okay, if you're sure." She found the plastic sleeve and slipped it over my arm. "I'll be in the kitchen with Chip, but I'll leave the bedroom door open a crack in case you need me."

When she left, I shed Jack's old pajama top and stood. As I made my way to the bathroom, the lightheadedness disappeared. In the shower, shielding my left arm from the spray with my body, I let the soft, warm water wash away the hospital odors and the ache in my muscles, along with my brief lapse into self-pity.

Now if only I could rinse away the fear and tension. What a situation I'd been thrust into—my shop vandalized two weeks after I discovered a multimillion-dollar art theft and a murder victim, and now, to top off everything else, as many stitches in my arm as in a Chinese tapestry.

At least I knew who the shop vandal was. But what about the murder and the Monet? The perp could be someone I didn't know, or worse, someone I did. Even someone as obvious as Trevor, though he and Ilona had been in Europe at the time of the robbery. Still, they could have accomplices. I'd seen bank heist movies…

I turned off the water and, wrapped in a towel, sat on the bathroom stool to dry off and think. The possible role of Morgan Jones and George Farragut in all this still bothered me. The connoisseur and the financial analyst. What one didn't know, the other did. Who was to say they hadn't cooked up a plot. And what about Simon? He'd recommended me to the Alexanders in the first place. Funny, I'd never asked him if he'd actually been in the house and seen the Monets. Though he'd mentioned them…and Ilona's good looks. Then there was Merle, the rat fink. And though I hated dwelling on it, whenever the Alexanders had a party, Paulo tended bar.

No, I shook my head. I was being ridiculous. Targeting people I knew when someone I had never even met could have gained entrance. Maria and Jesus might have admitted anyone.

Jesus!

The name lifted me off the stool to my feet. Good God, could Maria's husband have killed her? Could she have caught him in the act of stealing the Monet and protested? A horrible idea. Something else to drop at Rossi's feet. But if I'd come up with that thought, no doubt the police had, too, and with every other half-baked theory I'd hatched. I'd better let them do their work and stick to mine. And God knows, I had enough to do. Even though Lee said the shop had done well today, what would tomorrow bring?

I tossed the towel over a rack and eyed my mirror image. Since Jack's death I was ten pounds lighter, my stomach flatter, my waist narrower. A terrible way to lose weight. With a sigh, I slipped on a billowy lime green caftan and let my hair riot around my head like crazy. It had a mind of its own, and for once I didn't argue with it.

After easing my arm into the sling, I padded out to the living room in bare feet. Uh-oh, company, and me without a bra or panties. Too late. Simon leaped off Nana's sofa and hurried over to kiss me on the cheek. As though I were a piece of Steuben crystal in danger of shattering, he gently led me to the sofa, all the tenderness in the world in his eyes. Since that was more than I could handle at the moment, I glanced away. A gorgeous arrangement of peach-colored roses with apricot hearts sat on the coffee table.

"They're beautiful," I said. "From you?"

He took my hand. "Yes. After I read the paper, I called the hospital, but you'd been discharged. I'm so sorry this happened. If you plan to press charges, let me know. I'm at your service."

If Simon noticed my lack of underwear, he didn't let on. His soft gray eyes never left my face, his hands clung to my fingers.

"No, no charges." I shrugged. "Who would I charge?

I have no idea who vandalized the shop. It makes no sense."

That proved I could lie with the best of them, although Simon's legal eagle eyes narrowed, telling me he was skeptical. Maybe I needed to brush up on my lying skills.

To change the subject, I said, "May I ask you something, Simon?"

"Of course." He smiled. "Pop the question."

"Were you ever in the Alexanders' house?"

"That's a strange one," he replied, his smile fading. "Well?"

"Well what?"

"Were you ever in the Alexanders'? Did you ever see their Monets?"

"Yes, several times, but why the third degree?"

"Oh, just curious. I wondered what you thought of them."

"They looked like money to me. Lots of it."

I laughed. "You're an honest man, Simon." I had always thought he was, but now, my confidence shaken, I wondered. Damn the thief anyway. He'd stolen far more than a multimillion-dollar painting.

The kitchen phone rang, and a moment later, Audrey-Ann came into the living room, the receiver in hand. "A Jessica Jones for you, Deva."

I mimed "thanks" and took the phone. "Hello, Jessica."

"Deva, your housekeeper just told me you're all right. I'm so relieved."

Housekeeper. AudreyAnn would kill her.

"I read about your shop in today's paper and figured you could use some good luck. Well, listen to this. Last night, I informed Morgan of our little tête-à-tête. He's relieved I know about the Bonita house. Best of all, it's paid for, lock, stock and barrel. No mortgage. No loans. No anything. He's been piling up investments for years. Imagine that. He loves his little secrets, don't you know? So not to worry about losing his account. That won't happen."

Jessica chatted on for a few more minutes, obviously relieved. It sure sounded like she had patched up her marriage. I was happy for her and touched that she had reached out to assure me all was well. But as I hung up, I wondered if all really was.

Morgan had kept secrets in the past, could he be keeping another one? Had he accumulated a fortune, or had he stolen one?

AT NINE THE next morning, Simon dropped me off at the shop, promising to pick me up at five. "Earlier if you need me," he said, before hurrying around his BMW to open the passenger door and help me out.

"Next you'll be tossing your cloak over a puddle," I said.

He laughed. "If that's what it takes."

What did it take? I waggled my fingers at him as he drove through the alley. I knew Simon was waiting for me to up our relationship from kissing good-night to staying the night. Truth was, since Jack died, I hadn't made love with anyone…was Simon the one? He was charming and thoughtful and witty and intelligent. Handsome, too, and successful. Still, I wasn't sure. Something more than an injured arm had to be wrong with me. With a sigh, I stepped into the shop.

The disaster crew had performed wonders. Not one shard of broken glass sparkled anywhere, the displays were all neatly arranged, and the sun shone through the new shatterproof window. As soon as I had a free moment, I'd contact a sign painter to reapply the store logo. The shop smelled of cinnamon and spice from the aromatherapy candles I sold, but the pine scent was missing. So was the Christmas tree. Had the hunk of concrete hit it? For the life of me, I couldn't remember.

I heard someone stirring about in the storeroom. "Anybody home?"

Lee popped her head around the open storeroom doorway. "Deva! You're back! I was just getting out the Christmas cookies." She hurried across the shop, arms outstretched, ready to give me a hug, but at the sight of my sling, she stopped and gave me an air kiss instead. "Y'all look fine, Deva. Just fine." She smiled, but her porcelain complexion was ashen against that one and only black dress. "I feel so bad about what happened. Who on earth would do such a crazy-minded thing?"

"I have no idea. But you know what? It showed me how many friends I have. Including you. Thanks for taking such wonderful care of the shop. I'm curious, though, what happened to the Christmas tree?"

"That rock? It plumb knocked the tree to the floor. A lot of those beautiful decorations y'all had hanging on it got broken. I saved the ones I could and told the salvage people to tote the tree away." A worry crease etched her forehead. "I hope that was all right."

"That was perfect."

"The good baubles are in a box out back."

I peered at Lee more closely. Her eyes were red. "Have you been crying?"

She shook her head so vigorously her hair whipped around her face.

"While it's quiet, why don't we sit down for a few minutes?" I asked. "Take your desk chair, and I'll sit here." I sat on a tufted bench beside the bureau plat, cradling my injured arm in my right hand. "I have some good news. A Dr. Morgan Jones wants me to design the interior of his new house. Which means as soon as he signs a contract, I can afford to pay you."

"But—"

I held up my right hand, palm out. "Retroactive from the first day. That's for starters. As soon as business picks up some more, you get a raise."

Her eyes looked suspiciously wet. "That's wonderful, Deva," she said, but her expression didn't match her words.

"There's something else. Off Shoots next door is having a sale. I want you to go there today and buy another dress. Any color you like. Charge it to me."

"But—"

"Nope. No more buts."

She looked down at her hands without speaking.

"Lee? Is anything wrong?"

She shook her head, the motion loosening a tear from each eye.

What a stupid question. The girl was only working two jobs plus struggling with college classes. Worse, she had a control freak for a father...and a love gone awry?

"It's Paulo, isn't it?"

Her head bowed, she said, "I've been phoning him since Christmas, but he isn't returning my calls. I've texted him too, every single hour, but not a word back. And he hasn't given an art class at the Von Liebig or been by the Irish Pub either, not once. I'm so worried. If I knew where he lived, I'd pay him a visit, but I don't." She covered her face with her hands. "Oh Deva, I'll never see him again."

"Oh, yes you will," I said with more assurance than

I felt. "Why don't you give me his phone number and let me try?"

She knew it by heart. As I wrote it on a desk pad, the first customer of the day strolled in, and Lee fled to the back room to dry her tears.

Twice before noon, I found a moment to dial Paulo's number, but got no answer. I left a message each time, avoiding Lee's inquiring glance when I hung up.

By midafternoon, I knew I owed a huge debt of gratitude to the *Naples Daily* for their front page story. The sleigh bells jangled all day long announcing curiosity seekers mainly but a good sprinkling of buying customers as well. We were so busy I don't know what I would have done without Lee. She wrapped purchases, ran the cash register and, during a brief quiet spell, unpacked fresh merchandise to flesh out our depleted tables.

An hour before closing, I shooed her next door to shop for a dress. She left reluctantly; should Paulo return my call, she wanted to be here. But I insisted and, too polite to refuse, she did as I asked. The minute she left, I dialed Rossi at the station.

When he picked up, his voice rough and gravelly, my heart skipped a beat before settling into its usual rhythm, though I should be used to that reaction by now. It happened every time we spoke.

"Lieutenant, this is Deva Dunne."

I kept my voice all business. The call might be monitored. Who knew? There could be a kernel of truth in that old saw, "Just because you're paranoid doesn't mean they're not out to get you."

"I have a favor to ask, Lieutenant."

A pause. "And that is?"

"Lee Skimp and I haven't been able to reach Paulo St. James. Lee's been trying for three days. All we have

is a cell phone number. No address. I was wondering…
could you possibly tell us where he can be located? It's
important."

"You want me to give you Mr. St. James's address…
in other words, violate his privacy?" I could have made
a weapon out of the steel in his voice. "That is not the
function of this office. If you think there's a problem,
call back to the front desk. Ask for Missing Persons."

The dull flat humming in my ear told me he'd hung
up. Rude but right. I shouldn't have bothered him. The
man had his hands full trying to solve a murder and
find an art treasure.

But somehow, I wasn't sorry I'd called him. I'd been
fighting the possibility that something had happened
to Paulo. Every time he looked at Lee, his love for her
came shining through his eyes. So why wasn't he returning her calls? I hoped that Rossi, knowing Paulo
worked for the Alexanders, might be worried enough to
check on him. In fact, the more I thought about it, the
more I was sure he would, and it was only a matter of
time before the phone rang with Paulo on the line. Or a
police officer with bad news darkening the shop door.

By closing time, I hadn't heard a thing.

Just before five, carrying her new cornflower blue
dress in a pink Off Shoots bag, Lee left for home to
change into her Irish Pub uniform. She'd be up until
all hours serving drinks and food and then back in the
shop at nine. A grueling schedule.

"Sleep late in the morning, Lee," I said as she was
leaving. "I'll manage alone until you get here."

She shook her head. "I can't sleep, Deva. See y'all
at nine."

Before I could protest, she left with a little wave and
a shaky smile.

Heeding Rossi's advice, I locked up and turned the window sign to Closed. Faithful as a sunset, Simon pulled up outside my door at five on the dot.

I slid into the BMW's passenger seat with a grateful sigh.

"Tough day?" Simon asked.

"Tough but good." I held up a leatherette bag stuffed with the day's receipts. "Can we swing by the Sun Trust Bank and drop this in?"

"Of course. And then an early dinner?"

I forced myself to tune out the hopeful note in his voice. "The surgery's taken more out of me than I expected, Simon. I need to get home."

Chip had left some minestrone in the fridge. That would be dinner and then early to bed with two aspirin for company.

Simon gave my knee a squeeze. "Our time will come."

Would it? Too tired, suddenly, to reply, or to respond to his warm hand on my leg, I leaned back on the leather head rest without answering. From under half-closed lids, I watched his fingers slip from my knee and return to the wheel.

At my door, Simon gave me a brief kiss. "Good night. Rest well."

Once inside, I kicked off my shoes and padded out to the kitchen to micro the soup. Before I opened the fridge, the doorbell rang. Had Simon returned? I hurried into the living room and peered through the plantation shutters on the front window.

Rossi. He must have news about Paulo.

"You listened to me for once," he said when I flung the door wide.

"Meaning?"

"I drove by the shop. It was locked tighter than a drum. You left at five. As I suggested."

"On the nose, Lieutenant." I peered at him. For some reason, he was showing me a rare sight, his big white teeth. What a change from his attitude on the phone. Paulo must be okay. The knot in my stomach eased.

"How'd you drive with that arm?" Rossi asked, checking me over and frowning.

"Is this a social call?"

"Yes and no. I've still got the chief to consider."

"Then it's a no. So I guess I can't ask you in."

"Yeah, you can," he said, stepping into the foyer and closing the door behind him. "I'm here in response to your inquiry about a Mr. Paulo St. James."

"You found him?"

"That wasn't a problem."

"He's well?"

"Yes. Physically."

"Rossi, do I have to pull those teeth of yours? What happened?"

"Can I sit?"

I slapped my right hand on my hip. "In the six months I've known you, you've smiled once, maybe twice, and now, after sounding like the Ice Man when I called, you're grinning like the Happy Buddha. What did you find out?"

"He's in love with the girl."

I blew out an exasperated breath. "Tell me something I don't know."

"He's Jamaican."

"Keep going."

"She's not."

Heavy as a bag of groceries, my arm in the sling dragged on my shoulder. Waving Rossi to a club chair,

I sat on the sofa and rested my wounded wing on my lap. "Go on."

"That incident Christmas Day with Merle Skimp…"

"Yes?"

"…it made him realize there's a divide between himself and Lee that can never be bridged."

"That's ridiculous."

Rossi shrugged. With his toned torso, always an interesting move to watch. "I'm only the messenger here. He's not afraid for himself. He's afraid of involving Lee in a biracial relationship. Those are his exact words."

"He wants to marry her."

Rossi cleared his throat. "The M-word didn't come up, but, yeah, that'd be my guess."

"Now what?"

"Well, I am off duty, so—"

"That's not what I meant."

Half off his chair, he dropped back into it. "What happens next depends on just one thing. Love, Mrs. D. Love." He looked away as if chagrined by his own admission. "Hey, the Bible tells us love is stronger than death," he added, plowing on. "So, surer than hell, it's stronger than racial prejudice."

I nestled into the sofa. "Why, Rossi, you're an out-and-out romantic. I didn't know you had it in you."

"Sure you did." He showed me those big white teeth again. "You're looking at Cupid here, Mrs. D. The god of love."

Somehow that sounded about right, but Rossi was the last one I'd tell.

He stood. "Since I'm off duty, if it's okay with you, I'll go get something I left in the car. Be right back."

I sat quietly, relieved to know nothing bad had happened to Paulo. As soon as Rossi returned, I'd ask him if Lee knew all was well.

In a minute or two, he sauntered in like he lived here, with a bottle of Chianti and a Leoni's pizza box topped with a bouquet of multicolored flowers from a Publix market. He eyed the exquisite arrangement Simon had sent. "I guess you can't have too many. You want to take these off the pizza box? If you've got a jelly glass, I'll put them in water."

I reached out for the flowers, sniffed the blooms and laid them on the coffee table. "They're beautiful, Rossi. Thank you."

"My pleasure."

"You planning to stay for dinner?"

"That was the general idea." His eyes narrowed as he studied me. "If you're feeling up to it. You look a little pale. The arm hurting?"

"Now that I know Paulo's okay, I'm feeling much better."

"He's more than okay." Rossi looked great when he grinned. It transformed his face, like sun coming over the mountain. "He's been cleared in the Alexander case. So have you."

"Paulo and I are both off the hook? You're sure?"

"Enough said. We're working on all our leads. That's as much as I can tell you. You sounded worried about the kid, and I figure you've had enough tension for a while. Which is why I brought some relaxation with me."

Was he kidding? Rossi was Tension City personified. Just being in the same room with him had my adrenaline surging. Maybe that's why I wasn't tired anymore. Either that or the good news about Paulo had me pumped up.

"Did Paulo call Lee?"

"No."

"Then she doesn't know he's all right."

"Yeah, she does. I called her."

"Did you give her his address?"

"You know better than that."

I ignored the reprimand. "Did you ask him to call her?"

He waggled a finger at me. "I'm the detective. I ask the questions."

"Did you?"

"Of course not. Guys don't ask other guys to do stuff like that."

"Then she hasn't been in contact with him. She's still heartbroken."

"For now, but not for long. That's a Dr. Rossi prediction."

"What makes you so sure?" I found his certainty irritating. Lee's happiness was at stake here.

"The kid's going to crack. They always do."

"Who's 'they'?"

Rossi cocked an eyebrow. "Lovers, Mrs. D. Lovers. Now is it all right with you if I bring the pizza out to the kitchen? My hands are all over grease."

"Sounds delicious." I went to get up off the sofa.

"No, don't move. I'll open the wine and bring you a glass."

"You don't know where the opener is."

He lowered the Chianti onto the coffee table and, balancing the pizza box on the palm of his right hand, he reached into a pants pocket with his left, withdrawing a lethal-looking opener, the kind with a sharp spiral corkscrew. I relaxed back against the cushions. I should have remembered I could rely on Rossi.

"Aren't you afraid you'll castrate yourself walking around with that thing in your pocket?"

He stooped to pick up the wine and glanced over at me. "You wouldn't like that?"

"I'm taking the Fifth."

"That's tantamount to an admission of guilt. What are you hiding, Mrs. D?"

A good question I had no intention of answering. I was hiding the fact that I wished he'd put down the greasy pizza box and come over and kiss me. But all he gave me was a wink. Damn him, he *knew*.

The juices that had dried up when Jack died were liquefying, swirling around inside me, ready to rise and froth and bubble out. Stunned by the suddenness of this realization, I sat without moving a muscle and listened to Rossi slamming kitchen cupboards in his hunt for wineglasses. How could I be feeling what I undeniably was? Rossi was Jack's polar opposite—gruff, terse, irascible, unpolished as the hunk of concrete that had slammed through the shop window...and just as steady as stone, just as strong and constant. I suspected that, hidden within, he harbored a capacity for love that once tapped would sweep both him and some lucky woman away. True though it might be, I wasn't ready for such an emotional tsunami. Not yet. Maybe someday. Maybe never. But I had to admit, in the meanwhile, Rossi had me intrigued.

While I sat there immobile, entranced by thoughts that were turning my face hot, he returned, thrust a glass of Chianti into my hand and plunged the flowers into a glass of water. Then he disappeared for a moment and came back with his own wine in hand. *"Salute!"* he said, sitting on the club chair across from me. "I put the pizza in your oven to warm up."

"I didn't know you could cook."

"Oh, yeah. My specialties are sandwiches, pizza and cold cereal."

I sipped my Chianti, looking across at him with what I hoped were not hot eyes. He sat sipping his wine, looking completely at home, completely in control, one leg crossed casually over the knee of the other. He had no intention of making any moves on me. So why had I even wondered about drowning in a tsunami? To get a kiss out of this guy, I'd have to go after it. For all his he-man posturing, he wouldn't make the first move. That would be up to me. What an insurance policy he'd bought. For once I made my move, there would be no backing down. I kind of liked the idea. But draped with the sling, I was a wounded bird, in no condition to throw my wings around him and pin him to the floor. Or the bed. So for now at least, Paulo and I weren't the only ones who were off the hook.

CHAPTER FOURTEEN

NEEDING TO FLEX my independence muscles, cut arm or
no cut arm, on the third day after surgery, I slipped off
the sling long enough to drive to work.

Shortly before nine, Lee arrived, looking beautiful
in the new blue dress, her eyes faintly shadowed with
fatigue.

"You know Paulo's fine?" I asked.

She nodded and upped her chin. Her bottom lip quivered, and tears threatened at the corners of her eyes. So
he hadn't called her. Before I could mention my conversation with Rossi, a UPS truck clattered along the alley,
screeching to a stop outside the entrance.

From where I stood by the cash register, I could see
the driver stand up from behind the wheel and reach
into the back of the van. He stepped out of the cab carrying a large, flat carton. The dozens of china hearts
and cupids I'd ordered for Valentine's Day couldn't be
packed in a container that size.

After placing the carton on the floor in front of the
cash register, the driver held out a clipboard for my
signature.

I glanced at the shipping label. "It's for you, Lee."

She hurried over to sign for the package, her hands
trembling as she took the pen.

The door had hardly jangled closed behind the UPS

man when she disappeared into the storeroom, returning a moment later with a box cutter in her hand.

"I just have to open this up right now, Deva. I hope y'all understand."

"Absolutely." I couldn't wait either.

Kneeling before the carton, she carefully sliced through the outer cardboard then gently removed the bubble wrap. With something like a sigh, the padding fell away and slipped to the floor.

"Oh, God." Lee's hand darted to her mouth, as she stared at a miracle. Her portrait.

Awestruck, I stared at it, too. Paulo had placed her in the center of the canvas, and the painted glass of the shop window, a glittering frame within a frame, shimmered around her image. On either side of her face, her hair fell in a long golden curtain. Her eyes, as blue as in life, gazed fearlessly into the future. Her lips, parted in anticipation, smiled at all that lay ahead.

Paulo had captured both her beauty and her strength. A young man's masterpiece, it was a poem in paint. A love song.

Lee glanced up at me for the merest of instants, her eyes damp, her chin firm. "Actions speak louder than words, Deva. I don't know what all Paulo said to the lieutenant yesterday, and I don't care. This tells me what he *thinks*. It tells me what he *feels*." She swung her attention back to the portrait. "He loves me. That's all that matters."

A small white envelope had fallen out of the wrapping. I handed the envelope to her, and she removed a slip of paper. She read the message then gave it to me without saying a word.

Lee, This is for you. It was always for you. P.

She scrambled to her feet. "He can't hide from me

forever. He's out there somewhere, and I'll find him. I know I will." She balled her small hands into fists and paced the shop, weaving her way between the skirted tables, brushing against them, setting the fabric rippling. "If only I had me a clue. Lieutenant Rossi wouldn't give out Paulo's address. Said it was against regulations."

"It really is—"

She whirled to a stop in front of me. "Know what I'll do? I'll hire me a private investigator. Yes, ma'am!"

"They're expensive, Lee."

Her eyes clouded. "I'll sell Mama's silver. Daddy left it with my landlady the other night. He's moving back to Alabama and wants me to have it. I hate to see him go, but he's never been happy here. It's for the best."

Merle was leaving? Amen. I'd be glad to have him gone, but why now? And why so far from his beloved daughter? Running from the scene of the crime? Or crimes?

"The silver came from England a long time ago," Lee was saying, and I snapped my attention back to her. "Mama always said it was valuable. If it's all right with y'all, at lunch time, I'll go get it and bring it to that antiques mall."

Her mind made up, she lifted the portrait out of the welter of wrapping paper, gave the canvas a soft kiss and carried it into the storeroom for safekeeping.

I bent over to pick up the debris. My glance fell on the shipping label. *Of course.* An oversight on Paulo's part? Or a Freudian slip? My money was on Freud. Paulo wanted her to find him. "Lee, you don't need to sell your mother's silver. Look at this."

Her face, always pale, flushed pink. "Paulo's address."

"Exactly."

Before she could voice it, I saw the question form in her eyes.

"You want to go to him. Right now."

Unable to speak, she caught her lower lip between her teeth and nodded.

I peered at the label again. "Good heavens, Lee. He lives on Gordon Drive near the Alexanders. Millionaire row."

She took the label from me and studied it as if she were memorizing every word. "He said he lived over a garage. The owners travel a lot and want somebody on the property when they're gone."

"It's not far from here...but too far to walk."

"I'll call me a taxicab." Lee raced over to the service desk, removed her handbag from a lower drawer and pulled out her smartphone. She was about to call the local cab company when I asked, "Do you drive, Lee?"

She didn't glance up. "Yes, ma'am. Daddy taught me how. I had to take Mama for her treatments while he was at work."

"Then forget about a cab. Take my car."

"Your Audi?" She lowered the phone and looked at me, her eyes widening at my offer. "You're sure?"

No, I wasn't. Seeing that glow in her eyes, all my maternal instincts kicked in. "I'm sure you'll drive carefully, but I'm not so sure about..." I stopped. She wasn't my daughter. She was of legal age. Still, I held myself responsible. I was her employer, her friend, the older woman, supposedly a voice of experience. How would I react if the man I loved turned me into a goddess for all the world to see? Oh boy... "Um, you understand that when people are in love, they..."

She giggled. "Y'all talking birds and bees?"

I hugged the arm in the sling as if I were cradling a baby. "To use your phrase, 'Yes, ma'am.'"

"Please don't worry your head about me, Deva. First, I'll marry him in front of a preacher. Then I'll love him forever."

A steel magnolia.

I arched an eyebrow. "So you won't start loving him this morning?"

A shadow of doubt crossed her lovely features. "I don't think so."

I did think so. But I gave her the keys anyway. Tidal waves can't be contained.

"Take the rest of the day off," I called from the doorway as she ran down the alley to Fifth Avenue. But she must have been deafened by the beat of her own heart, for I don't think she heard me.

I turned back to the shop. A cluster of lookers followed me in and were circling the tables making little delighted "ohs" and "ahs" over their finds when the phone rang.

"Deva, where you have been hiding?"

Ilona Alexander.

"It's been a busy week, Ilona." Didn't the woman read the papers?

"Well, I have you now. Listen, Deva, I want you to plan important party for me. For wine festival. Trevor and I, we host one of the Friday night dinners. And it must be perfect. Those are Trevor's orders."

According to the *Naples Daily,* on the last weekend in February, the air over town would buzz with private jets ferrying in celebrities and oenologists and movers and shakers from around the world. Then on festival Saturday, vintage wines, exotic trips and classic automobiles would be auctioned at the Ritz-Carlton Golf Resort.

But it was the Friday evening before the auction that Ilona was calling about. That was when the four hundred and fifty paying guests Chip mentioned would mingle at intimate dinners at fifteen of Naples's most luxurious homes. And thirty of them would dine at Chez Alexander. Apparently, despite the crimes, Trevor and Ilona hadn't been dropped from the A list.

"And guess who is my celebrity chef?" Ilona asked.

"I know, he told me."

"Cheep."

"Thank you for asking him, Ilona. He's thrilled." And I was thrilled for him if also a bit worried. Chip's lasagna was legendary, but were his culinary skills really up to what amounted to a cook's triathlon?

"Of course, he's thrilled. Why not? I make him celebrity. I told you my family, the Szent-Gyorgyis, were kingmakers. So I say to Trevor, why I cannot make celebrity chef?" Her voice lowered to a whisper. "You see it is as I tell you. My family has fallen so far."

"Well, I wouldn't—"

"Never no mind. You come to my house tomorrow. Ten sharp."

"No, that's not possible."

She gasped at my refusal. "*Nem.* No?"

"I have to finish a proposal for January second, so I can't make any appointments until the third. Besides, I'm not a party planner. I'm an interior designer."

"You have gift, Deva, for making beautiful. That is what I want you to do. My theme for dinner will be Evening in Tuscany. How does that sound?"

Very Hungarian. "Ilona, listen to me. Call a party

planner. If you can't find one in Naples, call Miami. They're out there, trust me."

"*Nem*. I fire one I have. She no like my ideas. Besides, I want no more strangers in my house, not after what happened to painting."

The Monet. But still no mention of poor Maria. I'd be dipped. My Irish temper flared sky high as I grappled with the realization that to Ilona her cook had never been more than a household appliance and deserving of the same consideration.

"So no more strangers working here. That's why I want Cheep. And you."

So safety was what she was after, and compliance, not necessarily talent. Angry and insulted to boot, I was about to tell her to stuff it when she said, "For you, Deva, two thousand dollars flat design fee. Plus your hours to consult and whatever you buy to make beautiful."

A bonanza. Every woman has her price, and while it wasn't exactly prostitution, I sold myself on the spot for two grand.

"Done. You've seduced me, Ilona. See you on January third at two o'clock."

"Two-thirty. Sometimes after lunch Trevor likes…"

I didn't need to hear what Trevor liked after lunch. "Two-thirty is fine," I said and hung up singing.

For both Trevor and me, it looked like the New Year would be starting off with a bang. So to speak.

CHAPTER FIFTEEN

WORKING ALONE IN the shop, I had a busy day. Running the cash register with one arm in a sling was a challenge. Seeing my predicament, several of the customers wrapped their own purchases, acting as if they enjoyed helping me and hearing all about the vandalized window and my surgery. Around noon, I found time to call the two women who were interested in design work, got directions to their homes, and made appointments for the second week in January.

Throughout the day, I kept checking my watch. Two. Two-thirty. Three. Three-thirty. Where was Lee? At four, I paced around the tables to work off my anxiety. In this age of casual hooking up, should I be so worried?

Yes, I should. I'd encouraged Lee to go to Paulo. Well, if not encouraged exactly, I definitely hadn't discouraged her. I'd even loaned her my car, for Pete's sake. And what did I know about Paulo except that he was Jamaican and well mannered and gifted? Had the gifted part swayed me?

Calm down, you're not the girl's mother. Besides, the attraction between them was like a bolt of lightning. I couldn't have stopped it if I wanted to. *But you didn't even try.*

Ten past four.

Something must have happened by now. What that

something might be, I could well imagine. The first time with Jack had been...

The sleigh bells jangled. My glance darted to the door.

Yes.

Hand in hand, easy and relaxed, Lee and Paulo strolled into the shop, happiness surrounding them like an aura. If I had said, "Beam them up, Scotty," they would have risen out of sight. They were already ten feet off the floor.

"Deva, we want you to be the first to know," Lee said, her face aglow, all signs of fatigue wiped away.

"Do I need to sit down?"

Paulo laughed. "We're getting married." A frisson of anxiety sprang into his eyes as he waited for my response.

"Come here, both of you," I said, and holding out my good arm, I gave them a lopsided bear hug and dropped a sloppy kiss on each happy face. Then I held them at arm's length and studied them—Lee, armed with a love no problem could surmount, and Paulo, so terribly aware that love could be lost in a heartbeat. For I felt sure that was the worry I read in his eyes. How well I understood.

"When?" I asked.

"As soon as we can get a license," Paulo said. "We don't want to wait."

Ah. I shot a quick peek at Lee. She turned rosy red. I suppressed a smile. What had or hadn't happened between them was none of my business.

"Surfside Condominiums has a clubroom. If you like, my wedding gift will be a celebration dinner. I even have a celebrity chef to do the honors. His specialty is Italian soul food. What do you think?"

They glanced at each other and grinned.

"Okay, that's settled then," I said. "But since you've confided in me, am I allowed a personal question?"

"Anything," they said in unison, then looked at each other and laughed.

Already they were a single, united whole. I suspected they always would be, and at all I had lost, a sudden spurt of pain shot through me. But I squelched the self-pity before it could take root. The memory of a perfect love was mine to cherish forever. How many people have as much?

"What I was wondering is, where will you live? How will you manage?"

"We've been talking about that all day, Deva," Lee said. "Paulo's place over the garage is perfect. So small and cozy. As soon as the owners return for New Year's, he'll tell them about me. He doesn't think there'll be a problem. He has a Volkswagen, so we'll have a car."

"But money will be a problem," Paulo acknowledged. "I teach a few classes a week at the Von Liebig Art Center, and bartend whenever I can, but—"

"I have an idea." It was one that had been simmering in my brain ever since I saw Lee's portrait.

Looking surprised, they both stared, waiting for me to go on. "Suppose we put Lee's portrait on an easel here in the shop? Put some business cards next to it. Maybe a flyer with your picture, Paulo, and a little bio information. People coming into the shop would see it—"

Nodding and smiling, Lee finished my thought. "—and order paintings from you, Paulo. Deva, y'all have such wonderful ideas. Doesn't she, Paulo?"

"Yes, but…"

"But what?" Lee asked, her smile dimming.

"The portrait was a gift to you. Not a sales device."

"Oh, honey," she said. "Y'all need me so bad." With that she flung her arms around him, kissing him with an expertise she must have picked up that afternoon. Then she released him, glanced down and said, "I'm going to quit day classes."

"Oh, no." The words escaped my mouth before I could stop them.

At my outburst, Paulo gave me a startled glance then looked over at Lee. "That's the downside of our plans," he said quietly.

"No, it isn't," Lee insisted. "I'll take classes two evenings a week. I only have three semesters to go. It'll take a little longer to get my degree, is all. That way, Deva," she added shyly, "if you want me, I can work more hours."

"Of course I want you," I said slowly. "I've been dreading the day you'd leave. But to be honest, I'm sorry to see you drop out of school. Night classes are difficult after you've worked all day."

"Deva's right, Lee," Paulo said. "Maybe we should wait until you get your degree."

"Darlin'," she replied, with a tremor in her voice, "I don't believe I *can* wait." Then she flung her hands over her face, hiding her need and her bright pink cheeks.

Paulo looked across at me, and we both grinned.

"Well, I do have four design projects in the works," I said. "So having you here to keep the shop open would be wonderful."

Lee lowered her hands to her lap. "See," she said, smiling at Paulo. "What did I tell y'all? Everything's going to be just fine."

As soon as Lee arrived the next morning, starry eyed and smiling, I left for Michael Mesnik's Art Frame and

Restoration Studio. I had six ladies' fashion prints from the nineteen twenties that needed framing for the new powder room I was designing. Located next to Tin City, one of Naples's bayside tourist attractions, Mesnik's was the best framer in town.

The minute I walked in, someone said, "Well, fancy meeting you here, Mrs. Dunne."

The voice was familiar, as was the tanned, bald pate that had been polished like an apple.

"George Farragut. What a surprise." Actually, surprise was an understatement. I never expected to see a numbers cruncher like George in an art frame shop. Though come to think of it, he was supposed to have met Simon that night at the Russian art exhibit.

"I'm on my way to work," he said, "but I had to stop by and see what Michael has done with my last acquisition. And to drop off another one."

George rested his Hermès briefcase on the counter and shook my good hand a little too vigorously.

"This is one of my favorite places in town. Being next to the Riverwalk Bar doesn't hurt, either." He laughed, and eyes darting to my sling, said, "You've been making the headlines."

"To my regret."

"Any idea of who the vandal might be?"

"None at all."

"Unfortunately, the local police are less than efficient."

"Oh, I don't know—"

Michael, the shop's owner, a tall, thin man who always looked rushed even when he wasn't, came out from the back room. "Mrs. Dunne. Mr. Farragut. Pleased to see you both. Your etching is ready," he said to George. "I'll get it, and be right with you, Mrs.

Dunne." He hurried behind the curtain separating the shop from his workroom.

"Etching?" I asked. "So you're interested in art, George?"

He nodded, his attention on the opening to the workroom, his fingers drumming on the countertop. Like Morgan Jones, another obsessed art lover?

A moment later, an actor on a stage, Michael parted the curtain and emerged with a small framed image in his hands. About twelve by sixteen inches, the etching was French matted in cream and framed in ebony. He held it up for George to inspect.

"Ah, nice, Michael. Very nice, indeed."

I agreed. Flemish perhaps, or Dutch, it depicted a woodland scene, its incised lines crisp and clean. The deep ivory paper told me it was old. Eighteenth, or even seventeenth century.

"What do you think?" George asked, tearing his attention from the image long enough to ask my opinion.

"It's incredible."

"That's the word precisely. Not like those lurid abstracts Morgan chases down."

Uh-oh, an art snob.

"Abstract art has its admirers," I replied.

"You're not one of them, are you?"

I shrugged. "Modern art is a mirror of our time. And mirrors aren't always flattering." I sighed and let truth win out. "That said, I admit this etching is the choice of a very selective connoisseur."

George smiled as if I'd said something amusing. So my opinions were funny, were they?

"You're an intelligent woman, Mrs. Dunne. I'll be interested to see what you do with Morgan's place. All that blue. And all those huge acrylics in those garish colors." George indulged in a little shudder.

So the man thought I was intelligent? I supposed I should be flattered but wasn't. Somehow his compliment had sounded like a patronizing crack.

Working quickly, Michael laid the etching over a sheet of bubble wrap and secured it with tape.

"I have something else for you," George said, unzipping his briefcase. He reached in, withdrew a folder and opened it with a flourish. Inside lay a drawing of a female nude, sponge in hand, bathing in a tub of water.

Michael gasped. "Is it?" he asked in a hushed tone.

George nodded. "A Degas. The provenance is above reproach."

"The same framing? Ebony?"

"Exactly."

"I'll get to it right away. An honor, Mr. Farragut."

"Don't rush. The delay will give me something to look forward to. I trust we'll meet again, Mrs. Dunne," George said, giving me a little two-fingered salute. Then picking up his briefcase and tucking the etching under an arm, he exited Mesnik's with a swagger.

"One of my best customers," Michael said when we were alone. "His office is in the building next door, and he's in here all the time. A nice man with a very refined taste."

"So I noticed."

"He scours Europe for those old master drawings, and some of them are priceless. Judging from the number I've restored for him over the years, he must have a world-class collection by now."

"How interesting," I said, taking the fashion prints out of a manila envelope and laying them on the counter. After the Degas, I had to admit they looked pretty tame, but they'd be a colorful conversation piece once Michael matted and framed them. Together we made our selections, and I said goodbye, crammed the receipt in my purse and headed for the door.

What I'd learned about George *was* interesting. Another man with ties to the Alexanders who was obsessed with collecting. I hurried across the parking lot. The instant I got inside the Audi, I'd call Rossi and tip him off. My pace slowed. On second thought, maybe not. I'd promised myself I wouldn't play amateur sleuth, and that was a promise I needed to keep. I also needed to concentrate on my own business, and that meant completing the renderings Morgan Jones would expect to see on January second.

Besides, so what if George liked etchings? Everyone who collected art wasn't a thief. And everyone who knew the Alexanders wasn't a killer.

No, I wouldn't call Rossi and annoy him with my half-baked suspicions. Not about Merle's flight and not about George's etchings. Sink or swim, Rossi was on his own.

CHAPTER SIXTEEN

NEW YEAR'S EVE. Midnight, and all the bells and whistles at Times Square were going crazy. I pushed back from the drawing board and watched CNN record the frenzy. The glittering ball descended on the screaming crowd at the exact moment my kitchen phone rang. Who could this be? A reveler bringing in the New Year?

I stood, arched my back, and hurried out to the kitchen, hoping, hoping...

A little breathless, I picked up. "Hello."

"Deva! Happy New Year!"

Simon. My pulse, soaring a moment before, dropped down to its normal rhythm. "Where are you?" I asked. "You sound like you're partying."

"Upstairs. Alone. Want me to come down for a nightcap?"

Was I wrong, or was he slurring his words? "I'm in bed, Simon," I lied.

"All the better."

"Very funny. Thanks for the good wishes, but—"

"Don't hang up. Have you finished that Jones project?"

"No, but I've made a good dent in it."

"Translated that means dinner's out again tomorrow?"

"'Fraid so. I really need to spend the day working."

"Of course. I understand."

"Thanks for calling. It was sweet of you, Simon. See you in January."

"Wait—"

I hung up, but gently, and went back to the living room to watch the excitement in Times Square. People shaking noisemakers and shouting "Happy New Year, everybody!" Couples kissing and hugging and waving at the cameras…

I turned off the set and flung the remote on a chair. What was wrong with me? Sitting here alone on New Year's Eve without a friend for company, without anyone to hug or kiss, in a silence that suddenly pounded in my head like jungle drums? I could be in bed now with Simon…I could be partying, champagne flute in hand…I could be out somewhere, anywhere, with Rossi.

Wait a New York minute. This wasn't the first time Rossi had popped up out of nowhere. Why? *Why?* Without stopping to analyze the reason, I jumped up and dashed out to the kitchen. It wasn't too late. The ball over Times Square had hardly hit the ground.

I picked up the phone and dialed. Maybe Rossi had to listen to the chief, but I didn't. My pulse pounding in rhythm with the rings, I held the receiver to my ear, eager to hear that raspy voice. It would be on the cusp of irritation when he picked up, and then a heart-stopping pause when I said "hello" and he knew I was on the line. Yes…I had to hear that stunned pause. I had to have my fix.

On the fourth ring, I knew he wasn't home. On the fifth, I held the receiver at arm's length, staring at it as if it could tell me where he was. Did homicide detectives work at midnight on New Year's Eve? Sure they did. 'Round the clock. Twenty-four/seven.

And they had dates on New Year's Eve.

I hung up and said "Happy New Year" to the fridge. Disgusted with my own longings, I snapped off all the lights, tossed the sling into a corner and tumbled into bed. Sure, I was lonely, but did I have to turn pathetic and needy, making weird phone calls at midnight? My first New Year's resolution: no more calls like the last one. Not to any man on earth.

Before I could settle under the covers, the phone on the bedside table rang. Probably Simon again. I didn't want to answer, but the ringing wouldn't stop.

Annoyed, I grabbed the receiver off the hook. "Yes."

"Happy New Year, Mrs. D."

I bolted upright.

"I was asleep when you called," he said.

A likely story. "You have caller ID? I didn't say anything."

"You sound lonely."

So he could detect that, too? "You're a psychiatrist now?"

"I told you what I was."

A lover. "Under the circumstances, Rossi, it's hard to remember everything you say."

"For now, maybe, but not forever."

"What does that mean, exactly?" I'd just vowed not to make any more middle-of-the-night phone calls, but asking middle-of-the-night questions wasn't part of the deal.

"Are you in bed?" he asked, ignoring my question completely. Rossi did that a lot.

I gripped the phone tighter. "Why do you want to know?"

"I have some news that might help you rest easier. I would have called earlier, but I thought you'd be out with that neighbor of yours…that…what's his name?"

Rossi never forgot a name. I was beginning to enjoy myself. "His name is Simon. And for your information, he did invite me out." I lay back against the pillow. "What's the good news you have for me?"

"Your assailant has left town. The shop should be safe now."

"Oh?" So that was the reason he'd returned my call. Not because he needed to hear the sound of my voice or to say how much he missed not seeing me. "How did you find out about Merle?" I asked, trying to keep the disappointment out of my voice.

A growl pulsed through the line. "Go to sleep, Mrs. D. Sweet dreams."

The steady hum of a dead line sounded in my ear. Damn. He'd hung up. He did that all the time. It drove me nuts.

JANUARY SECOND. The holidays were over, thank God. So were my days wearing the sling. Dr. Lemoine removed my dressing and declared the angry-looking red scar "Healing beautifully. Two months from now, you'll barely notice it. In six months, it will have disappeared."

With only a light dressing covering the wound, and both arms fully functioning, I was a new woman. Armed with a portfolio of drawings, I drove to Bonita Bay and rang Morgan Jones's front doorbell confident he'd love my design ideas. Until he yanked open the door, greeting me with a face full of frowns.

"Good morning, Morgan," I said, forcing my voice into cheerful mode.

He checked his watch. "Let's make this fast, Deva."

Back to that attitude, were we? I saw red. Crimson with slashes of magenta. "I can do fast," I said, stepping inside and slamming the door so hard the bang echoed throughout the vast, empty rooms. "I can also do very fast. And I can do super fast. Which one is your pleasure, Dr. Morgan?"

Tripod in one hand, portfolio in the other, handbag slung over my shoulder, I glared at him. Not an auspicious beginning. Maybe I had just blown the account. So be it. Every once in a while, everything took a backseat to a temper tantrum. I'd just had one a two-year-old could be proud of and enjoyed every second of it.

Like challenged bullies everywhere, Morgan backed down. "It's been a stressful few days, Deva."

That and that alone would be his apology. I nodded. It would do. I was there to make a sale—not love or war.

In the center of the great room, empty except for the paintings stacked to one side, I set up the tripod and placed the drawings on it. The morning light poured through the wall of glass, illuminating the first one, a rendering of this very room with the palest whisper of blue on the walls, the huge Rosenquist facing the windows, and the other oils on opposite walls, each one dynamic, each one demanding attention. To offset that demand, I'd introduced minimalist furnishings, a pair of long, linear sofas in white leather. The only jolt of color, a cobalt blue ottoman that could double as a coffee table. Clear Plexiglas for the narrow console tables behind the sofas, and the end tables; they took up no visual space, leaving that to the exciting wall art.

Morgan studied the concept carefully, his gaze darting from one detail to the next, missing nothing.

Finally, too nervous to keep still, I said, "Everything is designed to showcase the paintings."

He glanced at me briefly then turned back to the drawing. "I can see that. Your conception is exactly what I had hoped for."

A bead of perspiration trickled down my back. It felt good. "I'm delighted that you're pleased, Doctor." I uncapped my pen. "Would you initial this sheet?"

His frown returned, as scowly as ever. "Is that necessary?"

"It's a standard formality." Why bother to point out that his initials protected me should he decide, once I'd ordered the case goods and other materials, that he didn't like the concept after all? If he were acting on good faith, he wouldn't object to signing.

Holding my breath, I handed him the pen with a shaky hand. His lips tightened a bit, but he took the pen and scribbled his initials on a corner of the page.

I exhaled that pent-up breath and showed him a sketch of the foyer that multiple coats of cobalt blue lacquer had transformed into a jewel box. Together with the great room ottoman, they were the only two vivid touches in my scheme.

As Morgan studied it, the merest wisp of a smile raised the corners of his mouth. He tapped a fingernail on the page. "I like the drama."

Good. I handed him the pen again. He quickly initialed the page before glancing at his watch. "I really am pressed for time. Let's get to the bedroom. It's the room I'm most concerned about."

I flipped through the sketches, found the one for the master suite, set it in front of the others and stepped back.

"Aaaah."

No need to ask if he liked it. As he stared at the satin bed linens, the piles of pillows, the velvet chaise and the concealed lighting that bathed everything in a soft glow, he smiled—an all-out, cheek-cracking smile. So he could do it when he wanted. I'd have to remember that the next time he frowned.

"It's all as I imagined." Without taking his attention from the drawing, he asked, "Are there dimmers on these lights?"

"Of course."

"Excellent. And I like the bed linens. The blue-gray satin is lovely, very subdued. Very alluring." He cleared his throat as if he had, somehow, revealed too much of himself.

I wondered if Jessica knew how important their bedroom was to her husband. It was nice to know a couple who had been together for years had kept the romance alive in their marriage. But I backed away from that thought—fast.

"Where do I sign?" Morgan asked.

I handed him the pen with a steady hand.

"The sooner I can move in, the better. So get started immediately," he ordered.

Some things never changed. I indulged in an audible sigh, but otherwise tamped down my temper. I couldn't afford another tantrum. Besides, you had to pick your battles, and right now I tasted victory.

"I won't waste a moment," I assured him. "The drawings will be in the shop. So if Jessica would like to see them—"

"That won't be necessary."

"Really? She's not interested?"

"That's irrelevant." He glanced at his watch again. An excuse not to look at me? "We're getting divorced. In fact, I'm late for an appointment with my attorney."

"Divorced? Oh? Jessica never let on."

"She didn't know. I informed her yesterday. A new start for a New Year."

So the satin coverlet and the dimmer switch weren't for Jessica after all. Nor the musky cologne drifting around him. Probably not the new-looking blue silk tie, either. Too bad. Jessica, hearty and unpretentious, had, I suspected, put up with a lot from Morgan over the years. I hoped she'd get a good settlement. Dumped after a lifetime, she deserved one.

Hey, wait a minute. What was I thinking? Divorce in Florida meant a division of assets. Even Steven. What a divorce would do to Dr. Jones's financial health wasn't any of my business. Whether he could afford to pay me for my work was. Deva Dunne Interiors couldn't afford to take a hit.

My heart in my mouth, I said, "I'll work up a proposal for you this afternoon and fax it to your office. Once you approve of the purchases, I'll require fifty percent down before filling any orders."

I hardly dared breathe as I waited for his answer. Red or green? Stop or go?

He didn't hesitate. "Not a problem, Deva. Just get the project in the works. I'm anxious to begin my new life."

Green.

With so much emphasis on the master bedroom, I doubted Dr. Jones would be living that new life alone. Not my concern, neither was the source of his funding. But I couldn't squelch the question that kept popping into my head. Where had he found the means for so much spending? From his investments? From his surgeon's skill? Or from the sale of the Monet? I decided on the spot that this time I *would* tell Rossi what puzzled me. For Maria's sake, the murderer had to be found, the Monet recovered.

And I'd call for another, less noble cause—until the police solved the case, I couldn't begin even the semblance of a new life. And I was starting to realize I needed a new one—whether it had dimmers and satin in it or not.

CHAPTER SEVENTEEN

ON JANUARY THIRD at two-thirty sharp, I called at Chez Alexander. A few minutes later, perched beside Ilona on one of the yellow brocade sofas, I watched Trevor stomp around his living room, his hand-sewn loafers slapping against the marble floor.

"Whattya mean, you want a grapevine?" he shouted. "Twenty thousand square feet under glass, and now I gotta build you a grapevine? No, absolutely not."

"But darling, is for wine festival dinner," Ilona protested.

"That damn dinner's costing me a fortune. With everything else that's going on, I don't need the aggravation. Or the expense."

"But Trev, we agree. You want everything perfect. Remember, our Evening in Tuscany."

"No grapevine. *Nem.* Come up with another idea. A cheaper one." Trevor stopped mid-stomp to point a finger at me. It quivered in the air in front of my nose. "And that includes you. She doesn't have any common sense, but I thought you did. I must've been wrong."

He stormed out of the room. "Don't wait up," he yelled before disappearing in the direction of the kitchen wing. A distant door slammed.

Ilona listened then ran on her pink slides to the front window. "I bet he take my Boxster just to be difficult."

Sure enough, a moment later a silver Porsche, sleek

as a high-speed panther, zoomed down the curved driveway.

"I knew it. *Te diszno!* You pig!" Ilona turned from the window and flipped her hair over a shoulder. "Whenever I say 'no sex' he act this way. A little boy. Never no mind. Maybe he get ticket." Her face brightened at the prospect. "Is all right, Deva. We forget grapevine. We come up with another plan."

What was this "we" stuff? The grapevine idea had been hers. Personally I thought it was too obvious to be tasteful and had told her so. But that moment of truth was about to be buried. Why bother to resurrect it?

Interesting, though, to hear Trevor complaining about the party's cost. So maybe he wasn't Midas rich. I gave a mental shrug. Even kings had a limit to their coffers. This one I wouldn't run past Rossi. When I called him yesterday, he hadn't been too impressed with my Morgan Jones story and in no uncertain terms told me to stick to my decorating and let him do the detecting. Off and on since then, I'd been trying to decide if I was seriously pissed at him or not. *Not*, actually. He was right, and I knew it.

"Deva, we have tea while you give me ideas for party. I tell Jesus."

Ilona wiggled her way across the marble floor to the kitchen wing. From the rear, she looked fabulous in her hot pink pants. In no time, she clicked her way back into the living room. Despite the frown lines stressing her normally smooth forehead, she looked fabulous from the front, too, in her hot pink sweater.

"Jesus will bring tea. And cookies," she added with a guilty smile. "After Trevor, I need sweet. Now, Deva, what will we do?"

We again. Okay, for two thousand plus extras, she'd bought the right to ask.

"Ilona, Tuscan means contrasts. Monks and aristocrats. Peasants and nobility. That's what your party should play up." I made sure my voice sounded decisive, for ultimately, decisiveness was what I sold. Clients hired me to make decisions that if left on their own they'd agonize over. I eyed Ilona, pausing to let my words sink in.

"Go on. I like," she said, shifting to the edge of her down sofa cushion.

"Okay. How about this? We serve dinner outside, overlooking the Gulf. The loggia can easily accommodate thirty diners, and it has the columns and arches of a medieval cloister. Torchlight on the lawn and rustic lanterns on the tables. Heavy tapestry tablecloths to the floor. For centerpieces, cornucopias spilling fruit and veggies."

Ilona wrinkled her perfect nose. "Veggies?"

I laughed. "Not potatoes or onions. Gourds and squashes. Pomegranates. Apples and pears. Grapes, too."

"Ha, grapes! I like."

"We'll costume the staff. Put the bartenders in brown monk's robes, the servers in peasant dress. Jesus in britches. That sort of thing."

Ilona waved her diamond-studded hands, sending an aurora borealis flashing through the air. "Where we get such clothes?"

"From a costume supplier. It shouldn't be a problem."

"Music, Deva. Music we must have."

"Yes," I agreed, warming to the theme. "Nothing too loud. A chamber ensemble during cocktails, so people can chat. At dinner, Italian love songs with the main courses, operatic arias during dessert. End the evening on a vibrant note."

"Your ideas, all of them are wonderful, Deva. You see, it is like I said, I need you to plan."

A soft footfall sounded on the marble floor. Jesus entered carrying a serving tray laden with a silver tea service and an assortment of cookies. A tall man, with the sad bearing of a deposed aristocrat, he had lost a noticeable amount of weight in the three weeks since Maria's death. His heavy eyes spoke of suffering. Three weeks and still no arrest. I could only hope Rossi and the Naples P.D. were working around the clock.

Jesus placed the tray on the coffee table. "Will that be all, señora?"

"For now, Jesus." He left us, and Ilona reached for a chocolate-frosted morsel. "Jesus wants to bring Maria's ashes to Guatemala. Can you believe that? At time like this, with wine festival so close? Have cookie, Deva. Maria made them. They're *finom*. Delicious."

The impulse to mash a cookie in her face told me I had to get out of there fast. I'd already had my temper tantrum for the year. I fake peeked at my watch. "Oh, I'm late. Must go, Ilona. As soon as the proposal is ready, I'll fax it to you."

"That is good. Tomorrow, Cheep comes to discuss menu. He has family recipes from many generations just like my *anya's* cooks. All will be well."

"Right." I grabbed my fake Chanel handbag and hurried toward the foyer, not even stopping for a loving glimpse of the remaining Monet. Air, I craved air and yanked open the front door. "As soon as possible, I'll drop off some samples for you to see," I called over my shoulder.

Ilona scrambled off the couch, a second, or maybe a

third, cookie in hand. "Wait, Deva, there is something you should know."

What now? She hurried toward me on tiptoes, all the while glancing left and right as if someone might be watching. Who? Jesus? The cleaning staff?

She came close enough to whisper in my ear, "I am not supposed to tell, but security code is changed. You will need new one."

"That's all right, I'll just give the samples to Jesus."

"Suppose he go to Guatemala? One minute only, I write number for you."

"But—"

She disappeared through the archway into the kitchen wing, returning with a folded slip of paper that she pressed into my palm. "Hide this," she ordered. "Trevor should not know."

"Ilona, why don't I phone you after I collect the party supplies? We can settle on a meeting date then."

She shook her head. "*Nem.* In two days, Trevor and I, we leave for Hungary. I promise my *anya* we come right after Christmas. Trevor no want to go, but I tell him I no come back if he refuse." She heaved a sigh that did great things for the hot pink sweater. "Is not easy, Deva."

"What isn't?"

"Being Mrs. Trevor. Tonight I give him sex. Only then will he stop the pout."

"A girl's got to do what a girl's got to do," I said, easing toward the door.

"Correct."

I cleared my throat. Ilona had her problems and I had mine, and one of them was money. While I loved the creative challenge of designing, I hated dunning people for fees. But with even the slightest chance that she might not return, I had to plunge into girl talk with a purpose.

"Ilona, I have a request." I squared my shoulders and looked her straight in the eye. "Before you leave for Europe, could you see that my design fee is paid? Or at least half of it. I'll need it to cover expenses."

She greeted this first from me with a fluttering of her luscious eyelashes. "Of course, I understand. You are working girl."

I huffed out a breath. *So are you, Ilona.*

"But Trevor is such a bear these days, I ask him for little. So I pay you myself from my, how you say, mad money. Wait." While I stood chilling in the foyer, she ran up the stairs, bouncing back down a few moments later with a sheaf of bills in her hand. "Two thousand. Correct?"

"Well, yes, but this is the full amount."

"Never no mind. I trust. Send other expenses to Trevor. He will be in better mood by then, I promise."

Designing, I decided on the spot, was an easier gig than some marriages.

"Thanks, Ilona. I'll see that the party materials are here when you return. *Bon voyage.* Don't do anything I wouldn't do."

"Oh, but I must," she said, no smile in her tone, or on her face, either.

For the first time since we'd met, Mrs. Trevor Alexander had my sympathy.

Poor little rich girl. In comparison, clutching the two grand, I felt like a rich little poor girl as I jogged down the stone steps to my car.

THE MONEY WENT fast, on rent, phones and payroll, but what a wonderful reprieve. Because of it, I didn't have to dip into my skimpy reserves, at least for another month. Then when Morgan's payment kicked in, Deva Dunne Interiors should be well on its way.

All week long, I found myself humming. What *was* that tune? An Italian love song, "That's Amore." Figures. Ilona's Tuscan theme had to be the inspiration. Not Rossi. Ha! With an effort, I banished him from my thoughts and concentrated on making a list of items needed for the Alexanders' party.

Fabric. Cornucopias. Fruit and gourds. Rustic lanterns. Costumes. Music. Engraved invitations.

With luck, when Ilona returned in two weeks, I would have booked the staff and musicians and purchased the party materials.

Overnight, Kravatz Fabrics in Manhattan priority-mailed me a carton of possible tabletop swatches. All medieval in feeling, in deep russets and greens with flashes of burgundy. To see which one looked best on the loggia, I telephoned the house, hoping Jesus would pick up. I'd rather he let me in than use the new security code. But he didn't answer at ten, twelve or two. On the chance that he might be enjoying a rare day off, I rang him again the next day. Only the answering machine kicked on.

While waiting for Jesus to return my call, I made a quick trip to the Miromar Design Center in Ft. Myers to pick up the party supplies. Then I scoured the local antique stores for vintage linen napkins. The largest I could find for dinner and smaller ones for cocktails. They didn't have to match, but they did have to look like old family heirlooms.

Each guest should also have a token gift waiting at the dinner table. Something Medici in feeling. Poison rings for the ladies? Faux antidotes in tiny pillboxes for the men? No doubt in poor taste after what had happened there, but Ilona might like an outrageous gesture like that.

As soon as Morgan's retainer arrived, I ordered his case goods and hired Oceanside Finishes to paint his interior. I also called on the two women who had come into the shop during the holidays, one wanting a new bathroom, and the other a revived family room. When I snagged both sales, I did a mental jump for joy.

Without Lee's help, all the scurrying around would have plowed me under. She kept the merchandise neatly arranged, charmed the customers and, I suspect, made selling Paulo's paintings a special interest. In a single week, she had lined up a commission for him.

Watching her, I realized how wondrous happiness is, and with a pang, understood that what I saw in Lee—the shining eyes, the effortless smile, the glow of a woman well loved—had once been mine in those days when Jack vowed I centered his universe. In the days when he couldn't wait to rush home to me at night. When he started undressing inside the front door, scattering his clothes from room to room, and mine as well…transforming me with his adoration into a goddess…

Rossi, you've got your work cut out for you.

The thought made me laugh, and to Lee's surprise, I went over and hugged her. "I'm so glad you're so happy," I said.

"Y'all mean it, I know, Deva," she said, hugging me back. "And I'm glad I'm so happy, too."

We laughed, startling two customers who walked in searching for sofa pillows in purple.

That afternoon, I rang Jesus again. Still no answer. He must have taken advantage of the Alexanders' absence and gone to Guatemala with Maria's ashes. No point in waiting any longer. I packed everything in the Audi's trunk and headed for Gordon Drive.

To be certain the house was empty, I rang the front door chimes. They echoed loudly to no avail. Satisfied that no one was inside, I entered the new code and carried one of the boxes into the silent, chilled interior.

"Anybody home?" I called. No response. I had the place to myself.

In the dining room, I worshipped the Monet for a while then brought the fabric swatches out to the loggia. As I suspected, the muted shades of the vine pattern had the vintage look I was after. I'd call Gwen at Kravatz the minute I got back to the shop and order enough to cover five tables of six to the floor.

Satisfied, I wandered back into the great room. Chez Alexander had never been a noisy house. Not once, in all the times I'd been here, could I recall a radio or a stereo playing, but today the quiet was positively eerie. Nerves, I told myself, plain and simple. I'd had so much stress lately I was jittery for no reason at all. So why was I tiptoeing across the polished great room floor? No one was around to hear me. Yes, definitely nerves.

Still, something was a little off. No gardenia scent wafted in the air. And usually when the Alexanders were out of town, the blinds and draperies were closed, shutting out the sun and its effects on the interior. But not today. Beyond the windows, out to the horizon, I could see the Gulf water sparkling turquoise and serene, and the sun's rays glinting off the occasional shallow whitecap.

The box of party supplies weighed a ton. I lowered it onto a chair and plunked my purse on top. On the coffee table, the bowl of gardenias that were changed every day had wilted, the faded blossoms drooping over the rim, brown petals scattered across the tabletop. No wonder no gorgeous scent perfumed the air. I sniffed. Actually a musty, closed-up odor had replaced it. Strange. Even if Jesus were left alone for days, he wouldn't neglect his duties.

"Hello," I called again, just to be sure. "Jesus, are you here? Jesus!" I half expected him to suddenly respond in that gracious, courteous manner of his, but he didn't. Maybe he had gone to Central America after all.

Oh, well. I gave a mental shrug and headed for the kitchen wing. I needed to scout out the garage for a place to stash the party supplies. As I passed the corridor leading to Trevor's study, I spied the glow of yellow lamplight. Maybe Jesus was working in there and hadn't heard me. Though he should have. I'd made as much noise as a Patriots cheerleader.

Led by curiosity, I started down the corridor to the study. When I caught myself tiptoeing along like there was something to fear, I forced my feet to step normally. Heel, toe. Heel, toe.

Still my heart pounded as I reached the open study door and peeked in. Empty. No Jesus. So why were the lights on over the desk? Ilona once told me that of the entire household, only Jesus, who had been trained not to touch Trevor's documents or move his papers, was allowed into the study. But I walked in anyway and strode to the desk. Might as well turn off the light. I leaned over and reached for the lamp switch then froze, an arm in midair, as a sheet of paper atop a pile caught my eye. A bank statement, it showed a massive withdrawal. Was I reading that correctly?

Leaving the lamp on, I picked up the statement. The account had been closed over a week ago. A Morgan-Stanley logo embellished the next sheet. I glanced at that as well. Another deep withdrawal, and underneath that statement a personal letter from the local Morgan-Stanley office urging Mr. Alexander not to sell at this point in the market.

The next sheet and the next, all stacked in that same neat pile, were much the same. Hmm. Stunned, I sank onto Trevor's leather swivel chair and rode it for a while. What was going on? Had Trevor found a more lucrative investment opportunity? One that required large sums of money? Or did the withdrawals signify trouble?

None of my business, of course, except that Deva Dunne Interiors couldn't survive a nonpaying client. Not with Ilona's demands accelerating as they were. And come to think of it, most of her payments to me had been in cash from her secret stash of mad money.

Tense as a wound watch, I swiveled like mad. Only one thing to do. As I'd done with Morgan Jones, before ordering anything more I'd ask for payment of my out-of-pocket costs up front. The downside meant that might delay the party plans. Well, either that or take a chance. The Kravatz fabric alone was seventy dollars a yard and for five tables, we'd need—

The phone rang suddenly, and I nearly jumped out of my skin, the paper in my fingers fluttering to the floor. As I bent over, heart thumping, to retrieve it, a familiar deep voice came through the line. I sat up, placed the paper back on the pile and listened.

"Trevor, this is Simon Yaeger. Want you to know I took care of that little matter. George wasn't happy about it, but I let him know where you stand. It's your money he's playing with, not his own. Don't think he'll retaliate, but you know George. I told him what he has in mind is definitely out of the question. You don't need any legal entanglements with the IRS, not on top of everything else."

Simon cleared his throat. I waited. Was there more? *Yes.* "One other thing, you know how women like to talk. You might ask Ilona to be discreet." A pause. "I heard the Dunne woman is in and out of the house a lot, so I'd make sure she doesn't get a hold of this. The fewer people who are in on it the better. I'll be in touch again soon."

A click and the phone went dead. I rode the swivel hard for a few moments then reached across the desk, turned off the lamp and slowly got to my feet. *The Dunne woman.* Is that how Simon thought of me? In that clinical, detached manner? So underneath that suave façade, Mr. Hot Lips was a man of ice. Nevertheless, he had just done me a valuable service. I would definitely ask Trevor for a serious retainer before ordering another thing. And I would definitely reassess my so-called friendship with Simon.

The urge to get out of this musty, silent tomb seized me. I walked out of the study, grabbed the box of party supplies from the great room and hurried down the hall to the kitchen. I didn't want to leave party paraphernalia lying around, sullying the hushed elegance of Chez Alexander. The workbench in the garage would do. Everything would be safely out of the way there.

The musty odor was stronger in the kitchen. How long had Jesus been gone, anyway? I rested the box on the island and opened the side door leading from the kitchen wing to the four-car garage. The instant I did, a strange odor smacked me in the face. I sniffed the air and wished I hadn't. My stomach clenched. What was that *smell?* Like an animal had found its way inside and been trapped.

I snapped on the garage lights. Their glare revealed the Mercedes SUV Jesus used for errands, Ilona's silver Boxster and Trevor's Cadillac Seville. The fourth stall held a rack of bikes and Trevor's prized toy, a glittering Honda Goldwing. All the household vehicles were here, so Jesus must have driven the Alexanders to the airport, returned the car, then gotten a ride from someone so he could catch his own flight. A trickle of perspiration slid down my back as I stood in the doorway sniffing the foul air, not knowing whether to go in any farther or not.

Well, I couldn't leave the boxes cluttering the house, so I picked up the one I'd carried in and stepped into the garage. Whatever had caused the odor must be dead. I hoped it was a squirrel trapped under the roof…or even, God forbid, a rat. The alternative didn't bear thinking about. Anyway, whatever had died in here couldn't hurt me, and the box was getting heavier by the minute.

I dumped it on top of the workbench next to a hammer and an open box of scattered tacks. The clutter surprised me. Jesus usually kept his workstation as impeccably neat as Maria had kept her kitchen. But not this time. He must have been interrupted in the middle of a task. As I turned to go back for another box, a dark stain on the concrete floor caught my eye. The trickle of sweat on my back chilled.

I bent over for a closer look. If the stain had once been wet, it was dry now. Mesmerized, I followed where its trail led—between the Cadillac and the Boxster.

And then I saw him. Not a squirrel. Not a rat. Jesus. Crumpled in death and glued to the floor with his own blood.

I grabbed the Cadillac's door handle to steady myself and stared, transfixed, at the corpse. First Maria, now her husband. It couldn't be, my mind shrieked. It is, my eyes insisted. Another death. Another murder.

I had to get to a phone, call 911, but afraid I'd pitch forward in a dead faint and join Jesus on the floor, I just stood there gripping the handle, staring at the horror of what lay before me...the gunshot wound in Jesus's chest, his wide, unseeing eyes, and, strangely, a handful of tacks in his open palm.

I kept inhaling, gulping, filling my lungs with the noisome air, but the gulping did little good. I couldn't breathe. My lungs weren't functioning. I'd pass out after all and fall to the blood-covered floor.

Before I could, the garage doors went into a noisy ascent, and my gaze switched from Jesus's corpse straight into Trevor and Ilona's shocked faces.

CHAPTER EIGHTEEN

"CHRIST! IT's JESUS," Trevor said, stepping into the garage for a closer look.

Ilona gasped and clutched his arm, tugging him back from the body. "No, Trev. *Nem.*"

He shook off her hand and edged farther in, stopping just short of the bloodstain.

In unison, we both stared down at Jesus, at his startled, unseeing eyes, at his mouth wide open, gaping at what? His murderer?

"Why did you kill him?" Trevor asked, glancing up from the corpse, pinning me with an accusing look.

"Don't be ridiculous. I didn't kill him. I just found him. He looks like he's been dead awhile." I didn't mention the way he smelled. Trevor had a nose of his own.

He grunted something unintelligible and, eyes once again riveted on the gruesome sight, yelled over a shoulder. "Call the police, Ilona."

Rooted to her spot by the open overheads, she didn't move, her face so pale under her golden tan, I thought she'd be the one who'd join Jesus on the floor.

"The phone, Ilona. The phone." Trevor snapped his fingers. "Hurry up." At his second barked order, she obeyed, sidling around the other side of the SUV and disappearing through the side door into the house.

"So why did you do it?" Trevor asked again.

"Don't be an ass." I was too irritated to be scared.

Or polite. "Do I have a weapon in my hand?" I pointed to the remains. "Is that a fresh corpse?"

His eyes flickered at my tone. "How the hell should I know?"

"The blood's dried on the floor, Trevor. Use your head." Screw the Mr. Alexander shit.

"You could have killed him and come back. Returned to the scene of the crime."

This guy had made millions in the stock market? Unbelievable.

"We're not moving until the cops get here," he said.

Egads. He must have seen every Eliot Ness film ever made.

Ilona returned and stood gripping the kitchen door-frame for support. As if I didn't exist, she avoided making eye contact with me, focusing solely on Trevor. "I call," she said in a dull monotone.

"Good girl. Now let's see how fast Naples's finest can get here." Then, as a sudden thought struck him, he glared at me. "Hey! How'd you get in? The code's been changed."

I shot a quick glance Ilona's way. She shook her head, the movement barely perceptible, but I caught it, nonetheless. Still leaning on the Porsche, I shifted my attention to Trevor. "I'll do my talking to the police."

A few minutes later, an NPD squad car pulled up in front of the open garage door. "Well, here's your chance to spill what you know," Trevor said as my shadow, Officer Batano, stepped out with his sidekick, petite Officer Hughes, close behind him. As usual, like a secretary in battle gear, she brandished a clipboard.

Before the cops could get in a word, Trevor announced, "I'm Trevor Drexel Alexander. My wife and I have been out of town. We can prove it." He waved an arm at the body. "This was our welcome home present. My butler, Jesus Cardoza. Or what's left of him." Trevor pointed an index finger at me. "She was standing over the corpse when we got here."

Batano pierced me with a keen glance as if he couldn't believe what he was seeing. "Are you Mrs. Devalera Dunne, age thirty-two? Address Surfside Arms, Gulf Shore Boulevard, condominium unit 104? Proprietor of Deva Dunne Interiors, Fern Alley, Naples, Florida?"

A flawless performance by Batano and I hadn't said a thing. "Yes."

Batano shook his head, either in disbelief or disgust, I couldn't be sure which, and shouldering his way in between the vehicles, he crouched over Jesus. "He's dead," he pronounced. The man had a gift for the obvious. Heaving his bulk to his feet, he turned to Officer Hughes. "Call Homicide," he instructed her. "Then stay with the remains. We'll be inside." He reached for her clipboard. "I'll take that."

The three of us trooped back into the house after Batano.

"This will do," he said when we reached the kitchen. It was then that the impact of what I'd seen hit me with the force of a sledgehammer blow. Only a month earlier, I'd entered this same room with its Smallbone cabinets and perched on this same wrought iron stool while Rossi interrogated me.

What would he think when he saw me here again? What would anybody think? Within a span of weeks, I'd found two murder victims. I'd stumbled on them, the poor things, only stumbled on them, but who would believe that? Who would continue to think I had nothing to do with their deaths? That I was simply in the wrong place at the wrong time?

No one, that was who. I glanced across at Ilona leaning against the center island looking positively ashen. I'd never seen her so upset, so moved, not even when Maria died. The sight caught me up short. So who was the selfish bitch now? *I was.* Thinking only of myself. Of my own welfare. What of the two victims? Earnest, hardworking people away from their families and their homeland, most days on duty around the clock, trying to please, trying to live…then murdered without mercy. But why?

There could only be one answer. For what they had seen. For what they knew. But what *had* they seen? What *did* they know?

My hands trembled. I couldn't control them and clenched them together in my lap. It didn't help. The cell phone suspended from Batano's hip holster shrilled, and I flinched. He answered the caller with a series of yes and no then stashed the phone back in its holster. "The lieutenant's on his way," he said.

The lieutenant. I prayed he meant Rossi.

"High time." Trevor upped his chin at his wife. "Make some coffee, Ilona."

"Me?" Ilona pointed a French-manicured fingertip at her chest. "I no make coffee. You want coffee, darling, you make."

"I don't know where the hell the pot is."

Ilona shrugged. "Nobody does," she said. "Not now."

Trevor grunted, a sound so deep he must have dredged it up from his belly. "As soon as Homicide gets here, they'll question the ass off us, and I've been up all night. I need some goddamn coffee. Find the pot. Make yourself useful."

Stiff-backed, Ilona began a fruitless rattling of the cypress wood drawers and cupboards. Pen poised above the clipboard, Batano looked over at Trevor. "While we wait, I'll take some information. Your full name, sir."

"I thought I told you that already," Trevor said.

"Ah, I find!" Ilona announced. Triumphant, she held up a gleaming stainless steel Cuisinart Coffeemaker. "It has another piece." She put the pot on the counter and lifted out the heating element. "There. That is all of it."

"Well?" Trevor asked.

"Well what, darling?" Ilona gazed at him, a puzzled expression on her lovely face. She was dumb as a fox, but Trevor bought it.

"Jeez, you really don't know, do you? Give me a minute here, officer."

Trevor elbowed Ilona out of the way, marched over to the Sub-Zero refrigerator and yanked it open. He removed a bag of Starbucks Medium Blend, plunked it on the shelf and untwisted the tie.

"Shit. Whole beans. Where's the grinder, Ilona?"

"I want to leave," she said to Batano. "To sit in living room."

"We'll wait here until Homicide arrives. Have a seat, Mrs. Alexander." He gestured to a stool.

As Batano questioned Trevor, Ilona glided to the stool beside me, sat and crossed her legs. Not an ounce of her admirable derriere oozed over the seat cushion. I gave myself a mental slap on the knuckles. As if, at a time like this, the shape of her ass was important. Trained to notice details…like the tacks in Jesus's dead hand…I couldn't turn off the habit when it didn't matter. An occupational hazard.

Maybe doing something helpful would calm my

nerves. "I'll make coffee, Trevor. I remember seeing where Maria kept the grinder."

He shot me a look—half gratitude, half exasperation.

My knees wobbled when I stood, but they held, and while Batano jotted down the Alexanders' answers to his questions, I went through the motions—grinding the beans, measuring the water, turning on the coffeemaker.

With every move, I was conscious I had stepped into Maria's shoes, carrying out the wishes of a demanding man. And when I found the mugs and silverware and arranged them on the island with sugar and cream, and, finally, poured Trevor his coffee, I became Jesus in that moment…silently serving…I only hoped to God I wouldn't end up sharing his fate. Or Maria's.

Voices from the garage broke into the kitchen's moody atmosphere. "Stay here everybody," Batano said. "I'll be right back." He left for the garage, leaving the kitchen door open. The smell of death wafted in, competing with the Medium Blend. Or was it my imagination? The Alexanders said nothing about it, appeared not to notice.

I went back to the stool, wrapping my legs around it so I wouldn't fall off, and took shallow breaths. Ilona sat sipping coffee, examining her perfect manicure, still refusing to make eye contact. Why couldn't she bear to look at me? Did she think I was the killer? And would everybody else in town think the same? Even Rossi? I'd know in a minute. His gravelly voice poured in through the open door. And then he was there in the kitchen, a cell phone pressed to an ear, issuing orders that sounded all too familiar.

"Yeah, the forensic team, ASAP, and notify the ME. You got the address? I'll be here for a while."

He ended the call and strode into the center of the

kitchen as if he, not Trevor, owned it. But my heart, which had leaped up at the sound of his voice, sank to my wobbly knees. Like Ilona, he didn't make eye contact with me, merely inclined his head. I was a stranger, a witness to murder, nothing more. My disappointment told me I had expected something other than an official interrogation from him—something warmer and more personal. Far more personal. I forced down my dismay to concentrate on what he was saying.

"Mr. and Mrs. Alexander. Mrs. Dunne. We meet again under unfortunate circumstances." With his thumb and forefinger, Rossi reached into the pocket of his shirt—yellow plumeria blossoms on a navy background today—and extracted a notepad and pencil stub. "We'll start at the beginning." He spread his legs wide in what I had come to recognize as his note-taking stance. "Who found the victim?"

"I did," I answered, my voice breaking like a brittle twig. I'd used those same words before and for the exact same reason. The trembling returned, sweeping through my body, shaking me like a palm frond in the wind.

"Grab her," Rossi shouted to Trevor who stood beside me. Startled, Trevor dropped his mug so fast the Medium Blend sloshed onto the island's marble top. His arm shot out and held me in place.

Hazily, through a fog of emotion, I saw Rossi rush to the garage door. "Hughes," he called. A hand on her holster, she hurried to the kitchen. "Accompany Mrs. Dunne into the living room and stay with her. She needs to lie down."

"But I also wish—" Ilona protested.

"We'll begin questioning with you, Mrs. Alexander," Rossi said, his eyes swiveling away from me to Ilona. "Describe what you saw when you first arrived home."

"But—"

That was all I heard as I left the room with Officer Hughes's surprisingly hard-muscled arm wrapped around my waist.

LIKE AN ARTIST's model—but fully clothed—I lay on Ilona's yellow brocade sofa. Rossi had pulled up a delicate French bergère and sat facing me. The interrogation had gone on for quite a while. I had related everything I could recall about what I'd found in the garage and what I had seen and heard in Trevor's study.

"Will this take much longer, Lieutenant?" I finally asked. "I've told you all I know."

His voice noncommittal, his attitude still all cop, he said, "One last question, Mrs. D. How much time would you say elapsed between when you saw the body and when the Alexanders came in?"

"Several seconds. A minute at the most."

"Anything else you want to add to your story? Any detail, however small, that you can recall?"

"Nothing." My skirt had slid up my thighs. I smoothed it down with a damp palm. "May I remind you, Lieutenant, that noting details is part of my business."

Rossi nodded, flicked a glance at my legs and put his notepad back in his shirt pocket. Ditto for the pencil stub. "That's it, then, Mrs. D."

I sat up straight. "There is one more thing."

Instantly alert, he said, "Yes?"

"I didn't do it."

He exhaled as if he'd just heard stale news. "I have no reason not to believe you, Mrs. D. But you do have an uncanny knack—"

"—for being in the wrong place at the wrong time."

"Exactly."

He stood, moved the bergère back to its original position on the pastel Hebriz, his face as impassive and noncommittal as stone. I swung my legs over the side of the sofa and got to my feet. The room tilted for an instant then righted. I slipped into my Jimmy's, tugged my white silk skirt into position and settled the taupe sweater over my hips. Rossi did his best not to let on that he noticed, but as I said, details are my stock in trade. I saw how his hooded eyes followed my every move. I suppressed a smile. So he wasn't all cop, after all.

We were alone in the Alexanders' living room, the house eerily quiet, just as it had been earlier when I coded my way in.

"Where is everyone?" I asked.

"Forensics is in the garage. The Alexanders have gone to bed."

Was that a smile lifting his lips? It looked like one, but with Rossi, it was hard to tell.

"If you've recovered from your shock, I'll have Officer Hughes drive you home," he said.

Something in his tone irritated me. Okay, seeing Jesus lying in a pool of dried blood had unnerved me. I'll admit that. Still, I wasn't some damned basket case who needed to be hand-driven to her front door.

"I'm perfectly capable of driving myself, Lieutenant. Don't worry about providing me with an escort service. Worry about solving the crime."

At my sarcasm, Rossi's dark eyes took on a glitter that I couldn't read. But I've never been good at body language. Paint, furniture and fabric is what I really understand.

I glanced around the room. For the life of me, I

couldn't remember where I'd left my bag. "All I need are my keys."

"I think you need more than that, Mrs. D. Come on. Come." He waggled his hand, beckoning me. Though he was no Pied Piper, I followed him out of the living room into the kitchen anyway. My bag awaited me on the marble-topped island. One of the cops must have put it there.

"Give me your keys," Rossi said. I was about to refuse when he beat me to it. "I insist."

I could have fought him but didn't. It would take too much energy. Energy I didn't have at the moment. "Here."

I dropped them into his outstretched palm. For an instant only, my fingers brushed his skin. He didn't try to take my hand or hold it but turned away with a curt, "Wait here. I'll be right back."

Telling myself his coldness didn't matter, I slumped on a kitchen stool until he returned with Officer Hughes in tow.

"Officer Hughes will drive you home," Rossi said.

"First I need to empty my trunk."

"Not a problem. We'll exit through the front door." The events of the past few months had taught me quite a bit about police procedure. I knew the garage was out of bounds.

Squad cars, a hearse and the forensics rolling lab—a retro-fitted panel truck that I remembered seeing a month ago—thronged the driveway, boxing in my car.

"Have Batano help you clear out her trunk, then drive across the lawn," Rossi told Officer Hughes. "I don't want the guys inside disturbed."

"Yes, sir."

After carrying out Rossi's orders, Hughes slid behind the wheel of the Audi, and I got in on the passenger side. At the entrance to the property, Batano stood guard, waving curiosity seekers away, keeping chaos at a distance.

"You have the address?" Rossi asked Hughes, as if I weren't sitting there perfectly capable of giving her directions myself. The nerve of him.

"Surfside Club on Gulf Shore."

"That's it." He turned to Batano. "Hughes will need a ride back."

Batano gave Rossi a noncommittal nod and, striding out to the middle of Gordon Drive, held up traffic long enough for Officer Hughes to gun the Audi across the grass and pull out onto the road. I wondered if the tires left tracks in the pristine lawn, but dismissed the thought as soon as it flared up. What difference did it make?

"Buckle up, Mrs. Dunne," Officer Hughes said and then drove silently all the way to Surfside. I laid my head back on the tan leather cushions, happy, actually, not to have to fight the traffic. At the height of the tourist season, the Naples roads were as congested as clogged arteries.

At Surfside, she parked in my assigned parking slot in the carport, and we both piled out of the car. Officer Hughes snapped the locks and handed me my keys. So she planned to walk me to my door. Fine. Police procedure? I shrugged and trudged across the parking lot, tired and depressed. Today Rossi and I had been total strangers. Though he said he believed my story, the easy camaraderie we shared the night he brought pizza and grocery store flowers had completely disappeared.

At my door, I inserted the key in the lock and extended a hand. "Thanks for the lift, officer."

Instead of taking my hand, Officer Hughes reached into her hip holster and removed her service pistol. "Open up and step aside, please."

"You've got to be kidding." I pointed to the gun. "What's that all about?"

"Lieutenant's orders. I'm to make sure your house is secure. Wait outside here till I return."

Egads. I leaned against the stucco wall and stood in the fading sun. It didn't take long before Officer Hughes was back, tucking her gun into its holster.

"You check under the bed?" I asked.

No smile. "Your house is secure, Mrs. Dunne. Have a good evening."

She strode off to the waiting squad car. "Hey," I called after her, "thanks for checking."

If she heard me, she didn't turn around to wave. Resigned, I just shrugged. I'd struck out all day long. But Jesus, Jesus had struck out big time.

CHAPTER NINETEEN

THE SHORT WINTER day had lowered into dusk. I kicked off my heels and peeled out of my sweater and skirt, replacing them with a Florida uniform—white T-shirt and denim cutoffs.

Too demoralized to eat or drink a thing, too world weary to even snap on the evening news, I flopped on one of the club chairs and stared at the living room wall. As the gloom gathered around me, I gave myself a halfhearted pep talk.

So what if Rossi had treated me like a piece of wood all day? A consummate professional, he had concentrated on his job, and, without question, that was the right thing to do. I was annoyed with myself for letting his clinical attitude bother me. What I needed to do was suck up my disappointment and believe that once the case was solved, he would come after me like gang busters, no holds barred, and love the breath right out of my body. Easier said than done. The day's trauma and the loneliness I'd been holding at bay for a year overwhelmed me, and I heaved out a sigh that echoed in the quiet room. I might have sat like that for hours, not moving a muscle if the doorbell hadn't chimed.

Da da da DA.

Whoever it was could damn well go away. I wasn't in the mood for drop-in company. I wasn't in the mood for anything.

Da da da DA. Da da da DA.

"Open up. Police."

Rossi. What did he want?

"Open up! Police."

I gripped the chair arms. Maybe this wasn't a social call at all. Maybe Rossi was here on official business. The man *was* a homicide detective. I *had* just found a murder victim.

My breath caught in my throat. Only one way to find out what he wanted. Slowly, as if my bones might be mush when put to the test, I got to my feet and dragged out to the foyer.

Da da da DA.

For some reason, he couldn't wait for me to open up, and I tensed for a moment. Then my Irish flared. I was innocent, for Pete's sake. Why act like I was approaching the gallows? Straightening my shoulders, I held my head high and flung the door open.

Ready to press the bell again, Rossi's finger hovered in the air before he lowered his hand to his side. Some part of my mind registered that he looked harassed and irritable, not surprising in light of what he'd had to deal with today, but I was too irritable myself to cut him any slack.

"Why are you here, Lieutenant? It was my impression the interrogation was over," I said, damned if I'd let him get past the foyer.

He waved his hand forward, impatiently nudging me back into the living room. To put a few inches between us, I retreated a step. That was all the edge he needed. Slamming the door behind him, he shot the bolt and strode past me into the living room.

Hands on hips, I followed him in. "I don't remember inviting you. I have nothing more to say to the police."

"Well, I have a few things to say to you." With a couple of strides, he covered the distance between us, pulled me to him and wrapped his arms around me. "It could have been you on that garage floor. The thought's had me crazy all day. You could have walked in on the killer. Caught him in the act. Then what?"

Too stunned to protest, I nestled against Rossi's chest, inhaling aftershave and a faint trace of something else. Male pheromones? Whatever it was, I liked it. I liked it a lot and didn't even try to pull out of his embrace. This was what I'd been wanting him to do for a month. What I'd been longing for. My irritation melted like icicles in April.

"I could have lost you before we ever…"

This was all so unbelievable. A hundred-and-eighty-degree turn. I wanted to hear more. Had to hear more.

"So sorry," he whispered into my hair.

"For what?"

"For what you found last month. For what you found today. For everything that makes you unhappy."

I tried loosening his embrace so I could see his face, but as I tensed in his arms, he held me even tighter.

"Let me go, Rossi. I want to look at you."

He relaxed his arms a bit. I drew back, still in the circle of his embrace, and glanced up at him. This was no joke. He was utterly serious.

"And I'm sorry for something else—for not being here to keep you safe all these weeks."

"But, the chief—"

He lowered his mouth to mine and, unthinking, as if it were the most natural thing in the world, I opened to him and slipped my tongue between his lips. He growled and seized me so close he sealed us together from thigh to hip to chest, his mouth hardening, pressing, his tongue teasing, his breathing labored and quick, as was mine. Why were we breathless? We hadn't climbed any mountains, had we? No, not yet. But somewhere in my fevered brain, I knew the Matterhorn loomed ahead.

When we finally parted so we could both inhale, his hands cupped the back of my head, his fingers probing deep into my hair. "I couldn't wait any longer. Not after today. Not after walking into that fancy kitchen and seeing your face all white and frozen. When your freckles pop out, I know you're in distress. I hate seeing you like that, Mrs. D."

I looked up into his face. "Say my name. You never have. I want to hear it from your lips. Say it."

He smiled into my eyes. "Deva. Devalera." His smile widened. "Devalera. That's a hell of a handle, Mrs. D."

Dammit, he'd wrecked the moment. "I happen to love my name," I lied, wriggling out of his arms. "You've got some nerve, Rossi."

"Honey, I've got more than nerve." He cocked an eyebrow. "Interested?"

A challenge. "I haven't decided yet."

He nodded and raised his hands in the air, palms out. "Okay, play it safe. Swim in the shallow end of the pool. For a long time, I've been that way myself. But I think I'm getting ready to change. So let me ask you something. When's the last time you went to the moon?"

"The *moon?*"

"Yeah. Since you lost Jack, that is."

"Three, four times last week. Twice yesterday."

His jaw dropped.

Aha! A hit.

"Yup. I've been the town pump, Rossi."

He waggled a finger at me. A metronome. Left, right.

Left, right. "Not a chance. You loved Jack too much to sleep around."

A surge of emotion flared through me. "My feelings for Jack are none of your damn business."

Serious again, he looked me straight in the eye. "I know you loved him. There's no need to erase that, ever. Or to pretend that you don't want another man in your life. Maybe I'm the guy." He shrugged. "Maybe not. But think it over."

"Let me ask *you* something, Rossi."

"Shoot."

"How many times have *you* been to the moon?"

"You know something, Deva. I used to believe I'd been there a lot, but lately I'm not so sure. I think those trips I took were to minor planets." He cocked an eyebrow and waited.

I smiled. Who could stay mad at Rossi?

The cell phone in his pocket began an insistent chirping. *Always at the wrong time.*

He fished the phone out of his pocket and growled into it. He listened for a moment, his fingers tightening on the receiver. "I'll be right in," he said. "Leave the report on my desk." He repocketed the cell. "Duty calls. Have to go." He gave me a hurried, unsatisfying peck on the cheek and was halfway out the door when he turned back, a wicked gleam in his eye. "One last question, Mrs. D. You ever hear of the Big Bang Theory?"

CHAPTER TWENTY

AT EIGHT THE next morning I woke with a start, flung back the covers and leaped up, amazed that I had slept like a baby for hours. With my life in chaos, how could I have been so relaxed? The conversation with Rossi? Maybe. The kiss? More than likely.

I stretched, long and luxuriously, reaching for the sky, then took a quick, cool shower and scrambled into some clothes…a white string sweater and a bright orange skirt. Strappy tan leather sandals with four-inch heels. In them I'd look tall and towering—to match my mood.

On my way out, I left the *Naples Daily* lying on the front step in its plastic sleeve without even glancing at the headlines. I knew what I'd find. Why torture myself? What I didn't know was what I'd find at the shop—a throng, a mob, or worse, deadly, empty silence.

I found Lee alone with worry lines creasing her forehead. No wonder. Having your employer discover two murder victims in less than a month didn't add up to job security.

"Morning, Deva," she said, forcing a wan smile. "Daddy just left. He told me what happened. I'm so sorry."

"Daddy?" About to stash my handbag underneath the sales counter, I straightened in disbelief and the bag fell to the floor. "Isn't he in Alabama?"

"He's on his way back there today. He sold his place over in East Naples and was here for the closing."

So Merle Skimp had been in town yesterday. I doubted Merle's presence was enough to cause the tension I had seen coiling in Rossi's back when he answered his cell phone yesterday. But who knew? If Merle had been in Naples at the time Jesus was killed, were the cops aware of that? And if not, would pointing out the possibility be the action of a rat fink? Or the best thing I could do for Lee and Paulo? Exasperated, I retrieved the bag and placed it under the counter.

With a tired sigh, Lee sank onto the chair behind her desk. "Daddy gave me a nice check from the sale. I know he worries about me…I didn't tell him Paulo and I are getting married." Her eyes filled with tears. "I'm afraid he'll try to stop me." She looked down at her lap. "But I took the check anyway."

"Of course you did. Your mother would have wanted you to."

"That's what Daddy said. So I took it." She glanced up, tears brimming under her lids. "In case…in case…"

"The shop fails," I finished.

She nodded. "There's just no way of tellin', Deva. I'm so scared. Paulo knew that Jesus man. They worked together. He'll be questioned again. Under suspicion again."

She was right, Paulo would be under suspicion again, and so would I. I could think of no words of comfort for either of us. All we could do was play the waiting game. And pray. But somehow I felt far from defeated even though the shop was dead all morning, even though by one in the afternoon not a single customer had come through the door, not a single phone call through the line.

The truth was Rossi was keeping despair at bay. I knew Jack would understand. Months earlier, in my dreams, he had told me not to let his death keep me from living. I could still hear his voice with its lilting brogue: "When life closes one door, it opens another. A pretty marvelous phenomenon, don't you think?"

I do.

Troubled about the lack of business, yet buoyant, I was such a contradictory bundle of nerves that when the phone finally rang in the middle of the afternoon, my hand shot out and I grabbed it before the second ring.

"Deva Dunne Interiors."

"Deva," Rossi said. Not Mrs. D. Pleased, I pressed the phone to my ear, bringing him in a little closer.

He cleared his throat, his voice lowering. "I appreciated your honesty during my…ah…interrogation yesterday." His discretion told me he was calling from the station.

"I would never lie to the police."

He laughed, an honest-to-God, deep belly laugh. I held the phone away from my ear and stared at it. That was a first. Grins, yes. Smiles, rarely. Smirks, definitely. But an out-and-out laugh? Never.

I brought the phone back to my ear. "I mean it, Lieutenant. I'll cooperate whenever I can be of service."

"I'll keep that in mind. In fact, I may have some further questions for you."

"Whenever you're ready, Lieutenant."

"I'll be in touch."

I hung up positively energized. Though business was dead, killed by all the lethal publicity, I was more alive today than I'd been since Jack died. Today nothing would defeat me. Nothing.

I glanced across the shop to where Lee sat behind her

desk, patiently waiting to greet the first customer of the day. It was two o'clock. We had been open since nine.

Screw it.

"Lee, how would you like to have lunch at the Ritz Carlton?"

Her eyes widened into blue pools. "Oh, my. I've never been to the Ritz."

"Well, high time then. Grab your purse and let's go. We're celebrating."

"What all are we celebrating, Deva?"

"The good men in our lives."

She rewarded me with the only real smile I'd seen on her face all day. Brighter than Ilona's diamonds, it lit up the whole shop. "It's the lieutenant, isn't it?"

The bells on the door jangled, and we both turned toward the door.

Uh-oh. Mrs. Jessica Jones. In funereal black from head to foot.

She bounded into the shop, slamming the door so hard the bells jangled for another thirty seconds. "Did that bastard tell you what he did to me?"

"Which bastard is that?" I asked, taking the Fifth.

"Don't pretend, Deva." With a nod at Lee, Jessica took a seat on the zebra settee. "He served me with divorce papers, the son of a bitch."

I heaved a sigh. This wasn't going to be easy. "You handle anger well, Jessica."

Her eyes narrowed at me, but she rested the Ferragamo tote on the floor next to her feet as if she planned to stay a while and crossed her legs at the knee.

At the knee. "Not to change the subject, Jessica, but have you lost weight?"

She ran her palms down her sides. "Ten pounds since Christmas. It's the best thing that's happened to me in years. Only forty more to go. I hope you don't have any of those Christmas cookies left. I can do without the temptation."

"You're safe. They're long gone."

Lee dropped her purse back into a desk drawer. I guess she recognized that Jessica needed to vent, and that meant girl talk, lots of it.

Jessica picked up the Ferragamo and rummaged in it for a tissue. I hoped she wasn't about to burst into tears. But no, she gave her nose a vigorous blow, tucked the tissue in a jacket pocket and said, "I like you, Deva, so I came to warn you, woman to woman."

"Warn me? About what?"

Lee stiffened. I caught her alarmed glance and smiled, but her troubled expression didn't change.

I pulled up a folding garden chair. Whatever Jessica had to say would be easier to take sitting down. I leaned forward. "What is it?"

"Don't trust Morgan. He's a bloody liar."

"But—"

She held up a hand for silence. "Let me finish. I have proof. Wait till you see this." She reached back into the tote, yanked out a bank statement and thrust it at me.

One glance and I knew. "All his accounts have been cancelled."

"Right. And that's just the Sun Trust Bank. The others are the same. He's stripped every account. At least those I could find."

I handed her back the statement.

"I had to take a hammer to his desk drawer to get this much information. Wait till he sees the damage. Not that I give a damn. What infuriates me is that he changed the password to his PC. God knows what he's hiding in there. But one thing for sure, he's holding out on me, Deva."

This didn't bode well for Jessica. Or for Deva Dunne Interiors, either. "I'm sorry to hear all this. You sounded so positive the night you telephoned."

"Yeah. Well I was a fool to believe him. He knew you and I had talked about the new house. So he figured he had to tell me the truth about it. That kept me off his back until he could move his assets where I wouldn't find them. And that little weasel helped him."

"Weasel?"

"George Farragut. God, I can't stand the creep. He's as bad as Morgan with his precious collections. All those drab etchings. Not a one with any color to it. Just like him. The little prick."

George's etchings may be drab, but your language sure is colorful.

"I used to be such a lady." Jessica uncrossed her legs and, spreading them apart, dropped her hands between her knees. "Now I'm a piranha. Out for blood. That's why I'm here. I don't want Morgan to screw you over—" with a wink to a wide-eyed Lee, "—metaphorically speaking, of course, the way he screwed me. So get your money upfront. Or else leave him hanging with a half-finished house. Slap a lien on it if you have to. He'll have a tough time impressing his bimbo then."

A housewife forever and now sliding down the fifties hill, Jessica had my sympathy, even though punishing Morgan, not protecting my interests, was her motive in coming here today. I couldn't blame her for her fury, but she should be concentrating on her fiscal interests, not revenge. Anger must have her blindsided. I wondered what marketable skills she possessed but didn't dare ask. Her ace in the hole was her husband, and it looked like she'd played that card. Unless?

"Have you seen a lawyer, Jessica?"

She looked up from her knees and shook her head. "A divorce lawyer? Not yet. First I'm talking to Morgan's tax attorney. See if I can get the truth out of him. We always filed a joint return, so I know how much Morgan earned but not where it went. Simon Yaeger better not hold out on me." She pounded a fist on the settee arm. "I have a right to know. Once I learn what's what from Yaeger, I'll contact a divorce lawyer. You know a good one? Somebody who'll go for the jugular?"

I shook my head when what I wanted to do was slap myself on the forehead. Sometimes you can't see the forest—too many trees in the way. Of course, they all knew each other. Simon, the Alexanders, George Farragut, and now the Morgan Joneses.

So not only did Simon handle legal affairs for Trevor and George, he apparently did so for the Morgans. That was something I didn't find out the day I rifled—I mean glanced at—the documents on Trevor's desk. The day Simon called and left that chilling message on Trevor's answering machine. And of course both Simon and George did business with Trevor.

Now that I thought about it, there were a lot of loose ends, too. George had recommended the Russian art show to Simon. They had planned to meet there that night so Simon could return George's briefcase. A briefcase Simon had been storing in his office for a week—the very week after Maria was murdered. For some unexplained reason, at the last minute George had skipped the art show. Had he seen Rossi lurking in his car outside the gallery? Could that have kept him away? It had to have been something serious. The next day he had arrived at Morgan's house practically panting to get his briefcase back. Whatever it held had to have been valuable.

Not a laptop. It had been too light. Client records, then? Facts, information? Possibly. Or money. No. Suitcases full of cash only cropped up in B movies...

Somewhere, in the background, Jessica nattered on about how rotten Morgan was, how *she* was going to operate on *him* for a change. Her words were gnats buzzing in the distance. A cold sweat broke out on my skin, for in that instant, I *knew* without proof, without evidence, without anything except a growling in my gut that could not be denied—

George had rolled up the Monet and hidden it in his briefcase. And Simon had stored it for him. What better hiding place than the office of Naples's most respected law firm? Which left me with two burning questions: Had Simon known what was in the case? And where was the painting now?

"...furthermore, Deva, I'll bet that bimbo is a bag of bones. Wait till he bangs into her in the dark. Ha! He'll miss me then."

With a start, I came back into the moment. "I'm sorry, Jessica. What were you saying?"

THE PHONE RANG shortly after Jessica left. Rossi again? Or maybe a customer. I picked up fast.

"Deva. For you I have bad news. It is bad for me, too."

"What is it, Ilona?"

"Our Wine Festival dinner is no more. It's *halott*. Dead."

Surprised but not stunned, I asked, "You've cancelled? Why?"

"Everybody we invite refuse. They will not come to my house. No matter how old my family, they do not come. Tonight, Trevor and I, we go to Port Royal Club for dinner. If no one sit with us then I know we are finished in Naples. Finished. It is not fair, Deva. We own two Monets, so we are victims." A Hungarian sigh floated through the line. "No longer do we even own two. I go now. I must inform Cheep."

"Your retainer, Ilona?"

"Never no mind, Deva. You keep. For aggravation."

"Thank you. I appreciate that." Especially since I had already spent it. Actually, Ilona was kind to excuse the two thousand. Maybe, after all, I had misjudged her. "What of the party supplies I stored in your garage? They're all returnable."

"Come get whenever you wish." She lowered her voice to a conspiratorial whisper. "The last number on code is three now, not five. But you may not need code. Tomorrow, our new housekeeper arrive. Another Maria, she is. I tell her to let you in whenever you call."

"I appreciate your trust, Ilona." I meant it. If the situation were reversed and I lived in a house where two people had been murdered, I wouldn't trust a soul with my security code. I wondered why Ilona did.

"We are girls together, Deva. Of course I trust. It is the mens I no trust."

Ah. My answer?

"Now, I hang up phone. I am too upset to talk more."

I cradled the receiver. Poor Chip. He would be devastated. I glanced around my silent, empty shop. Deva Dunne Interiors already was devastated. I had a feeling it would remain so until the Alexander case was solved. That had better be soon. My pockets were too shallow to hold out much longer. With that thought, my temper flared. I hated feeling like a victim.

"Let's call it a day, Lee. This place is as dead as a teetotaler's party."

She laughed. "You have funny sayings, Deva. Are they Irish?"

"Well, that one probably is." I glanced at my watch. Three o'clock. Too late for lunch. "Come on, I'll drop you off at home. I promise we'll do a fancy lunch another day."

"Would y'all mind dropping me at Paulo's instead? He's home working on a portrait. His first commission. You should see it. It's beautiful. Two little children, a brother and a sister. Though to speak frankly to y'all, I think the momma should have asked for separate portraits. Someday, I declare, those two little ones'll be fightin' over who gets Paulo's painting."

Her love for her man shone in her eyes, on her skin, in the very way she pronounced his name. Shyly, as if her pride in him were pride in herself, she said, "When he has six or more portraits finished, the Von Liebig Art Center is going to give him a one-man show."

"How wonderful! After that, he'll be on his way."

She nodded, happy to agree. "Uh-huh. 'Course he needs more commissions to get to that six number, but he'll get them. Wait till people see those children."

"Of course he will. Let's go. After I leave you, I'll swing by Mesnik's frame shop. Those powder room fashion prints are ready."

Then I'd go home and wait for Rossi to call. Impatiently.

CHAPTER TWENTY-ONE

At Mesnik's, the front section of the shop was empty. I stood at the sales counter for a few minutes before calling, "Hello. Anybody home?"

Michael Mesnik popped his head through the green velvet curtain that screened his back workroom from customer view.

"Sorry, Mrs. Dunne. I didn't hear you come in."

"The six fashion prints?"

"Ah, yes. They're ready." He parted the curtain, holding it open with one hand. "Come have a look. I think you'll be pleased."

I circled the sales counter and stepped into the inner sanctum. Curious, I glanced around at the sizeable room. Michael had centered it with a massive wooden worktable and lined it with shelves holding various lengths of framing in every conceivable style and color. Sheets of glass waiting to be cut to size and matting materials in a rainbow array filled several slanted bins. Against one wall, a long workbench held electric saws, hand tools, paint cans and brushes. Overall, a sloppy, cluttered space for busy, creative people.

And then against another wall something else caught my eye and I gasped. A portrait of Ilona Alexander. Unmistakable and breathtaking, it could be no other. I stepped in closer. The cascade of honey blond hair, the sculpted cheekbones, the knowing siren's smile, the deep cleavage. She lived on that canvas, a lush, pulsating woman, a dream goddess.

Mesmerized, I stood staring, caught up in the image before it occurred to me to search for the artist's signature. Ah, there it was along the edge, scrolled in a thick bold lettering—Paulo St. James.

Lee hadn't mentioned Paulo's doing a portrait of Ilona. Did she know?

"She's really something, isn't she?" Michael said, startling me out of my thoughts.

"Yes. Something."

"It's here for framing. Brilliant young artist painted it. A Paulo St. James. Got a great future ahead of him." Michael stared at the portrait smiling as warmly at it as if Ilona would smile back. "She's the most beautiful woman I've ever seen."

"Right."

"Present company excepted of course."

I laughed. "Not necessary, Michael. I know Mrs. Alexander. She's a stunner."

"St. James sure thinks so."

"He said that?" I asked, my voice sounding squeaky even to me.

"Didn't have to. How else could he have done this?"

Poor Lee. I remembered the way Ilona had stared at Paulo the day he came to Chez Alexander to set up the party bar. But that didn't explain why he kept his portrait of her a secret from the girl he loved. Yet there had to be a reason, I told myself. A good, solid reason. As soon as I had a chance to speak to Paulo alone, I'd ask him.

Or would I? What right did I have? None.

No, until Lee mentioned the portrait to me, I wouldn't say anything about it to either of them. But I would tell

Rossi. I had to. While I didn't want to believe Paulo had done anything wrong—couldn't believe it—for Maria and Jesus's sakes, the police should know everything that had occurred in the Alexander household, no matter how trivial. Though somehow this didn't strike me as trivial.

"Your prints are over here," Michael said, jarring me back to the moment. He went to a side wall where, out of the line of traffic, he kept the newly framed and restored artworks. "Let me put them where you can get a better look," he said, picking up the prints and laying them on the center worktable.

"Very nice," I said. The prints weren't great art, but they were charming and would lend a delicate, feminine look to the powder room.

Michael's assistant nodded a greeting. Intent on restoring a Hudson River oil painting, he couldn't talk. Not with a mouthful of tacks. He popped out a tack from between his lips. Holding it with a thumb and forefinger, he carefully tapped it into the edge of the canvas he was smoothing over a wooden stretcher. Then he popped out another one.

I hoped he wouldn't suddenly have to sneeze.

"Usually we staple a painting onto a stretcher," Michael explained, "but on these old canvases we use tacks. Less stress on the artwork."

His assistant continued to pop out the tacks and secure them in place, slowly stretching the canvas so it would show no bulges, no sags, no wrinkles.

Tacks. I stared at the oil, seeing not the murky river scene but a garage workbench scattered with tacks, and a dead man's open palm filled with more of them.

Michael made a stack of the prints. "Let's go out front so I can wrap these for you, Mrs. Dunne."

"May I ask you a question?"

"Of course."

"Have you ever invited George Farragut back here?"

Michael laughed. "George doesn't wait for an invitation. He just makes himself at home."

WHAT I WANTED to do was go to Surfside and wait for Rossi's call. Instead, I drove back to the shop, unpacked the prints and phoned the customer to tell her they were ready. Then I dusted all the displays, rearranged the tablescapes and uncrated a box of crystal hearts for Valentine's Day. I was stalling for time. Tonight, while Trevor and Ilona dined at the Port Royal Club, I intended to make a house call on Chez Alexander. Seven o'clock struck me as the most likely witching hour. At best, it would be a narrow window of opportunity. Tomorrow a new Maria would be in the kitchen, and for what I had in mind, I needed the house to myself. If I miscalculated, and the Alexanders were home, I'd say I had come for the party supplies. Feeble, true, but the best plan I could come up with.

At five o'clock, I locked the shop, turned off my cell and drove to Lowdermilk Beach to hide from Rossi and wait. As much as I longed to see him, if he came to the condo after work, he wouldn't want me to leave, and he'd never agree to go with me. Not without a search warrant.

If I thought he'd order a warrant, I'd tell him everything, though my everything amounted to nothing more than a hunch. Nothing more than a suspicion that George Farragut had stolen the Monet, stashed it in his briefcase in Simon's office for a while and then, using tacks like those I'd seen in Jesus's hand, had hidden it behind the remaining painting.

Why should Rossi buy into a theory like that? I had no proof. Just a belief deep in my gut that I was right. I couldn't ask Rossi to share that belief. If he did and I was wrong, the chief would have his head.

No, better I go it alone. Convinced the gamble was worthwhile, I sat on the sand with one eye on my watch, the other on a glorious sunset, all peach, purple and turquoise, uncannily like the missing Monet. At quarter to seven, I brushed the sand off my skirt and drove over to Port Royal. To keep suspicion at bay, I parked on Thirteenth Avenue with its steady trickle of traffic. On elegant Gordon Drive, any unoccupied cars parked by the side of the road were suspect. Attention from a PD cruiser was the last thing I wanted.

I slipped off my high-heeled sandals, changed into the Nikes I kept in the trunk, and power-walked the few blocks over to the Alexander house. Lights twinkled in the downstairs windows, but not many. The upstairs bedrooms were dark. A Ford Taurus with a dented rear fender sat near the bottom of the drive, enough out of place in Jaguar Land to draw my attention. I didn't see anyone around. Maybe the driver had run out of gas.

I jogged up the stone stairs to the entrance. The evening air, redolent with sea salt, blew soft and warm, doing little to keep me cool. To be sure the house was empty, I rang the chimes. No answer.

Praying Ilona had given me the correct new code, I punched in the numbers on the key pad and tried the door handle. *Bingo.* A quick glance over my shoulders… left…right…no one on the scene…

"Excuse me."

Nearly startled out of my skin, I whirled around. An armed security guard in an official-looking dark blue uniform strode out from around the corner of the house.

"Can I help you, Miss?"

Not Naples PD. A private security cop. Still, the stern-jawed guy didn't look like a pushover.

"I'm Devalera Dunne, Mrs. Alexander's interior designer. I'm out for a walk, so I thought I'd check up on some party materials she ordered."

"Just a minute, please."

The guard reached into his shirt pocket, removed a sheet of paper and eyeballed it. Heart pounding, I hoped Ilona had given the security company my name.

He repocketed the paper. "I need to see some ID. A driver's license will do."

Sweating, and not just from the humidity, I reached into my canvas tote, removed the license from my billfold and handed it to him. In the light cast by the entrance lamps, he glanced at my photograph, then at me.

"It's a terrible likeness," I babbled, "but I never did take a good picture." Oh God, of all the things to say.

After a final eye check, he gave the license back to me without a comment. "Go ahead in" was all he said.

Trying not to look too grateful, I nodded and, easing the entrance door open, slipped into the cool, dimly lit foyer, disarmed the motion sensor and reset the locks.

No need for more light. I knew my way and crept toward the dining room on the balls of my feet. Something about this house always put me in tiptoe mood, and tonight was no different.

I had seldom been in here after dark and couldn't help taking a few moments to glance around and wonder, for a split second, what it would be like to live in such opulence. Though beautiful in the daytime, at night the house was pure magic with the lamps casting soft pools of light on the lush rugs, the gleaming floors, the crystal chandeliers…and, in the dining room, on *Sunrise at Royan*.

The beam from a recessed ceiling light illuminated the lapping water on that faraway shore and the images of three women who stood staring at Monet's perfect blue sea. I blew out a breath, intimidated by the sight. Just looking at the painting gave me a high, never mind actually touching it.

I dropped my bag to the floor. No need right now for the flashlight. I wiped my damp palms on my skirt, reached up, and lifted the Monet from its wire holder. Slowly, I lowered it to the floor, turned it to face the wall and knelt in front of it. For all of its size, the painting weighed surprisingly little, the frame's gilded wood old and dry. Another surprise, no brown paper dust cover protected the back. A good restorer would never have left an irreplaceable painting unprotected this way. My pulses throbbed. Was my hunch right, then?

Four wooden pegs, one at each corner, secured the canvas stretcher in the frame. I took a pair of snub-nosed pliers from my tote, pulled out the pegs and placed them on the floor. A clock sounded in the distance and my hand jerked. Seven-thirty. I needed to be careful. Poke a hole in this masterwork, and I'd end up in jail.

Despite the cool air, my palms were sweaty, and I wiped them on the orange skirt again. Then gently, like pressing on a baby's cheek, I ran my fingers along the edge of the wooden stretcher and eased the canvas out of the gilded frame.

Beads formed on my forehead and dripped down my cheeks. If that guard decided to come in and check around, I'd be dead meat. My breath came in short, fast pants, but air wasn't getting into my lungs. *Slow down.*

Slow down. Breathe deep. It's okay. You're in this far. Don't panic now. Look. Look at what you came to see.

I fumbled in the bag at my feet, grabbed the flashlight and hit the on button. The light flared, concentrating its energy on a single spot—the raw edge of the canvas. I peered closer, holding the flash in both hands to steady it. In its yellow beam, I saw what I'd hoped to find. A row of tacks, holding not one, but two raw edges. A second canvas *had* been hidden under the first. For a moment, the thrill of triumph shot through my veins. I'd been right, after all. I'd found the missing Monet. But reality swept in and brought me back to earth. I had no way to be certain of what I'd discovered. No time. No tools. No right to tamper further. If caught here tonight, I'd be in deep trouble.

Fingers shaking, I carefully pressed the canvas back into the frame and inserted the four wooden pegs into the corner slots.

A door opened. The garage door to the kitchen? Crouched in front of the painting, I froze, listening.

Omigod. The murmur of voices.

I stood quickly and picked up the painting. It was heavier to lift than to take down. Arms trembling with effort, I raised it, fumbled for the wall hook and settled it in place.

Click. Click. Click.

Ilona's high heels. The sound coming closer shocked me motionless.

Where to hide? I couldn't let them find me in their dining room with a flashlight in my hand.

Where? Where could I hide?

Behind the draperies. Ten thousand dollars' worth of silk fabric should be able to conceal one medium-sized woman. I snatched up my bag and, dropping the flashlight inside, tiptoed over to the curtain wall and huddled behind the bouffant folds.

High heels clicked into the dining room. "Deva is not here," Ilona said. "She must have left without guard seeing her. But party boxes are still in garage. I no understand—"

"I told you not to give out the code to anybody. But as usual, you didn't listen to me."

Trevor. I'd heard that annoyed tone in his voice before.

"She forgot to reset the motion sensor on her way out. Just like a woman." His tone had gone from annoyed to disgusted.

"Deva is no threat. She just want party supplies."

"Don't worry your head over that pile of crap. You've got other fish to fry. Tonight's the night."

"*Nem.* No, darling. Not tonight. I'm too upset. Not one person sit at our table. Or stop to chat. We must leave this place."

"The only place I'm going to is bed. And you with me."

"You no understand, Trevor. I want to go home to my *anya.* To Hungary. We have armed guard outside our door. It's like gulag. I no want to live here anymore."

"Oh, yeah? Well, I do. It's a goddamn paradise. What I no want is that *nem, nem, nem.* Always, it's *nem, nem, nem.* What the hell did you marry me for? No, don't answer that. I already know. Come on. Come on. Up the stairs."

In the stifling air behind that heavy fabric, my clothes stuck to my back as I strained to listen. A muffled slap floated through the draperies.

"I've told you no touch my *derriere* like that," Ilona

said, then the click of her stiletto heels on the marble stairs.

I waited, hardly daring to breathe, for what seemed like an eternity before creeping out from behind the draperies and inching toward the foyer. I'd disarm the security code and reset it, motion sensors and all. In the next instant, I'd be outside waving to the guard. Then I'd disappear down the driveway and out of sight before Trevor got his pants back on.

CHAPTER TWENTY-TWO

The instant I slid behind the wheel of the Audi, I groped for the cell and, heart hammering, phoned Rossi. For once, I had something important to tell him, something he couldn't dismiss for lack of evidence.

He picked up on the first ring. "Where are you?"

"On my way home. Will you meet me there? Fifteen minutes?"

"I'm already there," he growled. "In your parking lot."

"You're waiting for me? How sweet." I heaved out a sigh of relief. I could always count on Rossi. "Why don't you jimmy my door open and wait inside?"

"There's a name for that. Breaking and entering. It's against the law."

"Be home as soon as I can," I said, disconnecting the call and tossing the cell on the passenger seat. As I eased out of the parking space and onto Thirteenth Avenue, my heartbeat slowed to normal. A purist about the law, Rossi might not be as pleased with my news as I'd first thought.

Okay, so technically, I'd entered the Alexander mansion under false pretenses. But I meant no harm. If, in fact, I had found the stolen painting, I'd done some good, hadn't I? An irreplaceable treasure, the Monet belonged out in the world, not fenced into hiding by some sneak thief. Surely Rossi would agree to that.

Anxious to get to him and spill what I knew, I pressed on the gas pedal. With light traffic all the way home, I made it in ten minutes flat and zoomed into the Surfside carport, screeching to a halt next to Rossi's Mustang.

He greeted me with a poker face and a slight nod of his head. What a romantic.

Nightfall had cooled the salt-laden air a bit, but not by much, and we strolled into my air-conditioned living room with a sigh of relief. But the air didn't feel cool for long. He reached for me, and together we soon upped the temperature to a sweaty, humid, tropical haze.

Before my body could turn to flame, I eased out of his embrace. "I have to tell you something."

"It'll wait." He stroked my hair.

I took a step back. "No, I have to tell you or bust."

"Your timing is terrific." He frowned but let me take his hand and draw him onto the sofa. While I told him what I'd found, he listened without interrupting. But the more I talked, the more the scowl lines in his forehead deepened into grooves.

"That it?" he asked when I stopped, his voice dripping with ice. Or maybe with fire.

I nodded and sat hugging my knees in a corner of the sofa while he paced around my living room waving his arms. I'd never seen him so incensed.

"Breaking and entering is a felony. The Alexanders would be within their rights to press charges."

The anger in his voice sent my own temper soaring. "Why would they do that? The guard let me in. I'm on Ilona's good-guy list."

Rossi glared at me, his hooded eyes smoldering, but not with the passion I'd hoped for. I couldn't blame him for being furious. Now that I was safely back home, the chance I had taken swept over me, catching me up in a delayed reaction. If I dared get off the couch, I was sure my knees would buckle.

Rossi stopped pacing to stand over me, glowering. "A killer's on the loose."

"I know," I said.

"He struck twice in that house you just broke into."

"I didn't—"

"Don't interrupt. You could have been his next victim. You should have thought of that."

Seeing him so upset, with worry lines creasing his forehead and veins sticking out in his neck, I just nodded, all protest exhausted. But Rossi had more to say.

"Suppose he found you examining the painting? Maria was killed because she caught someone cutting it out of the frame."

"You're raving, Rossi."

"And Jesus was killed because he caught someone—"

"Hiding the stolen Monet behind the other one," I finished. "And the most likely candidate to have done so is George Farragut."

Rossi shut up and sank onto the sofa next to me. He held out his arms. "Come here."

I didn't need a second invitation to snuggle next to him. Warm and hard, his arms pulled me in close. I laid my head on his chest and listened to his heart. All that ranting had it pounding like crazy.

"There's something else you should know," I said after a moment.

He groaned and loosened his grip a little. "What now?"

"When I was in Mesnik's frame shop today I saw something."

"Yeah?"

"A painting of Ilona Alexander. Paulo is the artist."

Rossi frowned. "Why is that significant information?"

"No one has been told about it. I don't think even Lee knows."

"So?"

"There has to be a reason for the secrecy. I thought you should know."

"All right. It's probably not relevant to the case, but I'll follow up on it." He dropped a kiss on my hair. "There's something else I have to tell you."

He knows the thief's identity. He trusts me enough to confide in me. I leaned back in his arms so I could look into his face.

"I care for you," he said. "I don't want anything to happen to you. Understand?" He held me at arm's length so he could judge my response to his words "I can't stand it when you place yourself in jeopardy," he continued. "Like you did tonight. Like you have in the past."

"But—"

"No buts. Throw your arms around me and tell me something I want to hear."

"I care for you, too, Rossi." Before the words left my lips, I knew them to be true. I did care for him, Hawaiian shirts, gravelly voice and all. So Jack, God bless him, had known the truth all along. When life takes something wonderful away, it sends something wonderful in its place. "As my Irish grandmother used to say, 'That's no word of a lie, Rossi.'"

Rossi beamed out one of his signature grins. "Yeah, I figured you did."

"What!" I opened my mouth to tell him off, but he stopped me with his sassy, educated lips.

Soft and warm at first, his mouth hardened and opened. His tongue darted out seeking mine, seeking that small lovers' mating dance. But the growl, where was the growl? Finally, a feral groan escaped from between his lips, a wild creature that couldn't be contained. I loved causing that reaction in him and all the fight went out of me. When the kiss ended, I gasped for air.

"I liked that." I admitted. He looked so smug I bristled and tugged free of his arms. "How come you were sure I would?"

Something suspiciously like amusement caused his eyes to crinkle at the corners. "You really want an answer?"

I nodded and folded my arms over my chest in classic defense mode. I had a sneaky feeling I wouldn't like what he was about to reveal.

"Remember the day you came to my house?"

"I remember."

"You didn't want to go into the bedroom with me."

"So?"

"So I figured there was no way you were afraid of me. You were afraid of yourself. There could only be one reason why. You were nuts about me." He cocked an eyebrow as if waiting for my retort.

I didn't let him down. "Rossi, that is so egotistical. It's over the top, even for you."

"Granted. But answer me this. Am I right?"

"Absolutely. I've been nuts about you since day one. I think your Hawaiian shirts appealed to me first. Then your charm. Your elegant manners. And the fact that when we stand side by side, we're at eyeball level with each other."

"You sayin' I'm short?"

"'Course not. I'm saying you're just about perfect—your height, your taste, your impeccable style." I unfolded my arms and wound them around his neck.

"See, what did I tell you?"

"Okay, you win." I kissed him again. If it weren't for the Monets, I could have sat there and kept right on kissing him, but what I'd seen in that elegant dining room was coming between us. "Rossi," I said, in his ear, "Suppose I'm right too? Suppose that is the missing Monet I saw? Then what?"

He sighed, topping it with a frown. "You want me to believe you're on to something even the FBI missed?"

"The FBI? They're in on it? So the insurance company got its way."

He nodded. "They've brought in their international art investigator, Robert K. Wittman. You ever heard of him?"

I shook my head. "No."

"The chief's nose is a little out of joint, but the insurers wanted every possible resource on the case."

"Then tell them there's a painting hidden underneath the top one, because there is." To beef up my argument, I asked, "You ever read Poe's 'The Purloined Letter'?"

"This an English test?"

"No. I'm going to give you the answer. The criminal hid the missing letter on his mantelpiece alongside his other mail. Brilliant, huh? The same here. First, the cops search the house. Second, art experts examine the remaining Monet. Third, they return it to the Alexanders. What better place to hide the missing canvas? In the same room where it was stolen. Right under everybody's nose."

He eased his grip on me and heaved another sigh. "A better place might be with a fence. But, okay, stranger things have happened. I'll go to the chief with what you've told me. If you're right...still a big *if,* Deva... you've found a huge piece of the puzzle, and I'll see that you get recognition for helping crack the case. If you're wrong, well, I can always start my own P.I. firm."

My eyes must have lit up or something because Rossi's fingers tightened his hold, frowning so deeply his eyebrows meshed together. "Listen to me." He turned me so I faced him directly. "There's an aspect to this case you know nothing about. So even if you have found the missing painting, the feds are going to tread lightly."

"What aspect?" I asked.

He shook his head. "You know better than to ask. Also don't expect to know or hear anything about this in the immediate future." He gave my shoulders a little shake. "Got that?"

I nodded. He was serious.

"Above all, don't tell anyone else what you've just told me. If you're correct and word leaks out, you could be killed. Finally, and this is important, you have no proof, none at all, that George Farragut is involved."

"But—"

"What you have is a hunch. Agreed?"

I nodded, reluctantly. "You could be correct."

"That's not the answer I'm looking for."

"Yes."

He pinned me with those hooded eyes. "You will tell no one else what you've just told me."

"I swear I won't tell another soul."

"Now kiss me. I have to leave. I've got to call a federal agent."

CHAPTER TWENTY-THREE

THE NEXT DAY, life almost spun back to the time before my big break-in. Almost, but not quite. Rossi cared. That alone would keep me going, but not Deva Dunne Interiors. For two days, since the news about Jesus's murder had hit the papers, no one had come into the shop. If this continued much longer, I'd soon be out of business.

The shine in Lee's eyes dimmed with each passing hour, and her shoulders drooped as she stood by the counter.

"Paulo won't marry me till his name's free and clear."

For no other reason? She still hadn't mentioned Ilona's portrait. In the midst of arranging a Valentine's display of cupids and crystal hearts, I paused to glance over at her. "I'm sorry,"

"I know," she continued. "But we won't get married till after they find the murderer and the missing painting. No telling how long that'll take."

"Is he under suspicion again?"

Her face tense and drawn, she nodded. "He's been questioned twice. Didn't have much to say, though. He hardly knew that Jesus man."

I longed to tell her the FBI might be on to the painting's whereabouts but couldn't. The best thing I could do for both of us was to keep the doors open to Deva Dunne Interiors. I hoped that would continue to be possible. In the meantime, I had to keep busy with the clients I did have.

"I've got to get over to Bears' Plumbing and order fixtures for that powder room project," I said. "Think you can handle the crowd alone?"

She nodded and gave me a wobbly smile.

I got as far as the Audi when I remembered my measuring tape and notebook were back in the shop. I tossed my handbag in the trunk and, dodging traffic, jaywalked across Fifth Avenue and hurried down the alley.

"It's just me," I said over the cheery jangle of the sleigh bells. I hurried into the shop then careened to a dead stop at the sight of him. Merle Skimp. To my annoyance, a flash of fear shot through me. "I thought you were in Alabama."

"You thought wrong." The Devil Rays cap shaded his eyes but didn't conceal the anger seething in them. At least his hands were empty. No hunk of concrete today.

"What are you doing here?" I hung my hands on my hips, shrew fashion, daring him to cause a problem.

Behind him, Lee, in her little black dress, her curtain of yellow hair flowing to her shoulders, sent a glance darting from her father to me and then about the shop as if she were searching for an escape route and couldn't find one.

"Are you all right?" I asked her.

"Yes, ma'am."

From the look of her trembling hands, "No ma'am" would have been more accurate.

Easing past the two of them, I rounded one of the display tables and aimed for the phone on the sales desk.

"No need for making calls, missy," Merle said.

"This is my store. I go where I want."

"Don't reach for that phone and we'll be just fine," he said. "Alls I'm after is a few answers from my gal here."

"Lee?"

"It's all right, Deva. I'll answer Daddy's questions. It's time."

I had to smile. She was ready for him, no matter what.

"Yesterday, I got halfway to Birmingham," Merle said to her. "Then I turned around so's I could ask you a question. When I came by with that check, did you lie to me?"

She shook her head. "No, Daddy, I didn't."

"Sins of omission I'm talkin' about. Omission, like the Bible says."

I took a step closer to the phone.

Merle's peripheral vision must have been damned good. "Step away from the phone."

"Daddy." Merle swiveled his attention back to Lee. Her chin came up. "I'm getting married. I'd like for you to give me away."

Merle spread his legs and plunged his hands into his pants pockets. "Who to?"

I edged closer to the phone.

"To Paulo St. James."

"No, you ain't. You're comin' home with me. Back to Alabama where you belong. Away from that—"

"I'm not going anywhere. This is my home. I *am* going to marry Paulo. Just as soon as he'll have me."

"I figured that's what you had in mind." Merle's hand emerged from his pants holding a snub-nosed revolver. "You're comin' with me, gal."

"No, I am not," she said.

Never had I heard a voice so soft and yet so determined. Its strength put steel in my own spine.

I grabbed a crystal heart from the counter. As I slung it at him, I yelled "Hey, Merle!"

He spun away from Lee. Before he could take aim at me, the crystal heart, heavy as a good-sized stone, smacked him in the head, knocking him to the shop floor. The gun dropped from his grasp and went spinning across the room. A little poetic justice, I thought, pouncing on the gun before Merle could gather his wits.

He lay moaning next to a skirted table loaded with Valentine figurines. At least he hadn't smashed anything when he fell. A few moments later, he struggled to a sitting position and fingered his head.

"Watch your moves," I told him. "Or I'll shoot."

"You're bluffin'. You won't shoot. You ain't got the guts."

"Want to put me to the test?"

No answer.

"Well?"

Merle sat up and hung his hands between his knees. "She's better off dead than married to that—"

"You God now?" I asked. "Lee, call Lieutenant Rossi. His number is 555—"

"No, Deva. Please. I don't want to call him. Let Daddy go."

I glanced over at her. "*Go?* You've got to be kidding. This was attempted murder."

She shook her head, sending tears flying off her cheeks. "If he wanted to kill me, he would have. Daddy's a crack shot."

With a groan, Merle got to his knees then pulled himself to his feet and stood wavering. A thin thread of blood trickled from his forehead. "I meant you no harm, gal," he said to Lee, "but I can't abide your choice. Not now, not ever."

"Then go, Daddy, and don't come back."

Merle held out a hand to me. "Not without my property."

"You mean this gun? You actually mean this gun?" With my free hand, I beckoned him forward. "Come and get it. But before you try, let me tell you about *my* daddy. He was a Boston cop. He taught me how to shoot. Toss a coin in the air, and I can hit it dead center." I leveled the gun at his gut. "You want a demonstration?"

"I hate boastful women."

"That so? Get the hell out before I change my mind. If you ever show your face around here again, I'll sue you for assault. And attempted murder."

Merle shrugged and sauntered to the door. "It makes no never mind. I won't be back." He upped his unshaven chin at Lee. "I only tried to do what your momma would want." He yanked the door open and stomped out, giving the door such a vicious slam the bells flew into a frenzy.

Lee collapsed on the chair behind her desk. "I'm so sorry, Deva, but I know him. He won't be back. He's through with me. I'll never see him again. And you know something, I really don't care."

With that, she laid her head on the desktop and sat weeping her heart out.

I patted her heaving shoulders, trying to be a comfort, but Paulo was the one she needed.

"Shall I call Paulo, Lee? He'll help you to—"

"No!" She bolted upright in her seat, raising a tear-stained face. "I don't want him to know what Daddy said. That's why I asked y'all not to call the lieutenant. Paulo is so worried about our...difference...I'm afraid he won't marry me. Especially since Daddy's so dead set against it. And if he doesn't, Deva, I will die, just like Daddy wants."

"Nothing in the world will keep Paulo from you," I assured her. Though my better judgment told me to turn Merle in, Lee looked so sad I didn't have the heart to go against her wishes. "Okay, no police, but I sure hope you know your father as well as you say you do."

I spun the barrel and slid open the cylinder, holding out a palm to catch the bullets. Nothing fell out. I peeked inside the chamber. Empty. "I guess you do know Daddy well. The gun wasn't loaded. He never intended to shoot, just to scare you into leaving with him."

Sorrow flickering in her eyes, Lee said, "Daddy wouldn't hurt a flea, Deva. His bark's worse than his bite."

She could be right, but my prior experiences with Merle Skimp didn't have me convinced. Without burdening her with the knowledge, I intended to turn in the gun to Rossi. I doubted it was the one that had killed Maria and Jesus. Surely Merle wouldn't be stupid enough to wave it around if it were, but it wouldn't hurt to be sure.

"Besides, if we reported Daddy, the newspapers might find out," Lee said. "We don't want them printing any more bad stories about the shop, do we?"

"No." I had to laugh, gallows humor no doubt. "Aren't we lucky business is so bad? Nobody came in during our Wild West Show."

She rewarded me with the hint of a smile and answered the phone—our first call of the day—then held out the receiver.

"It's Mrs. Alexander."

I stiffened. Another call from Ilona? What now? Whatever she had to say, it wouldn't be good.

"Deva, you are my friend," she began. "We must speak."

"I'm listening."

"Not like this. In person. Can you come?"

I shrugged at Lee and said, "Well, I did have a call to make, but I suppose it can wait. What needs redecorating?"

"My life. My whole life."

Uh-oh. This had the ring of another client-to-designer tell-all. But this time, I'd welcome the revelation, whatever it might be.

"I'll be right there."

"Wait, Deva. Do not hang up. I'm at Ritz Hotel. On floor twelve. Ask for Ilona Szent-Gyorgyi."

"Your maiden name, why?" But only the silence of a dead phone answered my question.

CHAPTER TWENTY-FOUR

At the Ritz-Carlton Beach Hotel, ballyhooed as America's finest resort, I valet parked the Audi and strode across a huge, echoing lobby scented with tropical florals and the odor of money. Trying not to be impressed by all the fake European opulence, I rode an elevator to Suite 1209. The purpose of this visit had me puzzled, but to be honest, I couldn't wait to find out why Ilona had summoned me.

She answered the door to her three-thousand-dollar-a-night suite with her mouth in a pout, a lace-edged handkerchief dabbing at her eyes. "So good that you come to me," she said, leading the way into a coral and gold living room with a sweeping view of the Gulf.

"This is gorgeous," I said, glancing around at the faux, but well-done, eighteenth century décor.

"Is adequate," Ilona said. "Have seat, Deva. I must talk to another woman or go crazy. *Megbolondulok* we say in Hungary."

"Sounds the same in English," I answered, taking the seat she indicated, but my attempt at humor fell on deaf ears. I suspected Ilona only heard the sound of her own needs. "All right. I'm here. Now tell me why."

Ilona sat opposite me, one arm flung lightly across the back of her loveseat. "You, I trust with the truth."

"Which is?"

"I leave Trevor. We are no more. I already speak to divorce lawyer."

I bolted upright. And on down cushions that wasn't easy. "You just took my breath away, Ilona. It must have been a quick decision. You never let on."

"*Nem.* Not quick. I plan to leave him long time ago. Before Christmas. Now I no can stand any more."

"That's too bad, Ilona. Trevor loves you very much." I thought I'd toss that out, even though I had no idea, really, what Trevor did or didn't love. About what he liked, on the other hand, I had a really good idea.

Ilona threw her hands in the air, as usual sending light rays sparking around the room. Her marriage might be dead, but there was a lot of life left in those wedding diamonds. "Love? Love? You want to know what Trevor love? No, you innocent working girl. I no say."

"Let me guess. Cookies and milk at bedtime?"

She ignored my attempt at a wisecrack. "But I treat him fair. I ask only for what our, how you say, pre-nup contract say is mine. *Sunrise at Royan* belong to me. I ask for no more."

"That's fair," I replied, trying to keep the acid out of my voice. I glanced outside, the Gulf water, a soft aqua so like Monet's sea, shimmered in the distance. The painting had been appraised at twenty million. The hidden one—which I was convinced was *Sunset at Royan*—must be worth at least that much. Even fenced, the black market price would fetch plenty. Clever. Very, very clever. And high payment, indeed, for a mere two years of wedded bliss.

"Can you keep secret, Deva?"

I nodded. "Of course. Keeping secrets is part of my job."

"This one is serious. For rest of my life." She paused to think that over. "Well, for a while anyway. I have new man."

I wasn't really surprised. Goddesses like Ilona might go braless but not manless. At least not for long.

"My new man, he is so different from Trevor. He has cultivation. Sophistication. He can speak of music and art and medicine. Psychology, too. I have headache, he understand. I need pill, he give. I need back rub, he rub. Not like Trevor. All he know is money. And sex. So coarse. The things I could tell." She shuddered, a little ripple running from her shoulders to her hips.

I asked the only question that mattered. Actually, I went for the jugular. "You love this new man?"

"That question, Deva, it is so American."

"Really?" I tamped down my annoyance. "I thought everybody in the world needed love."

She waved a dismissing hand and shook her head. "To choose a man for love is ridiculous. Respect, that is ticket. But I tell you something else. Another secret."

I leaned forward on the overly soft down cushions. "I'm all ears."

"A man must love a woman. That is what matter. Then he is in palm of hand."

"An interesting concept," I said, leaning back and sinking so deep into the cushions my thighs disappeared. Love on one side and respect on the other. Like bathroom taps: hot and cold.

"My new man call just before you get here and insist I go to him today. He cannot wait to see me. To hold me to him. I say yes, though he should wait. But he cannot help himself." She glanced at her watch. "I ordered tea for us but I cancel. He expect me in little while. I would like you to meet, but is not possible. But you meet soon,

I promise. I trust you, Deva, with everything—even with my new love."

Humph, she did, did she? I guess she didn't see me as any kind of female threat. In that she was absolutely correct. In the looks department we were apples and oranges. Though come to think of it, while I might be a Macintosh, she was no navel orange. A luscious exotic would be more like it. In other words, no contest. Her boyfriend would be safe with me. The burning question was, who was he?

"Want to tell me his name?" I asked, striving for an arch girl-talk tone.

"I want to, but I no can. We must wait for divorce before we tell."

With difficulty, I pulled myself off the sofa and swooped up my handbag. "I have to run. Don't worry about the tea. You don't want to keep your man waiting."

"He wait," she said, utterly confident. "Something else there is. Before you go, I have little favor to ask."

"I'll help you if I can," I said. For that two grand, I did owe her a favor, and maybe, just maybe, she didn't know about the hidden canvas.

"My clothes, my jewelry, my shoes, even, are in house on Gordon Drive. I want you to go there, pack everything and bring it to me here."

I shook my head. "Ilona, that would be breaking and entering. I can't do that. I could end up in jail." The irony of what I'd just said wasn't lost on me, nor was the kernel of truth in it. "Why don't you go get your things yourself?" I'd seen the stuff in her closet. She'd need an eighteen wheeler to move all of it out of there.

"Trevor, he no allow. He forbid me to step foot in

house. He's such a pig. What can he do with my clothes,
I ask you?"

Burn them? "Bitter, is he?"

She nodded and sighed, deeply enough to send her
chest into a spectacular up and down boogie. "You sure
you will not do it?"

"I'm sure." I fake peeked at my watch. "Now I really must go."

"Well, I tell my new man I tried. I can do no more."
To my surprise, she jumped up and gave me a fare-
well hug and a kiss on the cheek. I resisted the urge to
wipe it off.

"I appreciate that you listen," she said. "I needed
to talk."

"Not a problem, Ilona. I'd help you with the other
but—" In the foyer, my hand on the doorknob, I turned
to her. "Just between us girls, I think it's damn sporting
of you to ask Trevor for the Monet and nothing else." I
paused, a Meryl Streep with perfect dramatic timing.
"But what a shame you can't have both Monets."

Ilona gasped. A quick intake of breath. Nothing
more. But it was enough to reveal what I had probed
for—*she knew.*

In a flurry of "Ta-ta's" and air kisses, I hurried to
the elevator and jabbed Down.

After a valet pulled the Audi up under the Ritz can-
opy with only a faint squealing of brakes, I tipped him,
drove along the horseshoe-shaped drive and parked at
the foot of the curve by Vanderbilt Beach Road. The
driveway was the only guest exit from the hotel. Ilona
would have to pass me to get to her tryst.

I jumped out of the car, popped the trunk and removed a sunhat I stored there with my Nikes for beach
excursions. More than once it had prevented me from

turning into Freckle City. Together with a pair of outsized shades, it would have to do as a disguise. I got back behind the wheel and, keeping an eye on the rearview mirror, watched for the Porsche. For I was sure Ilona would be driving "her" car. Her pride and joy... well, one of them, anyway. I didn't think she'd recognize the Audi. When I called on Gordon Drive, she had never greeted me at the door. That had been Jesus's job, God love him. My hands gripped the wheel as a flash of silver came streaking down the curved Ritz drive.

I ducked down as the Boxster sped past and took a right onto Vanderbilt. I followed, and when Ilona turned north on Tamiami Trail, I kept on her tail, a super sleuth in a sunhat.

The daytime traffic, always heavy at the height of the tourist season, ran bumper to bumper. I took my eyes off the Porsche long enough to glance at my watch. Four-thirty. Rush hour. The Boxster could outmaneuver and outrun most cars on the road, but like the rest of us, Ilona was hemmed in on all sides and subject to the same limit, fifty per.

Or was she?

Two cars ahead of her, the middle lane opened up for a millisecond. Her foot, no doubt in her usual backless, spike-heeled slide, must have tromped on the gas. She zoomed into the opening, took the high speed lane, then swerved to the right, passed a pickup and was back in the far left lane in the blink of an eye.

Watching her antics, I admired her daredevil driving and the Porsche's flawless performance. Its racing car suspension switched lanes with no rocking and not the slightest tilt of the chassis, as smooth as water over glass.

A minute later, I was swearing my head off. Ilona

had sped out of sight. I had lost her. Doing some fancy passing of my own, I picked up speed and eyeballed the crowded lanes for several more miles. No luck. Whether she'd headed for Ft. Myers or beyond, or driven off onto one of the dozens of side roads that intersected the Trail, I couldn't tell.

Damn. Now I'd have to wait for a formal introduction to The Boyfriend.

Some sleuth. I snatched off the sunhat, flung it in the backseat and slowed down. I had taken a chance chasing Ilona. With the Glock still in my purse, I was carrying without a permit. One more piece of bad publicity in the *Naples Daily* and I might as well set up shop in Bangladesh.

As soon as I came to a turnoff, I'd head for home. Under the speed limit. Disgusted, I snapped on the radio. Some kind of fifties elevator music clogged the airways. I was about to change stations when an announcer's voice interrupted what was passing for music.

"A breaking news bulletin. An hour ago, a prominent Naples citizen was found dead in his Fifth Avenue South office. Mr. George Farragut, well-known financial analyst to many of Naples's wealthiest residents, was shot to death in what is apparently a homicide. Police are now investigating…"

I switched into the low speed lane and turned off the radio so I could digest what I'd just heard. George? *Murdered. Unbelievable.* So I had been wrong about him. Perhaps, all along he had been the prey not the predator. Or maybe his death and Maria and Jesus's were totally unrelated. But somehow I didn't think so. With his close connection to the Alexanders, it was entirely possible that George had been the victim of the same killer. But why George? What had he seen? What did he know that had caused his death?

I pulled off the highway and parked in a Walgreens lot to think for a while. The day I was in Trevor's study, Simon had left a phone message saying he had dealt with George. Whatever the problem might have been, was killing George the ultimate solution?

CHAPTER TWENTY-FIVE

I DIDN'T GET any answers to my questions that night, though Rossi called to say hello and to tell me to keep the deadbolts on and the cell phone next to my bed.

"Then you think whoever killed the Cardozas killed George too?"

"That has not yet been determined. I'm just telling you to be careful."

"You're scaring me," I said.

"Good. Stay scared. Scared doesn't take chances. I'll call you again as soon as I can."

He hung up. That was midnight, and by nine the next morning, when I left for work, I'd heard nothing else from him.

"Deva, wait up!"

As I hurried toward the Surfside carport, I glanced over a shoulder, though I hardly needed to. I'd know that deep, lustrous voice anywhere.

Tall, tanned and handsome, in a charcoal gray Brooks Brothers suit, white shirt and silver striped tie, Simon came striding across the Surfside parking lot looking like every woman's dream guy. Why not mine? Truth be told, I was afraid of him. George had been a problem to him and now George was dead. And I was "the Dunne woman" as if I were a person he had met once or twice on a bus or something. Also because I was intrigued with a short guy who wore garish Hawaiian shirts with the tails out. Go figure.

"It's good to see you," Simon said, a smile lighting his eyes. "I've missed you."

"Sorry, Simon, but business has been terrible. I haven't had time to think of anything else." I was lying through my teeth. Multitasking was every designer's middle name. But I didn't know what else to say. The truth was definitely not an option.

"You've heard about Farragut?" he asked.

"Yes, it was all over the news last night. And on the front page this morning."

"Nice guy. Very capable. A shame."

"I know, scary."

"Sounds like you need a diversion. After all this bad news, I could use one too. How about tonight? I have some Pinot Grigio. A Michael Bublé CD. We can order Chinese takeout. Your favorite, Beef Szechwan."

Though I hated to kill his hopeful-looking smile, I shook my head. I should tell him I was interested in someone else, but couldn't. Besides, Rossi and weren't actually dating. At least not officially. He had said he cared for me and worried about me, and I didn't figure him for a liar, but caring and worrying weren't commitments, were they? Besides, if I said a single word, Simon would want to know who the lucky guy was. I couldn't go there. Not yet. Rossi knew I wasn't implicated in the crimes, but he had to contend with that line in the sand the chief had drawn. Any outing of our… ah…relationship would have to come from him.

I rolled back my shirt cuff and glanced at my watch. "I'd love to chat, Simon, but I'm late for an appointment with a plumbing supplier."

He nodded as if I'd just said something interesting.

"Then I'm meeting an art installer at Morgan Jones's new house. It's quite the showplace, or will be when it's finished. Have you seen it?"

He shook his head. "No reason I should. I hardly know the guy. He's a friend of George Farragut's not mine."

True or false? I wanted to believe Simon, but the thought of how he'd had me deliver that Hermès briefcase to Morgan's house rose like a specter between us. My trust in him destroyed, I pretended not to see the hurt in his eyes, said goodbye and hurried over to the Audi. After stalling out a couple times, the engine roared to life, and I drove off leaving Simon on the tarmac watching me go.

CHOOSING SOME ORNATE powder room fixtures at Bears' Plumbing Supply only took a few minutes. Selections made, I tossed my tote and handbag in the Audi's backseat, got behind the wheel and switched on the engine. Or tried to. It didn't even turn over. Whether the battery had conked out or something more insidious had happened, I couldn't tell. Tire kicking summed up the extent of my mechanic skills.

Now I'd have to contact Tom at Art Installations and reschedule. I climbed out of the car and stood tapping a foot on the tarmac as I thought things over. Pretty much a one-man operation, Tom had set aside several hours for the Jones project. I knew he needed the business and hated to waste his time over a no-show.

Instead of canceling, I could leave my car in the Bears' lot for now and call a cab. Consider the fare a business write-off.

I went back inside the showroom to tell Bears Plumbing about my problem. They surprised me, big time.

Said they'd drop me off at Morgan's house, would call a garage, and if my car could be fixed in the next couple of hours, they would deliver it to the same address. Making a mental note to give Bears all my future business, I went outside and kicked the tires anyway. You never know.

WHEN I WAS dropped off at the Jones house, Tom's pickup wasn't waiting in the driveway. Strange. I rechecked my schedule. Yeah, Tom and I were on for today. The traffic must have held him up.

I coded my way into the house. The lacquered foyer, a lapis lazuli jewel box, positively glowed in the midday sun, exactly the effect I'd been after. I wandered into the great room where the odor of drying paint lingered in the air. The whisper of blue on the walls was as subtle as a baby's breath—not my first choice, but a good foil, actually, to the abstract art—especially the blue-inspired Rosenquist.

I left my bags on a kitchen counter and checked my watch. Tom was a half hour late. Very unlike him. Maybe being dropped off out here hadn't been such a good idea after all. Restless and getting a tad more nervous by the minute, I wandered through the downstairs rooms, making notes and verifying a few measurements. A bit bored, I wandered upstairs. If Tom didn't show in the next half hour, I'd call him and find out what happened.

At the top of the stairs, the master suite, an empty shell, stood waiting for the satin bed Morgan had demanded.

Hmm. I let my imagination play with the finished room and all its sexy details. Would Rossi like a similar bedroom? We could add color, soften the lighting, buy some satin sheets. But somehow I could hear his gravelly voice telling me such frills didn't matter. The important thing...

What was that? Had I heard something? Yes. A man's voice. It couldn't be Tom. He didn't have a key to the house. I stood still, listening. Ah, I recognized Morgan's cool tone and then another voice. A woman's.

Uh-oh, there was no car parked in the drive. Having me suddenly burst out of the bedroom like a Jack-in-the-box would be an unpleasant surprise. Well, no avoiding it. The sooner they knew I was upstairs, the better.

I took a step toward the open bedroom doorway. Then I heard her, loud and clear, the only woman I knew with a Hungarian accent. *Ilona.*

What was she doing here? And then it hit me. Oh God, could Morgan be her new man? The one she had left Trevor for? Like a movie camera on fast forward, my mind raced with possibilities. Of course, that was why she was here. This was no casual house tour. She was checking out her soon-to-be home. Nothing else made sense.

Paralyzed with indecision, I stood in the center of the room, listening to her heels click on the marble staircase. For certain, they'd come in here. Right where Morgan planned to make love the instant he had his new satin bed. Right where I was standing. *Egads.* Without thinking, acting on pure instinct, I hurried into the walk-in closet and silently closed the shuttered door. A dumb move, actually. To a woman like Ilona, clothes closets were as vital as air. She'd want to see if it were big enough. For sure, it wouldn't be.

Damn. But at this point, what choice did I have? They'd reached the room. It was too late now to pretend I hadn't heard them.

"Darling," Morgan said, his voice throbbing. "Here it is."

They strolled in, along with a drift of Ilona's Opium perfume, their footsteps loud on the room's concrete sub-flooring. The plush, wall-to-wall carpeting wasn't due for installation until next week.

"Now imagine our bed on that wall, between the sconces," he said.

"An ultra king?" she asked.

"Of course, what else? It will be our private playpen. Luscious and soft. As you are, darling."

Resisting the urge to gag, I peeked through the door slats. Morgan had taken Ilona in his arms and stood nuzzling her neck. Finally, with what looked like reluctance from behind the slats, her hands reached up and, encircling his back, she clung to him as he embraced her.

After a month or so, he lifted his head from her throat.

"If only we had a bed," he murmured. "If only…" His voice broke, whether from passion or a head cold, I couldn't tell.

"But we do not," Ilona replied.

Damn, Hungarian women were so practical.

"We can improvise. There must be something."

"Nem."

Ha! Morgan had just heard the first of many *nems*.

"I want our joining to be perfect for you," Ilona added, softening the blow, so to speak.

A sigh. The sound of a kiss. Then, "Very well, darling. I've waited this long. I'll wait a little longer. Counting each day, each hour."

"And I count minutes, Morgan."

"Darling!"

"No more kisses now. We must talk. Like I tell you

yesterday, I am worried. I think Deva suspect something."

"Let her. She's under suspicion herself. You were wise to give her the new code to your house…it draws her in. I'm just glad she didn't decide to use it the day I—"

Ilona covered his mouth with a diamond-studded hand. "No, no say out loud. You did what you had to do. But I must tell you, Morgan, Maria was big shock, but not like Jesus. When I return from Hungary and find him dead, I almost faint. That was not part of plan."

"No darling, it wasn't. But he caught me tacking the oil in place. I had to kill him."

Hardly daring to breathe, my heartbeat pounding in my ears, I kept peering through the shuttered closet door.

"I have question," she said.

Holding her at arm's length, he looked down into her eyes. "Yes?" Was I imagining it, or did he sound wary?

"Last night, the news say George Farragut is dead. Shot. Do you know of this, Morgan?"

"Of course I know of this. The airwaves have been filled with it. Poor devil."

"That is not what I ask. Do you *know* of this?" She stepped back, out of the circle of his arms.

His hands fell by his sides. "Are you asking if I killed him?"

She stayed out of reach of his hands and nodded, just once, briefly.

"George knew. Or maybe I should say, he suspected."

"How is that possible?" For the first time since I'd met her, Ilona's voice didn't rise above a whisper.

"We were drinking together one night. I alluded to a theft. He was a smart man, he surmised."

"What this mean, surmise?"

"Guessed."

It wasn't easy, peeking through the slats, but still I'd take a vow that Ilona's face went ashen white. "You killed him for a guess?"

"I had to. He could have gone to the police. I had no choice. For you, I have broken all my oaths. The ones I vowed to keep. But nothing matters except possessing you. I'll be faithful to you forever."

Under different circumstances I might have snorted in disbelief, but not this time. That was a serial killer out there, and I had no desire to be his next victim.

"If only I had a pillow or something to lay you on," he murmured. "I'd prove how much I worship you. I know I promised to wait, but I haven't the strength. I need you *now*."

"*Nem,* not like this. So sordid."

Poor Morgan. He had trashed his life and killed three people all for a "No."

But he didn't give up easily. I should have known. "Wait a moment, darling," he said, his voice rising with anticipation, "I'll check in the closet. There might be a blanket in there or something, anything, to put down on that hard floor."

Uh-oh. A cold sweat broke out all over my skin.

He yanked open the double closet doors. At the sight of me, he went rigid as stone and stood staring into my eyes, a brushed pewter knob in each hand.

"You heard," he said, drawing in a ragged breath then blowing it out fast, right into my face.

"*Jaj Istenem!*" Ilona gasped, peering over his shoulder at me.

Without looking back, as cool as if being overheard confessing to murder were an everyday occurrence, he said, "Don't worry about a thing, darling. I'll take care of this."

He let go of the knob and those strong surgeon's hands came up, fingers flexed, ready to press into my carotids. Or crush my larynx.

I backed up a step. "Stay away from me, Morgan."

"I can't let you leave."

"I can't let you stop me."

He smiled in derision. The derision reached his eyes. The smile did not. "How are you going to prevent that?"

There had to be a way. I took another step back. And another. I hit the closet wall.

He reached for my neck. I swiveled my head, bobbing from side to side so he couldn't get a grip. What else could I do? What else? His hands shot out and grasped me. At his touch on my flesh, my adrenaline shot to the sky. With an impulse of its own, my knee came up. *Smack*. Right into his groin.

Morgan let out a shrill scream and dropped his hands to his crotch.

As he bent over, clutching himself, I darted past him. Ilona stood wringing her hands in the center of the empty bedroom.

"No sex today, Ilona," I told her as I rushed out of the closet. "You're off the hook."

"Deva, where you go? We must talk."

"Nem," I said, sprinting along the upper hallway. *"Nem!"*

I dashed down the broad staircase and raced through the empty rooms to the foyer.

Behind me, Ilona's heels kept up a mad pace. "Deva, wait. Wait."

As I fumbled at the entrance lock, she caught up with me, bosom heaving, perfect hair flying out of control.

I glanced at her hands. She had no weapon in them and none hidden in those tights and brights she wore, either. Unarmed, she was no threat. But I had to get out of there before Morgan caught up with me.

"I did nothing, Deva. Nothing. You must believe. The painting, it is mine. I have papers to prove."

"Excellent." How did this damn door lock work? "Save them for the jury."

She grasped my arm with a slender hand, her cerise-tipped nails digging into my flesh. "Morgan, he kill. I never harm nobody. I can prove."

The deadbolt shot back. I twisted the knob and flung the door so hard it sent a giant crack spider-webbing across the foyer's lacquered wall. So much for a great paint job. Heavy footsteps sounded on the marble stairs. I sent a harried glance over my shoulder. Limping along the stairway, Morgan was moving as fast as he could.

"Hold her, Ilona," he yelled. "Don't let her go."

"I no can," Ilona cried, as I pried off her hand and raced away.

Once outside, I gulped a lungful of air before stooping to yank off my shoes. I'd run faster in bare feet. The spike heels I'd use as weapons if need be.

Above all, I couldn't let Morgan reach me. Pulse pounding, heart going like a mariachi band, I raced down the stone steps and along the drive. No way would Ilona catch up to me in backless slides and skintight capris. All my years of jogging were about to pay off. Shoulders back, fists at chest level, the stilettos facing out like daggers, I soon broke into a sweat in the hot, hazy atmosphere. Too bad the houses were so spread out, each one nestled like a huge jewel in its own acre or so of lush gardens. My best bet would be to pound on the first door I came to. Or flag down a passing motorist.

A car. I glanced back. A blue Maserati was careening along the quiet road, aiming its long, sleek nose directly at me. *Morgan.* And gaining fast.

CHAPTER TWENTY-SIX

To MY RIGHT, a For Sale sign sprouted on a parcel of land filled with subtropical growth. No Maserati could traverse that. Without hesitation, I plunged into the tangle of untamed jungle, shuddering as my bare feet sank into wet leaves, fallen palm fronds and God knows what else. Scorpions. Snakes. Iguanas.

A branch snagged my shirt. I ripped it loose and ducked behind a sabal palm to catch my breath and listen. The Maserati's elegant purr had been replaced by a noisy slapping of tropical foliage. *Morgan.*

So he had recovered from my assault then. Too bad. In pants and sturdy shoes, he had an advantage over my miniskirt and bare feet.

Something crawled over my toes. Stifling a scream, I glanced down. Fire ants! They'd be all over me in no time. I leaped to the other side of the palm, my fast move rustling the fronds. Morgan must have heard. Only the chirping of the birds broke the silence now. He had to be listening for the slightest move. As was I.

I stood frozen, an ice sculpture in nearly ninety-degree heat. And then I saw it. Only a foot or so away, a black snake coiled in a patch of sunlight. I'd heard pythons were breeding in the Everglades. But that wasn't a python. Nor was this the Everglades. Black snakes were harmless, weren't they? Even to bare feet?

Blood pressure in the stratosphere, I stepped gingerly away from the tree and inched past the snake, my footsteps silent on the mucky bottom. Overhead, a blue jay flitted from branch to branch, cawing at my every move as though I were a vaudeville act cavorting across a stage. All Morgan had to do was follow the bird's lead, and he'd have me. A persistent little devil, the jay perched on a nearby scrub pine and screeched his head off. I had to get out of his line of vision.

Up ahead, I spotted a dense clump of low-lying shrubbery. No telling what might be lurking in there. Well, only one way to find out. I crept over to the shrubs, parted the branches and stooped underneath them. A mosquito dive-bombed my head. I swatted it away, relieved no bigger critters were in there with me. Praying the bird would lose interest, I crouched motionless, listening to the heartbeat of the land, the tiny skitterings of unseen creatures, the hum of insects, the brushing of leaf upon leaf. And the loud crackle of branches thrust aside with an impatient hand.

Should I leap up and make a dash for it? No, too late. Morgan's labored breathing sounded frighteningly near. I let go of the stilettos and hugged my knees, making myself as invisible as possible.

From under lowered lids, I saw the tips of two brown brogans. If Morgan reached out a hand he'd have me. But he didn't. He stumbled on, noisily whacking branches as he went. The jay must have spotted him. Its raucous cawing started up again.

My throat dry, I swallowed and tried not to breathe deeply of the rotting vegetation. Unless Morgan had kept the gun he used on his victims, I doubted he had a weapon. I inhaled a breath of the heavy air and let it out slowly. He didn't need a weapon. His hands alone were enough.

If I hadn't been so scared, I would have pitied the guy. A gifted surgeon, stalking a woman through jungle growth to keep her from telling the truth—he had murdered three people, including his best friend. For a Hungarian blonde whose favorite word was *nem*.

The poor guy. Yeah, right. A poor sociopath with a tendency to sadism was more like it. A surgeon who earned his bread cutting into human flesh, separating tissue with his fingertips, removing pulsing organs… I shook my head, disgusted at where my thoughts were taking me. Those same hands could heal. Had healed. So what had gone horribly wrong in Morgan's life? When had his obsessive need to possess works of art morphed into the need to possess Ilona? The perfect woman, a work of art in her own right. At least on the surface.

From what sounded like a few hundred yards in the distance, I could hear him swashbuckle his way through the undergrowth. No finesse there. No careful stitching around a damaged heart. He was out for blood. Mine. And didn't care if I heard him coming. What was he doing? Trying to flush out his game?

I wrapped my arms around my body to still the trembling. If only I had my phone, I could call for help. If only I had sensible shoes, I could run. If only pigs could fly, they'd be airplanes.

I needed a plan…okay…five minutes without Morgan thrashing about and I'd make a dash for it. But in which direction? Of the four points on the compass, three would lead me out of here, one would not. If I walked in as straight a line as possible, I had a seventy-five percent chance of hitting a house sooner or later, or getting back to the road. But in darting from tree to tree, I'd lost my bearings. Behind the acre-wide strip of developed lawns and gardens edging the road, the land gave way to subtropical jungle…like this untamed parcel. If I set off in the wrong direction, I could wander deep into the wild and be lost with no one the wiser. The thought made me shudder.

I squelched the rising fear and told myself to think. The Gulf lay to the west. The direction that led out of the woods. West, then. But where the hell was west? I should have listened to my father years ago and joined the Girl Scouts. Too late for that, but like every school kid, I knew the sun set in the west. So…I'd step out from this undergrowth, look at the sky and follow the direction of the sun.

Right.

I peered at my watch. Three more minutes.

The rain began as quiet as a whisper. If every pore in my body hadn't been on sonar alert, I wouldn't have heard a thing. Then the whispering picked up. *Plink. Plink.*

Boom! A streak of lightning flashed across the sky, followed by a clap of thunder that practically split my eardrums. A second later, the sky pulled out all its stops, unleashing everything it had.

I crouched in a tight ball, sheltered from the worst of the deluge but still, in no time, rain soaked my hair to the scalp and my wet clothes clung like a Hooters outfit.

I didn't even care. Where the hell was west, anyway?

My five-minute plan turned into a half hour. Decision time. Stay here and be mosquito food or make a break for it. Even in bare feet, I could move fast. I was younger than Morgan. Fleeter. And judging from his harsh breathing of a while ago, I had more stamina than he. So if I could keep him at arm's length, I had a chance—if I turned in any direction but east. A big if.

Problem was, I had no idea where Morgan might be. Lost, too? Or close by, waiting to pounce the moment he spotted me? Could be, but I'd have to risk it. If I stayed huddled here much longer, I wouldn't be able to move.

I picked up the stilettos, and brushing the scruffy fronds aside, I stood, exposing myself to view. Nearby, a squirrel, as agile as Tarzan, leaped from branch to branch, soaring from one tree to another. Way to go! If only I could do the same, instead of standing on bug-bitten legs clutching a shoe in each fist.

An eerie quiet had replaced the angry slapping of palm fronds. Even the jay had shut up. Maybe Morgan had fled. No, I immediately dismissed that idea. Not a chance he'd leave before he caught me or until I escaped, whichever came first. He was hiding like I was, waiting for me to make the first move.

That he would kill me if he could I had not the slightest doubt. But if given the chance, would I kill him?

Not if I could. If I had to.

Yeah, if I had to.

Arms raised overhead, I arched my back then stretched my hamstrings. No more hiding. No more crouching. But which way to run? I picked a card. *That way.* Whether it was the fatal east or not, I couldn't tell with the sky so overcast. I'd just have to chance it.

From behind me, a hiss as subtle as a snake's glide.

I gasped and whirled about, stiletto heels forward in each fist.

"Hello, Deva."

A shiver of panic swept through me. Did he have a gun? No, his hands were empty, but they were weapons enough.

Before he could lunge for me, I spun away from him

and ran, snapping branches in my haste, shoving palm fronds out of the way, feet stinging, heart pumping.

Over my noisy retreat, I could hear him staying the course. Fear shot hot blood through me as I raced, not sparing so much as a second to look back. Soon, though, the sounds of pursuit became fainter and farther away. I must be outdistancing him.

Something sharp pierced my foot. I yelped in pain and kept on. The pain meant I was alive. I'd outrun him yet. He had twenty years on me, a man who spent most of his days in a fluorescent-lit operating room. When had he jogged the beach last? Probably never.

I leaped over a fallen log, then another. I hit the third log with the ball of my foot. The pain shot up to my teeth, the shoes flew out of my hands, and I fell, face-first, into a shallow ditch.

Stunned by the impact, I lay there for precious seconds. Morgan came pounding through the undergrowth and careened to a stop at the edge of the ditch.

I leaped up and grabbed the log I had tripped over. Like a mad Musketeer, I brandished it in front of me.

Morgan stood facing me, gasping for air, clenching and unclenching his hands, keeping his weapons warm and agile.

"Why, Morgan?"

He didn't bother to ask what I meant. He knew. For a moment, poised for a leap at my throat, he looked like he wouldn't respond, but he surprised me. "You're too young to understand."

"Try me," I said, waving the log like a sword.

Sucking in some deep breaths, he waited, as if mulling over whether or not to reply, but finally he said, "Life was passing me by in slow, agonizing increments."

"Very poetic. But I nearly flunked English 101." Actually, I aced the course, but he didn't have to know that. "So make it easy for me. The bugs are murder. I've got to get out of here."

"I've spent years saving lives. Every life but my own."

Was I imagining it, or had his voice gone shrill?

"I'm fifty years old. If I let the next few years slip by without seizing them—" his fists tightened, "—it will be too late...and now I've met her."

"Ilona?"

He didn't answer. I didn't blame him. It was a stupid question.

"Since then, every day has been magic."

"Yeah, *carpe diem,* Morgan. There's ancient wisdom in seizing the day."

"You can scoff. It doesn't matter. She's the woman of my dreams." For some reason, he was whispering, though no one could hear us but the snakes and the bugs.

"Get real, Morgan. She's turned your life into a nightmare."

"No, she hasn't. You have."

He raised his hands to chest level. Getting ready for his big play, was he?

"Oh, really?" I goaded, letting the sarcasm drip. I'd be damned if I'd cower in front of him. "Was I the one who told you to kill three people?"

"I had no choice. The cook saw me the day—"

"—you cut the Monet out of its frame?"

He nodded, the slight slump of his shoulders the only acknowledgement of defeat. Or was it guilt?

"And Jesus caught you hiding one painting behind the other. And George? Well, George was just too smart. He guessed."

"Unfortunately, yes." He sounded calm and conversational now, as if we were having a pleasant chat in somebody's living room. "The *Sunrise* belongs to Ilona. But she was correct. We need both paintings to live the life we deserve."

"God, she's got good ideas. Good breast implants, too."

"Don't be crass, Deva. It doesn't become you."

Crass? This from a guy who killed three innocent people in cold blood? A toxic mix of anger and adrenaline seethed in my veins. I raised the club. I'd give him crass. But before I took my place at bat, I had to know something.

"After the robbery, where did you hide the painting?"

He smiled and lowered his hands, ready to chat it up. I guess he figured what the hell, I was never going to escape alive, why not tell me how diabolically clever he had been.

"I rolled the painting in a priority mail box, drove to Tallahassee and sent it to the Naples Community Hospital, care of myself. The mailroom held it till I picked it up."

"So when Ilona gets her divorce, she walks off with not one Monet but two. And no one the wiser. Very clever." I swung my club. Practice warm-ups, if you will. "Except your plan didn't work. I told the homicide detective about the missing painting. The cops know it's hidden behind *Sunrise at Royan*. So does the FBI."

He reared back as if I had struck him. Desperate now, I played my strongest card. "If anything happens to me, they'll nail Ilona, blame her for my death. Her only hope is if you let me go."

He stood motionless. Would he buy what I was selling? Did he love Ilona enough to sacrifice himself for her? Doubtful. Far more likely he'd kill me and make a run for it. But I pressed on. "Ilona and I are friends. You heard her say so yourself. Those killings have appalled her. What will she think…or do…if you kill again?"

"She'll think I'm *stroooong!*"

Showtime. Morgan jumped into the ditch beside me. Confident he had me, he didn't bother to pick up another log so we could duke it out, but lunged straight for my throat. As his arms reached out, I twisted out of the way. He shot past me, whirled around and, with a snarl, came at me again, a beast seeking its prey.

Muscles I didn't know I had sprang into action. Weaving, parrying, feinting, I circled the ditch, brandishing my log, never turning my back to him. One chance was all I'd get. I couldn't waste it. My best bet— go for his head, knock him out.

We circled, panting with effort, our harsh breaths mingling in the damp air with a cloud of buzzing gnats.

"You haven't got a chance," Morgan gasped. "Give up, Deva. It'll be swift."

"Damn right, Morgan." Who did he think he was? He'd kill me mercifully, would he? Well, screw him. "Come on," I taunted. "Come on. Come and get me. Let's see how much of a man you are. Come on."

He paused, not answering, sucked in a deep breath and rushed forward, arms extended, fingers flexed.

In the last split second before he grabbed me, I raised the log and held it in both hands, straight out like a battering ram. Too late to stop his forward thrust, Morgan crashed into it with his chest, the force of his rush splitting the log and jarring my arms clear up to my shoulders.

I screamed in pain, but Morgan didn't utter a sound. A look of stunned disbelief flashed across his face, and he slumped to the ground where he lay as peacefully as if he were in his soft, satin ultra-king bed.

I flung down the log and scrambled out of the ditch. Helter-skelter, not knowing where I was running to, I raced through the woods on sore feet, hoping for the best, hoping for the west, hoping for a manicured lawn, a ribbon of road. I was running from a dead man. And from myself. For now I knew what I was capable of, and I ran from that as much as from the thought of Morgan's lethal hands crushing my windpipe.

On tortured feet, I ran and ran, knifelike undergrowth slashing my soles, branches slapping my face and clawing at my clothes, until like a madwoman I burst through the undergrowth onto a lawn like a carpet.

Relief brought me to my knees. I sank onto the manicured grass, gasping for air, spewing out a prayer of gratitude. I lay there panting, listening for the sound of pounding feet and angry hands shoving away branches. Nothing.

I had to get help. I needed Rossi.

Pulling myself to my feet, I limped across the lawn to a huge Tuscan mansion sitting like a well-fed *duce* in the center of its elaborate gardens. My feet left a bloody trail on the stone entrance stairs. Wait till they see that, I thought, as I pressed the chimes. From inside the house, I heard a musical ring then the sound of footsteps. A few moments later, the door opened. A heavyset Hispanic woman in a white nylon uniform took one alarmed look at me and slammed the door in my face. No wonder. I probably looked like I'd been regurgitated.

I punched the chimes again. I'd keep doing that until someone inside called for help. And that's exactly what happened.

After an eternity, the Bonita Bay security car rolled

up the drive, and an elderly guard slowly climbed out from behind the wheel.

"Thank God you're here," I said, not giving him a chance to say a word. "Call the Naples Police."

"You're in Lee County, lady. Not Collier."

"No matter, ask for a Lieutenant Rossi. His number is 555-8000. I want to report a homicide. Tell him I just stopped a man's heart."

The guard's jaw dropped open.

"The man I killed was a cardiac surgeon. I got him in the chest. I don't expect you to believe me, but it's a case of poetic justice."

He hesitated, then, without taking his eyes off me, trying to look tough, he stood at the bottom of the stone steps and dialed the number.

"They'll be here in a few minutes," he said, hanging up and pocketing his cell. "What's your name, lady?"

"Deva Dunne." I slumped onto the top step and let my feet hang over the edge.

"Good lord, how did that happen?" he asked, pointing to them.

"It's a long story, sir. If you don't mind, let's wait for the cops. I've only got the strength to tell it once."

Wary but willing, he nodded.

While we waited in an uneasy silence, I glanced around at the stone planters flanking the stairs. "Remind me to tell the owner these planters are the wrong scale for an entrance this size."

"Okay, lady, sure," he said, shifting from one foot to the other and giving his pants a hitch.

I knew he wouldn't. I could tell he thought I was crazy.

CHAPTER TWENTY-SEVEN

THE GUARD WAS right. I *was* crazy. Crazy from guilt. I'd done the unthinkable—killed another human being. Fought like a wild animal to save my own life—to smash the life out of Morgan. When he lay crumpled at my feet, pure, raw triumph had surged through my veins. I could remember the very *taste* of it. *Omigod, mea culpa. Mea culpa.*

Keeping his vigil at the bottom of the stairs, the guard stood with his feet apart. Though he wasn't packing, he kept his hands on his hips cowboy style. Still trying to look tough, he stared at me without blinking, though in my current condition I was no flight risk. I couldn't have taken a single step.

I didn't know if he had called Rossi or not. Like he'd said, we were in Lee County and Naples police had no jurisdiction here. At this point, I was almost beyond caring. All I wanted was to lie down in a clean bed and lose the pain in my feet and in my heart.

Within minutes a Bonita Springs cruiser drove onto the circular drive. No Rossi then. Two officers emerged from the car and one approached the guard. "This her?"

He nodded. "Yes sir. I apprehended her right here."

"Hey wait a minute," I said. "He's got it all wrong."

The younger of the two, the one without the paunch, strode up the steps. "I'm Officer Casey. Why don't you tell me what happened."

I waved an arm at the wooded lot. "He's in there somewhere."

"Who's in there?"

"The man I killed. Dr. Morgan Jones."

"You killed a man?" Officer Casey upped his chin at his partner. "Take this down." He turned back to me. "What is your name, ma'am?"

"Devalera Dunne. Mrs. Devalera Dunne."

Paunch poised his pen over his clipboard. "Spell your first name please,"

"Oh for God's sake. I've been spelling that damned name my whole life. Forget about it. Just go find the body."

"Don't worry, ma'am. If there's a body, we'll find it." From the soothing tone of Casey's voice, I could tell he had gone into hysteria-control mode. It infuriated me.

"What's your address, ma'am?" he asked, his voice super soft.

"What are you whispering for?" I glanced over a shoulder at the quiet house behind us. "Nobody in there can hear a bloody thing. Not unless you bang on the door."

"Where do you live, ma'am?" he asked.

I turned back to him. "In Naples at the Surfside Condominiums. Gulf Shore Boulevard. Satisfied now?"

"Do you have any ID?"

"What's the matter with you people? Do I look like I'm carrying ID?"

The two officers exchanged glances. "Have the guard call an ambulance," Casey ordered.

"I don't need an ambulance. I need you to listen to me."

"We are listening, ma'am. You need medical attention." He pointed to my cut and bleeding feet. "How did that happen?"

"I already told you. In the woods over there. After I ran out of the house."

"What house?"

"The big deconstructionist one."

He frowned so deeply his brows collided. "What house is that?"

"The white one. Down the road on the left. Ilona is probably still in there." I gasped as a thought struck me. "Unless my car got fixed and Bears' Plumbing dropped it off. If so, she could have swiped my keys and left in the Audi. She's in on it, you know."

"In on what?"

"The art theft and the murders."

"I see."

"No you don't. You think I'm deranged."

The two officers exchanged another glance. One of *those* glances.

"Okay, you want proof? You want some ID? Go to 1900 Bonita Bay Road. You'll find my purse on the kitchen island. At least that's where I left it when I ran out of the house. I was fleeing from Dr. Jones. He had already killed three people, and I was next on his list.

"Anyway, look for a lime green hobo. A Kate Spade. It was expensive as sin, but not as extravagant as you might think. I'm an autumn on the color chart, so the green goes with a lot of my outfits." I glanced down at my soiled, torn skirt. "I probably shouldn't have worn it with this orange skirt, but sometimes a girl has to think outside the box."

That was when Casey's face got all fuzzy. Determined not to pass out and bonk my head on the stone landing, I leaned against one of the planters and listened to sirens screaming in the distance. Before I knew it, a medic was bending over me.

"This chair is hard," I told her. "It needs cushions. An indoor-outdoor fabric would be good."

"Yes, it is hard," she said, her voice soothing. "We're taking you where you'll be more comfortable."

"The gas chamber?"

"Close your eyes," she said. "You're going to be all right now."

The ambulance crew lifted me onto a stretcher. As I passed the guard, I said, "You didn't call Rossi like I asked you to." He looked puzzled as if he didn't know whom I meant, but he knew all right. "It's okay," I assured him. "These guys are doing fine."

"That's a relief, lady," he said as the medics slid my stretcher into the back of an ambulance.

The green, groomed landscaping of Bonita Bay passed by in a blur, and we were soon racing along the Tamiami Trail heading into Naples, sirens screaming, and no doubt blue roof lights whirling. What was the hurry? I wondered. Morgan was no longer a threat to anyone. What were we racing toward? My fate?

I WOKE UP in a hospital bed, my feet wrapped in bandages. A pair of liquid brown eyes were inches from my own. I knew those eyes and the stern, stubbled face they belonged to. I even recognized the shirt—lush hula girls swayed in the breeze clear across Rossi's chest.

"So they finally called you," I said.

"Yes. Sorry I wasn't there, Deva." He took my hand. "You did well."

Tears flooded my eyes and leaked down my chin onto the sprigged hospital jonny someone had dressed me in.

"How can you say I did well? I'm no better than Morgan was. When he came after me, Rossi, I lashed out with everything I had. I didn't know I was capable of…of…" The word wouldn't come out.

"We're all capable of the same thing, Deva," he said, yanking a fistful of tissues out of a box on the bedside table and wiping my eyes. But the tears wouldn't stop. "Keep that up and we'll be having a wet T-shirt contest in here." He grinned, giving me a flash of even white teeth. "Maybe you should just let the tears roll."

I grabbed the tissues out of his hand. "That's not funny, Rossi. I killed a man."

He sobered immediately. "No, that wasn't funny," he agreed. "But you haven't killed anyone."

I blinked and swiped a hand at the wetness. "No?"

"No. Morgan's alive. Bruised and battered, but alive. Two floors down, under twenty-four-hour police guard."

Relief like a drug flooded my soul. "Oh, thank God. To have a death on my conscience was awful."

"I know," he said, his voice as soothing as the paramedic's. But this time, it sounded good to me.

"What about Ilona?" I asked.

"We found her on Alligator Alley, halfway to Miami. But not to worry. The Audi can be repaired."

I reared up on my elbows. "What? I *knew* it."

Rossi pressed my shoulders back onto the pillow. "Relax. I'll see that the repairs are made and Trevor's given the bill."

"Really?"

"Of course. He's legally responsible. Ilona's still his wife, technically anyway. The divorce hasn't gone through, and from what Trevor said it won't. He still wants her. He's hiring Alan Dershowitz as her defense attorney." Rossi shook his head. "I thought I'd heard everything, but this one tops all. Trevor said he bought her, lock, stock and barrel, for three hundred thousand dollars. And he has no intention of losing his investment."

I nodded. "Ilona told me all about the yenta who negotiated their marriage. I'm just glad he'll take care of the Audi."

"Repairing your car won't even be a blip on his radar. According to a piece in today's paper, he's an extremely wealthy man. Recently bought a huge parcel of land in Estero and intends to develop it. Simon Yaeger is his partner in the deal."

Ohhhh. I blew out a pent-up breath. So that was why Trevor had made those massive withdrawals I'd stumbled across on his study desk. And that's why when Simon called that day, he wanted no one except George to find out about the deal—not until it was consummated. Not even the Dunne woman, I sniffed.

But that was all right. Actually Simon had done me a favor. Since then I'd known without a scintilla of doubt that we would never be more than casual friends. As for Rossi standing by my hospital bed with that attractive all-night stubble on his face, who knew?

CHAPTER TWENTY-EIGHT

A WEEK LATER, back at the Surfside condo, my bandaged feet propped up on the living room couch, I watched Rossi stride in with a pizza box and a six-pack of Coke.

I sighed. *A pizza.* "Rossi, we need to talk. I don't think I can swallow another bite of pizza. I need a salad. Fresh fruit."

"You don't like my cooking?" he asked, lowering the pizza and the soda to the coffee table.

"I'm grateful for all you're doing, and I mean that, but in a word, no."

He waggled a finger at me. He liked doing that. "The rest of the stuff's in the car."

"The rest?"

"Yeah, the girl food. Be right back." He returned in a few seconds with two bags full of groceries. "Salad greens," he announced. "Strawberries. Grilled chicken tenders. Thin-sliced bread. Danish butter. Something called tea cookies." He cocked an eyebrow. "What do you think?"

"I think you're a genius."

"Correct. Let me stash this stuff. Give me a sec." The refrigerator opened and closed a few times before he reappeared and handed me a Coke. Then he sank onto a club chair across from the couch where I lay stretched out like a pampered invalid.

He smiled across at me. "You look nice sitting there, Deva, like Cleopatra on her barge or something."

I sipped the Coke. He had put ice in the glass just the way I liked it. "That was positively poetic, Rossi."

"Yeah, I've got a gift for words." His eyes narrowed. "The problem is what I'm doing is stop gap. You need somebody staying here with you." He cocked an eyebrow. "You know, somebody to cook. And help you shower and stuff."

My turn to cock an eyebrow.

He ignored it. "Somebody to get you to your doctor's appointments. Go for pizzas. You can't drive yet with your feet like that." He cleared his throat. "In case you haven't guessed, I'm volunteering for the job."

"I guessed, Rossi, and I thank you, but no thanks. Besides, the stitches should come out next week, and if everything's healed, I can ditch the crutches. Probably walk a little. At least long enough to stand up and do a few chores. Maybe even go into the shop part of the day. And Lee stops by, too. So no need to worry about me. I'm fine, really."

He shrugged a little. "About staying here...I was shooting in the dark, but thought it was worth a try."

"I have my Irish grandmother to worry about."

"I thought she had passed."

"Well she has, but you never know."

"That's logical," he said, but he laughed, and to my relief changed the subject. "The next few weeks are going to be difficult. So I hope you're right and that you'll be up to the challenge physically. When the trial starts, you'll have to testify. There'll be cross examinations, attempts to twist your testimony, shake your story. None of that's going to be easy. And of course, Jones is claiming he's innocent. That you're lying about what you heard. His testimony won't stand up under scrutiny, but it will make for a tense trial."

"How's Morgan doing these days?"

"He's well enough to stand trial. The force of that blow knocked his heart out of rhythm for a while, but he's pretty well recovered. Though I hear his whole chest is bruised black."

My relief that Morgan had survived was far greater than anyone knew. During the past week, Rossi had spent a lot of time telling me I had only done what I had to do. My God-given instinct for self-preservation had gone to battle for me. And had helped stop a killer. Still I grieved for all the lost and destroyed lives—most of all for Maria and Jesus and George. But for poor, misguided Ilona, and Trevor, too. He must be hurting. For ill-fated Morgan and for Jessica who was standing by him despite what he'd done. She'd even stopped her divorce proceedings, at least until the trial ended.

The Bonita police had believed me after all and had sent a search and rescue team into the woods, where they found Morgan wandering about, dazed and disoriented.

I guess he had never been a Girl Scout either.

"Any further news about Ilona?" I asked Rossi.

"She's out on bail and singing like she's on *American Idol*. We're keeping an eye on her. She's a flight risk. But that's nothing new. She has been right along."

"What's that mean? Right along?"

"Since the Monet was stolen. Her polygraph was inconclusive."

"You never let on. You held out on me, Rossi."

"Had to. That's my job."

"Well, she knew where the painting was, and she

knew who had killed Maria. No wonder she flunked the test."

"Well, flunk is strong. Let's say the results were cloudy. The technician thinks she did something to skew her answers."

"What could she do? I thought the answers were involuntary?"

"They are. But when you answer the baseline questions, if you bite your lip or your tongue, or step on a tack in your shoe, the pain can change your response."

"So it's harder to spot a lie on the graph."

"Exactly."

"I was at the house the day Ilona took the polygraph exam. Afterwards, when Trevor kissed her, he had a trace of blood on his lips."

Rossi nodded. "That could be the answer. Chances are the blood came from Ilona. Trevor passed the poly with flying colors."

"So you were on to Ilona from the get go?"

"Pretty much. The feds followed her to Hungary after Christmas. She called on an art dealer in Budapest with known ties to the Russian art world."

"A fence?"

Rossi shrugged. "Probably. We couldn't do a thing without proof. You supplied that when you figured out where they hid the Monet. Good detective work, Deva."

"But I was dead wrong about George Farragut. He was innocent all along."

"Told ya."

"Okay, you can gloat." I was too ashamed to mention I had also harbored suspicions about another innocent guy, Simon Yaeger.

But before I could beat up on myself anymore, Rossi said, "Not all leads are good, not all suspicions are correct. The thing to remember is that some are right on the money. You lose a few, you win a few. And Deva, you won the lottery—you found the painting and you found the killer. Those are A pluses in anybody's book."

What do you know? For the first time in my life, I was on the A list.

CHAPTER TWENTY-NINE

LIKE A NEATLY tied package, the affaire Alexander was all wrapped up with no dangling loose ends. Except for one.

Lee had never mentioned Paulo's painting of Ilona. The fact that I knew about it but she apparently did not weighed on me. Though Paulo had nothing to do with the murders or the theft, why hadn't he spoken about such an important commission? What did he have to hide?

Even with the notoriety swirling around the Alexander name—or perhaps because of it—the publicity could only enhance Paulo's career. That and a subject like Ilona, who was so very beautiful. A mystery for sure, and one I worried about for Lee's sake. Yet every time I was tempted to ask her if she knew about the portrait, I couldn't bring myself to pose the question. It was none of my business. Besides, Paulo would have many commissions over a lifetime. Lee wouldn't know of each and every one. Still…why the secrecy?

I expected them to drop by tonight. With their wedding just two weeks away, they wanted to meet with Chip and discuss the wedding dinner menu. My feet propped up on an ottoman, I sat in a club chair and waited for them, telling myself not to worry, everything would be all right. On the plus side, my right foot had completely healed, and I was down to a light dressing

on the left. Most of the time these days I didn't even
need the crutches.

Da da da DA.

"Come in," I called. "Door's open."

Chatting and laughing, Lee and Paulo burst into the
living room in a whirlwind of excitement.

"Look at this, Deva. Look!" Lee ran over to me and
held out her left hand. "From Paulo!" A diamond soli-
taire adorned her slim ring finger, its small, round stone
as brilliant as a tiny star. "I declare, I'm still in a state
of shock." Like the ring, Lee's eyes sparkled with star
shine.

"Some day when my commissions are better, I'll re-
place the diamond with a larger one," Paulo said with
a happy smile.

"Never!" Lee flung her arms around him. "I want
to keep this one for my whole life. And I want to keep
you for my whole life." She rested her left hand on his
shoulder and gazed at her new ring. "Mr. Alexander
was a smart man to pay you to paint his wife. You're
going to be famous."

"I hope so for his sake." Paulo laughed. "My portrait
of Mrs. Alexander is the only painting he's keeping.
He's selling everything else. Even the Monets. It's pretty
flattering to be preferred to a master." He shrugged
"The subject's the reason, not the artist. No matter, I
wanted to surprise Lee, and I did."

The front door opened, and Chip sauntered in, glum
as I'd ever seen him. Slump-shouldered and quiet, he
still hadn't gotten over losing his chance at being a celebrity chef.

Lee held out her hand to him. "Look at this, Mr.
Chip."

At the unmistakable happiness in her smile, Chip smiled back. "Paulo's a lucky man."

"I'm lucky too," Lee said. "I have Paulo, and now I have y'all cooking my wedding dinner. What could be better than that?"

I could almost hear the unspoken answer echoing in Chip's head. *Being a celebrity chef.* But all he said was, "That's a great compliment, Lee. So what would you like me to cook for you?"

"Italian wedding soup would be nice, if that's all right, Mr. Chip. Then maybe an antipasto."

"Lasagna?" Paulo sounded hopeful.

"For dessert, besides wedding cake, how about some spumoni on the side?" I asked.

Chip groaned. "Every grade-B spaghetti house has that stuff on the menu."

"It's what we all would love to have." Like a Southern lady, Lee uttered her request so sweetly, what man could refuse?

Though his shoulders remained slumped, Chip nodded.

"It's the bride's day, after all, Chip," I said, anxious to coax another smile out of him. "Besides, I know you'll do a wonderful job. Everybody loves your food." I tried to sweeten the deal. "If you have some cards printed, I'll put them out in the shop. Talk you up. I'll bet in no time you'd have a catering business going. If you want one, that is. You could be a celebrity chef right here in Naples." I spread my arms. "After that, who knows?"

"I'll think about it." He spoke in a monotone, but his face brightened as he turned to Lee and Paulo. They were sitting side by side on Nana's sofa, so close you couldn't slide a piece of paper between them. "Lee, for you I'll get out my mother's secret meatball recipe. It makes a killer lasagna."

"Y'all are such a sweetheart." She leaped up and gave him a hug.

His cheeks bright red, Chip fled my living room for home, and Lee sat back on the sofa holding Paulo's hand as if she never wanted to let it go.

"Just two more weeks till our wedding. I can't hardly believe it, and it can't come too soon. Paulo was in and out of that Alexander house every time they had a party. What if something bad had happened to him before we even…I mean, before we did…I mean, I want to marry him," she finished, running out of words. No more were needed. Her flushed face said it all.

Paulo grinned and kissed her cheek. "The only bad thing that could happen to me would be losing you."

"Did y'all hear that, Deva? Isn't he wonderful?"

"Without question."

He laughed and kissed her again.

"Will you be my matron of honor, Deva?" The shy note in Lee's voice said she wasn't sure I'd accept.

"I'd be thrilled to."

"Do you think the lieutenant would stand up for me?" Paulo asked.

"I think he'd love it."

Remembering the other reason for her visit, Lee reached into a tote and removed a sheaf of papers. "These are the week's receipts. I made daily deposits to the bank."

"Thank you, Lee. That's awesome. How did we do?"

"Business has been good. Better than good. Since the paper reported how y'all found the murder suspect and nearly got killed fighting him off, people have been jamming the shop. It's been so busy Paulo came in afternoons to help out. The accessories are pretty much gone, so I brought the manufacturers' catalogs for you to do some more ordering. And here are the names of several ladies who want you to design for them."

A worried frown creased Lee's forehead as she handed me the receipts. "I know the Dr. Jones job was a big one. What about the furniture and what not y'all ordered for his house?"

"The wholesale costs are covered, so I haven't lost anything. I'll have the furniture delivered to the shop and set it up for sale. We'll be crowded for a while, but I think the pieces will sell. The murder-mystery provenance might actually help. People love a story."

She nodded, sat back and reached for Paulo's hand. I smiled. It would be a long two weeks' wait for both of them.

Then out of the blue, I suddenly said. "I've made a decision."

"Y'all have?"

"Yes, Lee. I'm closing the shop—"

She drew in a quick shocked breath.

"For the next three weeks. You get time off with pay, and I get more time out to recuperate."

Delighted, she flung her arms around Paulo. "We can have us a honeymoon. Right in your apartment!"

What neither of them knew, would never know, was I owed Paulo big time, and this was my way of repaying the debt. For days I had suspected him of—yes, I'll admit it—cheating on Lee with Ilona. Shame all over me for such a suspicion. These two were so much in love no one could ever violate their devotion to each other. If I were Jimmy the Greek I'd lay odds on it. And so would Jack. I just know he would.

THE WEDDING MORNING dawned flawless and blue, not a
cloud in sight. With only one small Band-Aid covering
the last few stitches, my feet slid into low-heeled sandals without any trouble. I slipped on an apricot lace
halter dress and smoothed it over my hips. Yesterday
I'd had a manicure and pedicure. And I'd had my hair
cut short enough to tame my curls but long enough to
please Rossi. I screwed on pearl earrings and clasped
my grandmother's pearl bracelet on my right wrist. A
little blush and apricot lip gloss. Taupe shadow on my
eyelids and new super mascara guaranteed to make my
lashes look like bird's wings.

As a finishing touch, I spritzed on some Diorissimo
and stepped away from the bathroom's full-length mirror to view the effect. A happy, smiling Deva looked
back at me and winked.

I plucked my bouquet from the refrigerator where
I'd stashed it to keep fresh. For sentimental reasons, I'd
chosen a multicolored cluster of grocery store blooms
from Publix Market and cobbled them together with a
long apricot streamer.

The kitchen clock said five to ten. Rossi would be
here soon. Always punctual, he wouldn't be late, not
today.

Sure enough, the chimes rang at ten on the dot. I
opened the door to a Rossi I nearly didn't recognize. He
was all decked out in a navy blazer, tan slacks, striped
tie, and a starched white shirt. With the tail tucked in.

"Wow," I said.

His eyes widened at the sight of me. "The wows are
all mine. You're absolutely gorgeous." He peered closer.
"What's with the eyes? You look like you could fly."

"It's—"

"Whatever it is, I like it. I like everything." He

pointed to my bouquet. "That's the kind of flowers I buy."

"I know. I've always loved them."

He stuck out an elbow. "Well then, shall we?"

"Oh, yes, let's."

We reached Moorings Beach in plenty of time for the wedding. Like love birds released for the occasion, gulls soared overhead, riding the warm air currents; the Gulf water lapped softly on the shore, and the sun shone over all, flawless and golden. The bride had made her own gown and was a vision in a cloud of white tulle. On a minor note, I'm pleased to report I had no problem walking on sand. But Lee and Paulo? Well, throughout the ceremony Lee and Paulo were walking on air.

And later, for their wedding feast, just as he had promised, Chip served a killer lasagna.

Salute!

* * * * *

REQUEST YOUR FREE BOOKS!

2 FREE NOVELS
PLUS 2 FREE GIFTS!

WORLDWIDE LIBRARY®
Your Partner in Crime

YES! Please send me 2 FREE novels from the Worldwide Library® series and my 2 FREE gifts (gifts are worth about $10). After receiving them, if I don't wish to receive any more books, I can return the shipping statement marked "cancel." If I don't cancel, I will receive 4 brand-new novels every month and be billed just $5.49 per book in the U.S. or $6.24 per book in Canada. That's a savings of at least 31% off the cover price. It's quite a bargain! Shipping and handling is just 50¢ per book in the U.S. and 75¢ per book in Canada.* I understand that accepting the 2 free books and gifts places me under no obligation to buy anything. I can always return a shipment and cancel at any time. Even if I never buy another book, the two free books and gifts are mine to keep forever.

414/424 WDN F4WY

Name	(PLEASE PRINT)
Address	Apt. #
City	State/Prov.	Zip/Postal Code
Signature (if under 18, a parent or guardian must sign)	

Mail to the **Harlequin® Reader Service:**
IN U.S.A.: P.O. Box 1867, Buffalo, NY 14240-1867
IN CANADA: P.O. Box 609, Fort Erie, Ontario L2A 5X3

Want to try two free books from another line?
Call 1-800-873-8635 or visit www.ReaderService.com.